Amber in Autumn

SUSAN AYLWORTH

Published Internationally by Susan Aylworth
Chico, CA USA
susanaylworthauthor.com

Exclusive cover © 2022 Bright Book Media
Inside design and formatting by Teri Barnett, indiebookdesigner.com

PRINT ISBN 978-1-955056-12-0
EBOOK ISBN 978-1-955056-11-3

Like Susan's Facebook Page
Follow Susan on Twitter: @SusanAylworth
Follow Susan on BookBub
Follow Susan on GoodReads

For my dear sisters and friends who helped me develop this story.
Special thanks to Pat, Liza, Lorena, Judy,
Kathy, Sue, and Gail.
You're the best!

CONTENTS

Chapter One

The century-old stone church was at its best, simply but tastefully decorated for a grand occasion. If guests recognized the lavender bows repurposed from the last wedding, barely a month ago, no one mentioned it. The organist stood on the dais, filing through her music, ready to take her place.

A few guests arrived, telling the young men at the door whether they wished to be seated on the bride's or groom's side. Amber Reyes gave the scene a final once-over. *I believe we are going to pull this off. I had my doubts.* It was time for her to take her place with the bridal party, so she gave the chapel a final approving nod and walked down the hall to the bright classroom that served as a bride's room, redolent with the scents of fresh flowers.

A month ago, she'd served as maid of honor at the wedding of her girlhood best buddy, Paris Cutler, now married to Greg Frantz, Amber's colleague and friend. Now she returned in the same role for Sunny Ray, her cousin, who was like a sister to her.

Sunny and her younger sister, Skye, had lived with Amber's family since Sunny was eleven and Skye only nine. That was the year Amber's mother rescued the girls from the Children of Rah cult and from their loving, but addicted and neglectful, mother.

Amber, who had always wanted a sister, had been thrilled. She and Sunny were so close in age that they were sometimes mistaken for fraternal twins. With their straight, dark brown hair, dark eyes, and slightly darker complexions—the result of one Latin and one Anglo parent for each—the assumption made sense. Meanwhile, people often thought that Skye—with her darker complexion, full lips, and curly hair—was fostered or adopted. That assumption always burned Skye but amused the older girls. *That must have contributed to Skye's sense that she didn't belong. How I wish I could take that all back!*

Amber brushed that thought away as she walked down the hall. *I can't fix the past. Best to focus on the present. We have plenty going on right now.*

"I believe everything is ready in there," Amber announced as she entered the bride's room. "How are we doing here?"

Sunny turned to her with a smile as bright as her name. "Things are coming along," she answered. "I know you worried about pulling a wedding together this fast, but I always knew you'd manage it."

"You had more faith in me than I did. But I wanted you to have a lovely wedding. You deserve that."

"Turn this way for a moment." Olivia Reyes, who served as the mother of the bride, straightened the crown of white rosebuds and purple freesias. "There. Hold right there while I put some hairpins in."

The bride obeyed, a serene smile lighting her face.

Amber said, "It helps that you and Paris and Skye are all the same dress size."

"I fully agree." Sunny beamed at Amber. "It means that Skye and Paris can wear the bridesmaids' dresses from Paris's wedding. Then Paris made the generous offer to let me wear her wedding dress. If we hadn't all been the same size, we wouldn't have had that option."

"Good job that Libby has a dress of her own, one we hope will fit in with the color scheme." Amber bit her lip, choosing to keep her fussing from muddling Sunny's big day, but wondering about Sunny's friend. "Sunny, have you heard from Libby, yet?"

"Yes," Sunny answered. "She called from the cell phone pull-out. I told her that's the only place on that windy road where she can get a signal. I asked her to call when she got there."

"Super. How long ago was that?"

Olivia, finished with the hair pins, answered for the bride. "I checked my watch. It's been twelve minutes."

"Then she should arrive any minute, but she'll still have to get dressed." Amber shook her head. "That's cutting it close!" She tacked on a rather forced smile.

Sunny shrugged. "Libby just started her new job at that new boutique hotel in Sacramento. I'm sure she's getting here as soon as she can. If it takes a little longer for us to be ready, we'll just ask the organist to play another song."

"I'm glad you can be so cool about this." Amber slumped into a chair. "You're the one who's supposed to be nervous!"

Sunny responded with another sweet smile. "I've told you all along: I'm not worried about having a beautiful or perfect wedding. This is one day in our lives. It's the marriage that follows that's important…to both of us."

"I'm glad you feel that way." Amber straightened her own lavender dress. They'd pulled the wedding together In only three weeks, and Amber

"I'll be happy with however it goes, so long as I'm married to Evan when the ceremony ends." Sunny turned to look at the women who attended her. "I can't thank you all enough for what you've done. You know I never expected to have such a beautiful event. I always imagined that, if I married at all, it would be a simple ceremony in front of a county clerk."

"We couldn't allow that," Olivia answered. "You may not have a father or mother, but you have us. We're family and we want you to start this new phase of your life in the best way possible."

"You've been wonderf—" Sunny broke off as Libby swept into the room.

"Five minutes and I'll be ready to go." Libby carried her dress over her shoulder.

Amber looked at her watch. "I'm glad you made it. We were getting worried."

"I kept telling my new boss that I needed to roll. He kept adding 'just one more thing' and then 'just one more' after that. I got out as fast as I could."

"We wouldn't have started without you." Sunny's calm seemed to settle over everyone. "Go ahead and get ready. Take the time you need."

Libby changed behind the privacy screen and stepped out a few minutes later.

"Whoa." Amber's eyes widened. "You meant it when you said

your grape-colored dress would fit well with the purple and lavender we already have. It's almost as if we planned this."

Libby winked, her own smile sly. "Almost as if it was Destiny."

Amber rolled her eyes. Raised in Destiny, California, she'd heard those jokes all her life. "Enough with the Destiny jokes. Are we all set?"

"Give me another minute to do something with this hair." Libby tidied her bright red tresses into a thick braid. "This is as good as it gets," she said, looking in the mirror. "I'm ready."

"One detail." Amber grabbed a white rosebud from the container of blossoms she'd saved for 'just in case' and tucked it into Libby's braid. "There. All done."

"Thanks."

Amber grinned. "No problem!"

"Looks like we're all ready." Sunny said, looking around the room. "Amber, you can signal the organist to start the processional any time. Aunt Olivia, you agree?"

"Absolutely." Olivia led the way as the members of the wedding party lined up in the hallway, preparing to enter the chapel. Amber peeked in and nodded to the organist.

The music changed. The minister, with Evan and his brother-in-law beside him, entered from the front of the chapel and took their places at the altar, Evan in a well-cut dark gray suit.

Amber remembered the discussion they'd had over what Evan should wear. Sunny had agreed with him that his best look was probably his deputy sheriff uniform, but Amber had begged him to buy a suit for this occasion. When Sunny thought of the wedding pictures they'd want to keep forever, she agreed. After that, Evan was all in. "Anything for my Sunny," he'd declared. Now he stood waiting, looking toward the doorway with eager anticipation.

Aunt Olivia entered the chapel on the arm of her son, Amber's older brother Tyler, who came to share this day with the family. Tyler seated her in the place reserved for the mother of the bride and took his own seat.

The bridesmaids came next. Libby entered first, unescorted, her grape-colored, tea-length dress a perfect complement to her startling red hair. Behind her came Sunny's sister, Skye, in darker purple, with Amber following in lavender. They took their places beside the altar.

The music changed again, the audience stood, and Sunny entered, a vision in the wedding dress Paris had worn a month earlier, escorted by her proud *Tío* Rico, her Uncle Enrique, in the place of the father she'd never known. Together they made the stately walk to the front of the chapel. Enrique took Sunny's hand and placed it in Evan's. He leaned slightly toward Evan and, in a low stage whisper, said, "Take care of her, Son."

"I will," Evan answered soberly. "I promise." The ceremony began.

"Who gives this woman in marriage?" the minister asked.

Enrique spoke strongly. "Her Aunt Olivia and I do." He turned and took the seat beside his wife.

The minister welcomed everyone. The audience included a few friends of Evan's who had driven in from Butte County and others from his new job in the Sacramento County Sheriff's office. The rest of the room was filled with friends and neighbors from Destiny, most of whom had known Sunny since she was a little girl, all friends of the Reyes family.

After a few words about the importance of marriage and how traditional marriage created tighter family and community bonds, the minister offered an invocation. Then he invited Evan's brother-in-law to give the reading the couple had chosen from First Peter, chapter four. He stepped to the microphone and read, "Above all, love each other deeply—"

Evan and Sunny held hands and gazed into one another's eyes as the scriptural words swam around them. Beside her cousin and friend, Amber watched, barely hearing the few verses. *I'm so happy for Sunny. She and Evan hurried into this, but they're a good couple. They'll find they have some problems as they get more acquainted, but they'll work them out.* The thought came to her, *I wonder if this will ever happen for me?* She banished it quickly. *Stop it, Amber. This day isn't about you.*

But she found she couldn't help thinking about the possibility of her own marriage, especially when her reasoning kicked in. It wasn't as if Destiny was crawling with eligible men. Greg was about the only one left and he married Paris, not that Greg and she had anything going beyond the work both did. She tried again to focus on the reading, but her mind kept ruminating, remembering her former boyfriend, the one she'd thought she might marry. Chad had split the minute she took the Destiny job. Would she have to give up Destiny in order to find her own love story? The doubt hovered there, coloring her emotions as the reading ended.

The couple had written their own vows and had agreed on some of the wording, but large parts they'd left as a surprise. Evan reached into his inner coat pocket and pulled out a slip of paper. "It's been said that attraction is a biochemical reaction and that infatuation can flare and die in a moment, but love, real love, is a choice. Today I choose you, Golden Sunny Ray, to be my wife, and I promise I will continue to choose you every day for the rest of our lives and even beyond. I choose you to be my companion, my lover, my partner in all our worldly affairs, and the mother of my future children.

"I promise you my total fidelity, the complete commitment of my body, heart, and soul, and all my worldly goods. I promise to care for and cherish you, to support your strengths and strengthen your weaknesses. Even on the days when we disagree or struggle with difficult decisions, I promise to choose you every day, forever and always."

As he tucked the paper away, the wedding guests responded with "ahs" and "ohs."

Sunny turned to Amber, who handed her the folded paper from her dress pocket, but Sunny surprised her. "With the good reverend's permission, I have asked the Daughters of Destiny to sing the first half of my vows." The crowd erupted into excited applause as five women, well-known to this crowd but increasingly known to the world, came forward.

Still on hiatus before their first cross-country tour, the Daughters of Destiny used a pitch pipe to find their notes and began singing:

Today I choose to pledge to you to make your life my own.
Today I choose to love you and to make your heart my home.
I choose to live close by your side each day throughout my life,
To take you as my husband and to be your wedded wife.

I choose you-oo-oo. I choose you.
I choose to be your partner, your lover, and your friend,
To love you when you're feeling low and help your hurt unbend.
And when we disagree, my love, I'll hold you closer still.
We'll solve our problems patiently, let hot emotions chill.
I choose you-oo-oo. I choose you.

Sometime during the second verse, Camille Reed picked up her guitar to strum a musical bridge before the group sang its final chorus. Guests swayed to the music while Sunny faced Evan, her hands in his, her eyes shimmering with tears. When the women finished their number to loud applause, they took their places in the audience, and Sunny began to read:

"Today I choose you, Evan Michael Millett, to be my husband, and I promise I will continue to choose you every day for the rest of our lives and even beyond. I choose you to be my companion, my lover, my partner in all our worldly affairs, and the father of my future children.

"I promise you my everything. I will wear your ring on my finger, your name as my own, your love in my heart. I will share your secret joys and sorrows and support you as you make life choices. I will only honor you when we're on the same page and when we disagree, I will hold you closer still. I promise to choose you every day, forever and always."

The minister looked out at the assembled guests. "I think that about covers it, don't you?" Laughter rippled around the room. He turned to Evan. "Evan Michael Millett, do you take this woman, Golden Sunny Ray, to be your wedded wife, to have and to hold, forsaking all others, from this day forward, for better, for worse, for richer, for poorer, in sickness and in health, to love and to cherish always?"

Evan's voice was strong as he answered, "I do."

"Golden Sunny Ray, do you take this man, Evan Michael Millett, to be your wedded husband, to have and to hold, forsaking all others, from this day forward, for better, for worse, for richer, for poorer, in sickness and in health, to love and to cherish always?"

Sunny's voice was equally strong. "I do."

"Do you have the rings?" the minister asked. Evan's best man reached into his pocket and retrieved the two rings the couple had picked.

The minister picked up one band. "This ring has no beginning and no end. Let it stand as a symbol of your everlasting love for one another." He watched as the pair put the bands on each other.

"Now that Evan and Sunny have pledged their forever love for one another in the presence of this company and have formalized it with an exchange of promises and rings, I am pleased to announce that they are husband and wife, legally and lawfully joined together. Evan and Sunny, you may now kiss one another as husband and wife."

Evan wasted no time in sweeping Sunny into his arms. The kiss was quick, more urgent than sweet, and both husband and wife came up grinning as everyone applauded.

"Ladies and gentlemen, I give you Mr. and Mrs. Evan Millett!"

The applause continued as the newlyweds led the way down the aisle and into the sunlight outside. Guests followed them out, scattering birdseed over the couple as they stood on the walk in front of the church. Enrique, in his role as father of the bride, called out: "We'll be busy taking some pictures here for a while. Please feel free to cross into the park and start enjoying the reception. The wedding party will join you soon."

That brought another cheer and most of the guests filed across the street into the park.

Amber, who had posed for wedding pictures earlier that week and again that morning, knew they wanted a few poses that included Libby. She helped organize everyone.

"Thanks, everyone," Amber said as the photographer finished. "Those of us who are helping with the food can go change now. I'll see you all at the reception in a few minutes."

Approval rippled through the small group as they scattered to the various classrooms in the church where they'd left their less formal clothing. *I'll see you at the reception*, Amber thought again as she followed the other women inside. Then she permitted herself one small, self-pitying thought. Maybe she should have followed Chad instead of letting him walk away. Maybe he was the only chance she'd ever have. She imagined herself becoming that older single woman people talked about, the principal at the school who spent her time raising other people's children. She shook the thought away. *Enough of that,* she told herself firmly. *I'm twenty-six. That doesn't qualify me for spinsterhood yet. I need to go play hostess at the party. I can worry about my own life some later.*

If only she could make herself listen.

Chapter Two

The crowd swirled around Amber as she joined her parents to help serve the food. Although Sunny didn't know it, Enrique and Olivia Reyes had been planning to host weddings for both their nieces ever since taking them in as children. They'd established a wedding fund to which they added a little every month and they were prepared to take on the role of the bride's family when Sunny and Evan had announced, just three weeks earlier, that they wanted to marry before Sunny's graduate classes began.

"We'll do the same for Skye when her turn comes," Olivia said when her daughter asked. "And of course, sweetheart, we'll do it for you." Olivia blew a kiss to Amber as she took the first rack of chicken from its barrel and began separating it into servings.

"Thanks, Mom." Amber spoke as her mother turned away. *I hope there will one day be a wedding you can pay for.* She pulled a second rack of smoked chicken.

As often happened in Destiny, the wedding was a community event. Friends and neighbors brought salads and side dishes to go with the barrel-smoked chicken the Reyes family provided. Others volunteered desserts to go alongside the wedding cake, and the cake itself was a gift from friends who ran the local post office and decorated cakes on the side. This sense of community was a big part of what Amber loved about Destiny and one reason she wanted to stay. When she'd had to choose between Chad and Destiny, she'd chosen the town. If she hadn't loved Chad enough to leave here, had she loved him enough to marry him? Now she knew better.

She watched in satisfaction as locals gathered, chatting and hugging, to honor the newlyweds. The town of Destiny always celebrated momentous occasions together. The Reyes family had been there for as long as any, and the older residents remembered. When the family took in Sunny and her sister, Skye, so did the town. Sunny might never have felt secure about her role in this community, but Destiny had always known she belonged. The town had embraced her fully.

A tap on her shoulder jarred her from her thoughts and she turned to see her friend, Paris. She immediately wrapped her in a hug. "Hey there, girlfriend! Haven't seen much of you lately. I suspect you've been having a fine honeymoon."

"Exactly." Paris said with a grin. "But we need to get together more often."

Amber stepped away to serve more chicken. "I hope you had time for a real honeymoon before Greg had to be back at the high school. A principal's job is all year 'round."

"As well you know. But yes, we had time for a short honeymoon away, and, as you said, we're still honeymooners. She looked at the chicken and asked, "Would you like some help with that?"

"Sure. I'd be grateful." Amber scooted over, letting Paris in beside her. "I'm taking the smoked chicken, cutting it in quarters, and putting some on each plate. Then the plates go on the big trays. When the table in front runs low, Mom or Dad reaches back here for another full tray."

"I think I can handle that." Paris started cutting chicken.

"So? About the honeymoon?"

"Greg arranged a week in the city—nice hotel, great restaurants. We did the tour of Alcatraz and visited a couple of art museums. We wanted to see a play, but the good ones were all sold out. We talked about going to the San Francisco Symphony too, but they didn't open their season until a week or so ago. Don't worry, though. We found plenty to do." She ended her statement with a Mona Lisa smile.

Amber raised an eyebrow. "Is that all I get?"

Paris raised a brow of her own. "All I'm telling, girlfriend."

"Killjoy. So how are you adjusting to life with Greg away at school all day and you working from home? And what did you decide to do about changing your name?"

"I have changed it, officially. I'm now Paris Cutler-Frantz."

"And Greg's cool with that?"

"He fully appreciates why I might not want to be known as Paris

Frantz. The only request he made was that the children who come along will get Frantz, nothing hyphenated."

"Sounds fair. I'm guessing you won't be naming any daughters after yourself?"

Paris grimaced. "No-o-o. I don't plan—"

Olivia interrupted. "Hey, ladies. We're getting backed up over here."

"Oh. Sorry." Amber shifted into a higher gear. "Come on, Paris. Let's get some chicken for these hungry people."

Minutes passed while the women worked side-by-side. It felt good to work with Paris again. *I'm glad she's back.* When Amber felt a tap on her back, she turned, expecting to see someone in the family. Instead she saw a man, a short, but round, middle-aged man who seemed quite drunk. Something was off about him. Hair rose on the back of her neck. "Can I help you?"

"You the maid of honor?" The man's speech slurred. He swayed a bit, catching himself on the edge of the serving table.

"Yes, I'm Amber."

"I hear you were the maid of honor last month at another wedding. That right?"

"Yes." Amber took one step back. She gestured toward Paris. "Hers."

"Heh-heh. Always the bridesmaid, huh?" The man laughed, appreciating his own joke.

Amber suppressed a shudder. "Do you have a question, Mr.—?"

"Donald. Donald Rawlings. Just call me Don." He held out his hand.

Amber ignored it. "How can I help you, Mr. Rawlings?"

Behind Rawlings, Paris had begun gesturing, asking without words if she should round up some help. Amber gave a slight shake of her head, signaling Paris to wait. "Your question, Mr. Rawlings?"

He gave her the elevator look, starting at her feet and moving up to her face, pausing a little too long at her chest. "You're a good-looking woman. I'm available and looking for someone like you. Maybe after this shindig—"

Paris covered her surprised laugh with a cough.

Amber swallowed hard. She turned a forced smile, one she hoped looked both civil and determined, on the aggressor. "Thank you for your interest, Mr. Rawlings, but I'm not available. Good luck with your search." She turned back to the chicken.

Rawlings grabbed her elbow. "Oh? I heard you're single. Who are you with?"

Amber shoved his hand away. Adrenaline began coursing through her. "I'm—"

"She's with me." A deep bass voice spoke behind her. She looked back as the source of that voice—this man much younger and quite appealing—stepped close, putting his arm around her waist.

"Oh. Oh, sorry." Rawlings shrank before them as he backed away. "No offense meant."

Amber started to answer, but the stranger spoke for her. "You need to be on your way, Rawlings. Now. And I recommend you avoid the booze. You're drunk enough already."

"Drunk?" Rawlings puffed up, but his angry expression faded almost immediately as he looked up, way up, into the stranger's face. "Oh yes. Yes, I suppose…Well…" He turned and staggered away, still mumbling under his breath.

The possessive arm fell away from Amber's waist as the rescuer stepped to the side. "I hope you don't mind."

"Not at all." Amber faced him, the better to admire all she saw. He was quite tall, a few inches over six feet, and well-built, more like a man who worked than one who worked out. He was older than she— Amber guessed in his early thirties—with perfectly sculpted features, thick, dark hair, and dark brown, puppy-dog eyes. "Thank you. I believe we could have managed—"

"Oh, we would have!" Paris stepped next to Amber, in a protective gesture, but with a smile on her face. "But thanks for your help."

Amber waved off her friend. "As I started to say, I believe we could have managed, but you helped us avoid a more serious confrontation. Thank you, Mr.—?"

He grinned, showing off gleaming white teeth. "Call me Max. Good day, ladies." He nodded and blended back into the crowd.

"Whoa." Amber shook herself as if coming out of a trance. "That was unexpected."

"But I don't see you complaining." Paris gave her a sly smile.

"No-o-o-o-o. Not complaining at all. He can come to my rescue any time."

"Your family isn't serving alcohol at this reception, right?"

"No. It's part of the deal for any event in the park that's open to the public. Only closed events can have alcohol and even at that, nothing can be served in bottles."

"To avoid broken glass. That's what I thought. So, where did Rawlings get his booze?"

Amber shrugged. "No idea, but people sometimes bring their own. Folks tend to look the other way as long as they keep it to themselves."

Olivia stepped back to their table. "Ladies, we need more chicken."

"Coming right up!" Amber answered. They went back to work, Amber keeping her hands busy with chicken while her thoughts centered on the handsome stranger who appeared just when she needed him. That was the kind of rescue always appreciate.

Half an hour later, the crowd had been fed, Enrique had announced he had chicken left if anyone was still hungry, and Olivia excused Amber and Paris to get their own food. "Enjoy the party," she said. "We won't start clean-up until after the newlyweds leave."

"Clean-up," Paris murmured as Olivia left them. "Sounds like fun."

"You don't have to stay," Amber said. "But I'd appreciate both your help and your company."

"I know, but after all you did to help Greg and me with our wedding, I fully intend to help you. Greg is staying too. We both expect to be here until you, Olivia and Rico all leave."

Amber reached out to Paris, giving her arm a quick squeeze. "That's how we know who our true friends are. Thanks, girlfriend."

"You're welcome. Let's go get something to eat."

They filled their plates and sat at an empty table. Between bites, Amber asked, "That guy, Max, did he seem at all familiar?"

"No. I can't say that he did, and I'm pretty sure I'd remember that one. Did you recognize him?"

"Not sure. You remember the house where our family used to live?"

"Sure."

"When you and I were little kids, around ten or so, the family next door were the Burnetts, remember?"

"Right. Keith was in our class, and there was someone older, too," Paris replied.

"The guy who was a junior or senior when we were in fifth grade was named Max."

Paris nodded. "Right. I remember now. You and I used to watch him ride off on his motorcycle. We thought he was so grown up."

"He was. Compared to us, anyway. We were little kids."

"True." Paris paused, looking thoughtful. "Do you think there's any chance it's the same guy?"

Amber nodded. "Could be. Our school got eight new families at the start of this year and another that came in late. Those kids will start on Monday and the family name is Burnett."

"Hmm." Paris looked over the park. "This reception is open to the whole community. It's possible someone invited the new neighbor."

"Just what I was thinking."

They finished their dinner just as Enrique took the microphone to announce music and dancing. "I expect Greg will want to dance," Paris said, clearing away the dishes she'd brought from home. "You?"

"I think I'll avoid Mr. Rawlings." Amber began clearing her own dishes. "I'll get an early start on clean-up."

"I'm sorry you won't get to enjoy more of the party, but I can appreciate your reasons. Of course, you might get a chance to dance with Max." She grinned.

"Have you seen him around in the last little while?"

Paris shook her head. "Can't say that I have."

"I haven't either--and I've been watching." She saw Greg approaching. "Here comes your husband. Go dance while you can. I'll catch you later."

"Great. Can you get away for a lunch this week?"

"I don't know. Things are still hectic. We're only three weeks into the term—"

"I know. I get lonely working by myself all day, and Greg isn't able to get away for lunches, either." She shrugged. "Maybe next week?"

Greg reached them, wrapping his wife in a half-hug. "Hey, gorgeous. Dance with me?"

"I'd love to," Paris answered, but she lingered long enough to ask, "About next week?"

"Sure. Maybe you can pick up lunch in town. We can close my office door and manage a few minutes of girl talk before we both get back to the grind."

"Sounds good. Let's stay in touch."

"Will do." Amber did a quick survey of the park. Many guests had already given their gifts and good wishes to the newlyweds, cleaned up their tables and left for the day. Others joined in the dancing as the D.J. played crowd favorites. The only area where she could start clean-up was where she'd just been working with the food. That space needed plenty of cleaning. Her thoughts circled back to the man called Max as she went to work, secretly hoping she would get a chance to meet him again.

Chapter Three

Max Burnett growled as he drove his car into the pull-out at the side of the winding road. "What a day!" he mumbled aloud. First the load of ore delivered to the Sacramento plant had been credited improperly, and then his order for chemicals had failed to show up, apparently due to some mix-up on the other end. Both situations needed someone to clear things up in person and, because he was in charge of the mine's supply chain, he was the obvious choice.

Unfortunately, everything had taken longer than it should, which meant he was running late for the appointment at his kids' school. The twins had only been in school for a week. How much trouble could they be in? Starting late meant he'd been speeding, which was undoubtedly the reason for the siren and the bright lights he saw in his rear view mirror. Max pulled over at the side of the road, put on the emergency brake, rolled down his window, and waited.

The officer got out of her car and approached the driver's side, ticket book in hand. His heart sank when he saw she was a woman. Max had been dealing with unreasonable women all day, starting with the one who'd messed up the receipt for the ore.

Then he'd gone to the chemicals vendor and had been directed to another woman. This one insisted the latest order went out just as specified. He'd had to talk her through the whole process five times before she actually looked at the order and realized it had not yet been filled.

His ex-wife and her mother had given him enough of dealing with unreasonable women and his day had already been full of them, but he knew better than to hassle a police officer. She had nearly reached his window when he pasted on a pleasant smile. "Good afternoon, Officer."

She did not smile. "Do you know why I stopped you?"

Max chose to play dumb. "Uh, do I have a problem with a brake light?"

She pursed her lips. She seemed to be struggling to keep from rolling her eyes. "The limit here is forty-five. I clocked you at sixty-two."

"Forty-five? I didn't realize that. I've just recently moved to Destiny and—"

"And you need to understand the law," she said, cutting him off. The officer asked for his license and registration and began scribbling in her book. Precious minutes later, Max pulled back onto the highway, driving at a careful forty-five until he saw the officer turn the other direction, heading down the mountain. Even then he didn't punch it. Who knew if there might be more than one officer patrolling today?

Max blew out a breath in sheer exasperation and pushed his speed up to fifty. He was going to be *so* late to this appointment. He only hoped he wouldn't have to deal with another irrational woman.

AT HER DESK in the principal's office, Amber checked her watch. She stepped into the front office, glancing at the wall clock to be certain her watch was correct. "No word from Mr. Burnett?"

"Nothing yet." Liza, her secretary, glanced at the clock. "If he gets here now, he'll be nearly half an hour late."

"Good thing he's my last scheduled appointment. If he gets here soon, I may still be able to meet with him." She let out a sigh as she locked her hands behind her, stretching her back, arms, and neck.

Liza looked sympathetic. "Long day." It was a statement, not a question.

"Long week," Amber answered. "The days all seem so long at the beginning of the term."

"True, but I've noticed it's tougher on you when you're talking with the parents of troubled kids."

"You're right, of course." She smiled. "You know the parents I really feel for? The stepmothers. They always seem so nervous or even defensive. It's worse when they show up by themselves, without the children's fathers. That fairy tale cliché of the wicked stepmother seems to dog them all. The poor women are afraid to discipline a child who isn't their own or to make decisions about their schooling. Their husbands often stick them with both those jobs."

"Then, as the kids get older, they get mouthier and tougher for the stepmothers to handle," Liza said.

"You've noticed it too?"

"Oh yeah." The secretary grimaced. "If there's one thing I never want to be, it's a stepmother to a mouthy sixth-grade boy."

"Or girl." Amber shook her head. "But even the little kids can give a reluctant stepmother a wagonload of stink." She glanced at the clock. "I'm going back to my reports. If Mr. Burnett finally arrives, show him in."

"Will do."

Amber returned to her office, stewing on the thoughtlessness of some people. It didn't seem likely there could be more than one Max Burnett in a town the size of Destiny, so the very late parent of twins must be the same Max who had once been her neighbor and could also be the same Max who had come to her rescue at Sunny's reception. The various pictures weren't coming together well. Or at all.

MAX BURNETT FUMED as he pulled his car into the parking lot at Destiny Elementary. He was half an hour late. This was not the way he did things! He could have looked up a number for the school office and called to let them know he was delayed but doing that would have made him even later. Now he wished he'd taken the time to call. Better yet, he could have rescheduled for a different day. Why did he have to be here, anyway? The kids had been in school five days. They were first graders, for heaven's sake! Slamming his car door, he jogged to the front office.

The woman behind the desk had to be a secretary. She looked like a kid "Hello?" he said.

"Oh hello! Are you Mr. Burnett?"

"Yeah. Sorry I'm late."

"We've been hoping you'd get here. Ms. Reyes is in her office. Please tap on her door and go on in."

Max tried to squelch his sour expression as he tapped on the door. He didn't understand how his kids could already be in trouble, and he didn't want to have to deal with another woman, let alone a female principal.

He decided the woman behind this desk must be the principal's secretary. Like the first woman, she had her back to him, and she looked like a kid. "Hello? I'm here for Principal Reyes. Am I in the right place?"

"I'm Ms. Reyes." The woman turned to look at him and smiled in recognition.

Max and Amber spoke at the same time. "It's you," Max said.

"Well, hello," said Amber.

For a moment, they stared at one another in silence. Amber recovered first. She stood and gestured toward the empty chair beside her. "Please, have a seat. Let me start by thanking you again for your timely rescue last Saturday."

Max, still recovering from the surprise of recognizing this woman and realizing she was the principal, said, "Yeah. No problem. I guess you want to see me about my twins, Will and Kate?"

"Yes. Your children have interesting names, like the duke and duchess of Cambridge."

"Their mother's homage to the royals, but you didn't call me here to ask about names."

"No, I didn't. I thought it would be good to talk right at the beginning of the school year—"

"They're little kids," Max said. "How much trouble can they have gotten into already?"

Amber smiled. To Max, it looked like an indulgent, placating expression, which only wound him tighter. Principals were supposed to be cranky old men, not sassy, beautiful women. And this one was young. What could she know about working with children? And why was she giving him that look, like he was the one who didn't know what was going on?

"Mr. Burnett," she began.

"Max." He remembered how he'd said it under other circumstances just a few days ago.

"All right then, Max. I called you in here to talk about your children because—"

"Cut to the chase. What's the problem?"

He watched as the principal took a deep breath, clearly put out by his response—or maybe by his interrupting. She offered that tight, indulgent smile again. "Your children aren't in any trouble, Max. I wanted to talk with you about them because they seem so unhappy here and—"

"Wait! You dragged me In here because you think my kids are *unhappy?*"

"They're also behind the other children—"

"How can they be behind? School just started!" He could hear his voice becoming louder with his growing frustration, and he ordered himself to calm down.

"Three weeks ago," the woman said, correcting him. "School started three weeks ago."

"My job just changed a week ago." He hoped he wasn't glaring as hard as he wanted to. "We didn't really have a choice about—"

"Please understand," Amber cut in. "I'm not talking about the last three weeks. Kindergarteners here in Destiny are reading and writing simple words by the end of the year. They recognize all letters, both upper and lower case, practice learning to write those letters, and know their numbers up to 100. Your children are behind in all those skills. Did Will and Kate attend kindergarten last year?"

He swallowed down his first answer, recognizing that additional rudeness would not help. "They went to a private preschool. It was what their mother wanted for them."

Ms. Reyes straightened in her seat. "Perhaps I should be speaking with Mrs. Burnett."

Max swallowed hard. "That won't be possible."

"We can arrange a special time, make it easy for her to get here—"

"My ex-wife died last year." Max bit off the words.

"Oh. I'm sorry." Amber paused. The look on her face was apologetic—or was it straightforward pity? He'd seen that look way too many times. "That might explain their hesitancy and why they always seem so sad."

"Now we're back to you thinking my kids are *unhappy*." Max emphasized the word.

"Mr. Burnett," the principal began again, and this time Max let it go. "We pride ourselves on giving Destiny's schoolchildren the best. We try to keep them happy, well-adjusted, and learning at or above grade level. I believe we can catch your children up to the rest of their class if you can help us at home—"

"Fine." Max stood. "Send home whatever you want us to work on. We'll work it into our evening schedule. Not that it will be easy..." He stood and took one step toward the door.

"Please sit."

"We're not done? I need to get back to work."

"No, we are *not* done." He could see the temper building behind her eyes and hear it in her tone. He sat.

"We'd also like to help your children be more comfortable here. We have some exercises we do with children suffering from PTSD. Of course, what we do here is just a start. I also recommend you arrange for professional counseling. Since they lost their mother last year—"

Max stood again. "Are you a psychiatrist? Even a psychologist?"

The woman took a deep breath. "No, I'm not. That's why I recommend that you see someone professional. In the meantime, I'm an educator. We are trained to work with—"

"My kids aren't crazy, and they aren't unhappy at home. If they're unhappy here, maybe you need to fix that on your end." He turned, starting for the door.

"Max." The principal stood, her tone commanding.

Reluctantly, he turned. "We don't need your permission for the exercises we'll be doing here. They're simple art exercises. Please understand that I'm not asking. I'm letting you know what we will be doing starting next week."

Max cursed under his breath. "Then I don't know why you even bothered to ask." He was almost to the door when he heard her speak again.

"Max?"

He blew out an exasperated sigh but turned. "Yes?"

"Do you still ride a motorcycle?"

"What?"

"I thought perhaps you'd recognize me."

He almost growled his response. "You're the woman from the reception last Saturday, the one the drunk was hassling."

"I was also your next-door neighbor, though it's been many years."

"What are you talking about?"

"You are the Max Burnett who lived next door to the Reyes family when you were a teen, aren't you?"

"Yes." He could feel his forehead wrinkling. "Wait! You're Tyler Reyes's little sister?"

"That's right. I'm Amber Reyes. Your brother, Keith, was in my class."

He paused, considering his words, and then he said exactly what he felt. "I knew you were too young for this job." Growling to himself, he stomped from the office.

AMBER SAT AT HER DESK, stunned. She took a deep, cleansing breath, trying to calm herself. Had she ever met anyone as arrogant or as rude? And here she'd been thinking so well of him since his timely rescue in the park.

Liza stuck her head around the door. "Did he just say what I thought he said?"

Amber's voice shook as she answered. "I'm afraid he did."

"I've never heard anyone—"

"Me either."

"When did people stop respecting their kids' principal?"

"Around the time they started teaching their kids to disrespect all authority figures, I suspect." Amber steadied herself, finally able to stand. She shook herself, releasing some of the energy her anger had generated. "Starting Monday, we'll have Kate and Will Burnett in the office during the time the first graders are doing art projects. They can draw their art in here."

"Good." Liza made a note. "I'll tell Mrs. Nguyen."

"Thanks."

Liza stood. "Those kids sure are cute, all that coppery red hair. The little boy's hair is even naturally curly. So adorable! And they have those gorgeous brown eyes."

Like their father's. Appalled at herself, Amber said, "Yes, they are. They're adorable." She returned to her desk, still too upset to concentrate on her report. Instead she went to the books she'd gathered on children, art, and post-traumatic stress. She determined to help the Burnett twins settle in whether their father liked it or not. Calming herself, she looked up a chapter on healing after the loss of a parent.

More than two hours had passed since he left the principal's office and Max argued with himself as he left his office at the mine. *You didn't have to be rude,* his inner voice chided.

She had it coming, Max thought as he got into this car. *Who does she think she is, anyway, trying to psych out my kids?*

The kids did suffer when their mother left. Then, when they found out she died… Maybe they really could use some help. his inner voice suggested.

But from her? She looks like she could still be in school herself! Max snorted as he pulled out of the parking lot.

Admit it. She may look young, but she's a full-grown woman, and that makes her old enough to be a principal. You noticed how good she looked even when you were angry, his inner voice countered. *Maybe that's why you were so very rude? So you wouldn't show you are attracted to her?*

Yeah, okay. Max blew out a breath. *She's a beauty, no question. But she's Tyler Reyes' little sister, for heaven's sake! What is she? Maybe twenty years old? She shouldn't even be out of school!*

Do the math, his inner voice shot back. *Tyler was three years younger than you and his sister wasn't more than four years younger than that. Duh, Max. She said Keith was in her class. He's twenty-five. Then she's probably at least that old.*

Ugh. That's still young for a principal. Max merged onto the main road.

True, but maybe a town like Destiny doesn't have a lot of options. Maybe they hire good people even if they're younger and have less experience, his inner voice added.

Max scratched the side of his face as he waited for the light to turn green at an intersection. *I hadn't thought of that; it makes sense…*

He pulled into Mrs. Larsen's driveway where his kids attended an after-school program.

His inner voice still argued the point: *She did seem to have things in order in that office, and the school runs efficiently.*

Max cursed. *Okay, I get it. I should apologize.*

Yes. That would be wise, his inner voice teased.

Max cursed again, louder this time, and shut off the engine.

His inner voice had one more bit of advice: *Better put on a happier face before you see the kids. And try to act excited when you talk to them about— On second thought, better not talk about it at all. Let art therapy seem like a natural part of being in school.*

"Good point," Max growled aloud. He put on his happy face and went to pick up his children.

AMBER KNOCKED on the door of her mother's kitchen. "Mom? You busy?"

"Not too busy to see you, *chica.*" Olivia Reyes waved her daughter in. "You can keep me company while I roll these enchiladas."

Amber took a seat on the other side of the island and began helping with the process, putting chili sauce and cheese on each tortilla as Olivia put it into the pan.

Amber looked around. "Is Dad here?"

"Not at the moment. He went into town to run a few errands."

"Good." Amber sighed. "I need some girl talk."

Olivia grinned. "I'm all about girl talk. Tell me."

Amber began by talking about the wedding and reception. "Did you happen to see that drunk hassling me?"

"Yes, but I'm glad your father didn't see it."

Amber lifted an eyebrow. "Me too. Someone else noticed, though."

"I saw that too." Olivia looked speculative. "A nice-looking man. I didn't recognize him. Is he new here? Or a wedding guest from out of town?"

"He's new here, sort of."

Olivia raised a brow. "Sort of?"

"He's Max Burnett. His family lived next door to us when--"

"Oh yes. I remember the Burnetts, and I remember Max. He's moved back?"

"Yes. He has six-year-old twins in my school."

"So he's married now."

"He *was* married. He told me today that his wife died last year."

Olivia's expression lifted again. "You saw him today?"

"Yes, but I'd hardly call it a pleasant experience." Amber told her mother the whole story, starting with his late arrival half an hour after their appointment time and ending with the insulting way he left her office.

"Ouch. I'm glad your father didn't hear that."

"Right. Dad hasn't gotten used to the idea that his little girl is a big girl now and can fight her own battles. That's why I wanted to be sure he wasn't here before I said anything. Having Dad hunt this man down wouldn't exactly help the situation."

"You know your dad is like a chihuahua, right? All bark and very little bite?"

Amber chuckled. "Yeah, I know. Still, I'm glad—"

"Me too." Olivia rolled another enchilada. "You're sure he's the Max Burnett who used to live next door?"

"Certain. He remembered Tyler. He even remembered Tyler had a little sister."

"You sneered just now when you said that."

"He made me angry."

"Because of what he said? Or because you find him attractive—when he's not being a jerk."

Amber blew out a breath. "You do have a way of getting to the point."

Olivia raised an eyebrow.

"Maybe that has something to do with it," Amber finally acknowledged. "It's been a couple of years since Chad left and I haven't dated much. I haven't found anyone to date. This is Friday night and I'm planning to watch an old movie. Alone." She tried not to pout.

"The right man is out there. Maybe not this one—"

"Almost certainly not this one. And if the right guy is out there *somewhere*, that means he's not in Destiny, which is where I am."

"You're still young."

"And still single."

The kitchen door opened as Enrique Reyes stepped in. "*Hola, mija. Are you here for dinner?*"

Amber and her mother glanced at each other. Both answered, "Yes."

Chapter Four

Amber watched as the Burnett children responded to her direction. Handing each a large sheet of paper and a set of crayons, she asked Will and Kate to "draw a picture of how you're feeling right now."

Kate drew a round face with teardrops falling from large, round eyes. Will scribbled with black crayon. Both put down their crayons and looked up.

Will's black scribbling distressed her. She kept her voice steady. "Will, let's start with you. Can you tell me about your drawing?"

"You told me to draw how I'm feeling and that's how I'm feeling." The little boy pouted, defiant.

Even in this moody condition, Will was adorable. She couldn't help smiling. "Why don't you tell me how you're feeling? Use words this time."

Will pointed at the picture. "Like that."

Amber deliberately kept the smile on her face. She was about to try another tactic when Kate spoke up.

"I think my brother is feeling sad, just like I am," she said, smiling helpfully.

Kate is a people pleaser. "I'm going to give each of you a new sheet of paper and I'd like you to draw a picture of what makes you sad."

Kate looked eager. Will shrugged. With the paper in front of them, both began to draw. Soon Kate had a picture of a stick figure family. She began rounding out the figures: a man, a woman, a girl, a boy. Then she deliberately, carefully drew an X across the woman. Will took his time with his drawing, producing what looked like a person lying down on a bed. Then he added handles to the 'bed.' With a chill, Amber realized he'd drawn a coffin.

She worked to keep her voice steady. "Kate, let's start with you this time. Tell me about your picture."

The girl seemed eager to share. "First I drew my family, my old family before Mama left us." She turned the picture so it was right-side-up for Amber. "Then I crossed out Mama because she isn't with us anymore."

"I see," Amber said. "I also see why that makes you sad." She turned to Will. "Your turn," she said. "Tell me about your picture."

"It's our mom," he said, "like she looked last time we saw her."

Amber had taken a workshop last summer about age-appropriate behaviors and experiences for children. She remembered a lengthy discussion about the appropriate age for a child to attend the funeral of a loved one. The workshop only confirmed what she'd always believed —that it's better for the child to know what's happening. Now she wondered if that might not always be a good idea. "You saw her in a coffin." She tried to keep her voice neutral.

"Yeah." Will pushed the paper toward her. "I'm done with this. Can we go back to class?"

Amber patiently looked at her watch. "The art period isn't quite over yet. How about I give you another sheet of paper and you can draw anything you like."

Will shrugged again. "Yeah. Okay."

Kate said, "Can I draw a unicorn?"

Amber smiled. "Sure, or anything else you wish." She picked up the report she'd finished Friday and had just printed out for review, surreptitiously watching the children as she proofread her earlier work.

Kate's drawing really did look quite a bit like a unicorn. *She must have plenty of practice.* Amber watched as the little girl, her hair as red as her brother's, carefully lengthened the horn she'd already drawn and added a bright rainbow of color behind the figure's head. She wasn't exactly sure what Will was drawing.

Kate looked up, eager for Amber's approval. "That's a very good unicorn," Amber said with an encouraging smile, turning the picture one way and another. "Nicely done."

Kate beamed.

Amber turned her attention to Will. "Tell me about your picture, Will."

He bristled. "Can't you see? It's army guys shooting each other."

Amber licked her lips. *Remember nothing he draws can shock you—at least not as far as he knows.* "Let me turn it around so I can see it better." The army men were there, large groups of them facing each other. He'd also drawn blood, some on the arms or legs of the standing or kneeling men, more under the few that lay prone. "It looks like a hard-fought battle."

"Yeah." Will seemed disappointed.

Was Will deliberately trying to shock her? Amber guessed he might have expected her to be shocked. She checked her watch again. "Your class will be putting away their art projects now. You may join them. We'll do more drawing here on Wednesday."

"Great!" Kate stood. "Can I take my unicorn with me?"

"Yes, you may."

"Cool." Kate picked up her page. Will picked up his army men as well.

"Wait." Amber reached toward Will's picture and then put her hand back down. She couldn't justify keeping Will's picture when she let Kate keep hers. She scrambled for an excuse to explain why she'd stopped them both. Thinking fast, she asked, "Would you both like to put your names on your pictures? That way they won't get lost or mixed in with someone else's."

"Cool!" Kate said again. She picked up a dark marker and carefully began writing her name in the corner of her unicorn picture.

"Yeah. I guess." Despite his reluctant tone, Will seemed brighter now that he realized he could still take his picture with him.

"There you go," Amber said as they picked up their drawings. "See you Wednesday."

"I want to take my other drawings too." Will reached for the black scribbles and the picture of the coffin.

"Let me keep those," Amber said. "We'll work with them again next time."

"But I want to take them with me."

"Not this time." She tried to keep her smile warm while ushering the children toward the door. "See you on Wednesday."

Kate linked her arm through her brother's as they left the office. Given his attitude so far, Amber expected Will to pull away. Instead he put his hand over his sister's, stepping closer to her. Amber heard him mumble, "Are you okay?"

"Sure!" Kate said. "That was fun."

"For you, maybe."

Kate's face fell as she faced her brother's pout.

He brightened. "Yeah, part of it was fun," he said. He took his sister's hand. Together, they strolled down the hall.

MAX PARKED in front of the school. He'd worked through lunch so he could leave the office early. He almost wished he'd worn a hat. Then he could show up hat in hand, or maybe toss it in ahead of his arrival to see if she shot at it. He smiled at his little joke but thinking of the task ahead quickly sobered him. He straightened his back and marched into the front office. *Here goes nothing.*

"Hello, Mr. Burnett." The secretary couldn't keep her surprise from showing. "Do you have an appointment?"

"No. I wasn't sure how quickly I could get here. Is Ms. Reyes in?"

"Yes. Let me see if she can see you today."

"This won't take long." Max managed a pleasant smile.

The secretary tapped on the door of the inner office. "Ms. Reyes? Mr. Burnett is here to see you. He says it won't take long."

He heard the principal's voice but couldn't distinguish her words. The surprised tone suggested her attitude. That pleased Max. Better surprise than fuming anger.

The secretary stepped back. "Go right in."

"Thank you." He stepped forward but tapped on the door before entering.

"Please come in." Amber Reyes rose from her chair, smiling stiffly, extending her hand.

He took it. Her grasp was firm and confident. He liked a woman with a good, firm handshake. He noticed her expression too. Her forced smile reminded him that the last time they'd parted, they were not on the best of terms. He gestured toward the chair. "May I sit?"

"Yes, of course." She sat.

So did he. "Ms. Reyes, I want to apologize. My behavior last Friday was unconscionable. I'm sorry. All I can say for myself is it had been a very rough day and—" He paused.

"And you're a father who loves his children, who is very protective of them." Her eyes forgave him, even if she didn't say it aloud.

"You're putting words in my mouth," he said, but there was no heat in his complaint.

"I'm sorry. Go ahead." She sat back, waiting, her expression more guarded.

He smiled a little, feeling sheepish. "And I'm a dad who loves his kids and feels protective of them. You got it."

She smiled again. This one looked genuine. "No one can blame you for being protective of your children, but—"

"But I was unconscionably rude. I'm not usually like that. I behaved abominably, and I'm sorry."

"Thank you," Amber said. "I appreciate your apology." She took a deep breath.

He watched the motion, watching her chest rise and fall, and felt a quick jab of purely masculine interest, more than he'd felt in a while.

"Your children were in here during the art time for their class. Would you like to see what they drew?"

Despite his earlier judgment, Max's interest was piqued—and not just in the principal. "Yes. Sure. You can show me what you're doing with them."

Amber drew out the file where she had saved the children's pictures. She set them in front of Max one at a time, explaining what the children said about each.

Max winced when she showed him the black scribbles and told him how Will described them to her. "He said that?"

"Will knows his own mind," she said in a somber tone.

"I guess so." Max picked up Will's second picture. "What did he say about this one?"

"He said it's his mother as he last saw her."

"Oh." Max sat back. His opened his mouth to speak, but nothing came out. Finally, he said, "I didn't realize—" but left the sentence there.

"Kate's drawings weren't as dark." Amber pulled the other drawings and repeated his daughter's words. "After they finished these pictures, I gave them more paper and told them to draw whatever they liked."

Max grinned. "Let me guess. Kate drew a unicorn."

"She did. It was quite good, really."

"Should be. She's had lots of practice. And Will?"

"What he called 'army guys,' facing and fighting one another. Some were injured and bleeding. Some were—" She paused.

"Some were dead."

"Yes."

He blew out a sigh. "I see what you mean. That is, about the kids being unhappy. I knew this this past couple of years have been tough on them, but I didn't realize—" Again he left the sentence dangling. Then he said, "Kate seems to be adjusting better than Will."

"Or maybe she's just better at hiding it." Amber's hand reached toward him, although she stopped short of touching him.

His look darkened. "What do you mean?"

"Your daughter is a people pleaser," Amber said, her voice gentle. "She seemed eager to please me with everything she drew and what she said about it. It's possible she has feelings much like Will's, but she keeps them to herself because she knows it disturbs you, and the other adults in her life if she says what she really feels."

If Max had acted on his first thought, he'd have to apologize again, so he didn't ask the principal how she could know anything at all about what his daughter thought. Instead he said, "Kate does like to please—"

"That isn't necessarily a bad thing." Amber said reassuringly. "It only becomes a problem when the pleaser helps everyone else and functions, or even over-functions, for others instead of taking care of her own needs." She paused. "Of course, men can be people pleasers too. I'm using the feminine only because—"

"...because you're speaking of Kate."

"Yes. If Kate is trying to make you happy, maybe to fill some of the role her mother played in your life, she could be swallowing any negative feelings of her own."

Max felt himself on the verge of difficult questions again, but just then the woman reached for a book on a nearby shelf. "I've been reading up on it," she said, handing him a book about the risks of being a people pleaser.

Max recognized the name of the author, which surprised him greatly. He thumbed the first few pages. "May I borrow this?"

"Of course. I will have to ask you to return it though. It belongs to the faculty library."

"Yeah. Sure." He stood. "What can I do at home? You know, with the kids. What can I do to help with … all of this?"

She shrugged. "Talk to them. Get them to talk to you. Don't accept their first answers. Dig a little. Let them know that you care about how they really feel, even if it's sadness or anger."

"Especially with Kate," he murmured.

"With Will too. It's possible he's willing to act out here at school, with strangers, but will hide his real feelings from you. He doesn't want you to be disappointed in him."

"I hadn't thought of that."

"I wouldn't have either." She gestured toward the book he held. "The psychologists are educating me." This time her smile reached her eyes.

He returned the smile. "I'll let them educate me too. Thank you." He turned toward the door. "Oh, Ms. Reyes?"

"Yes?"

"Thanks for accepting my apology. I was out of line and I know it."

She nodded. "Thanks for being willing to apologize. I understand being protective of those you love. I've had some experience with that." She stood.

He started toward the door again.

"Mr. Burnett?"

He turned back, smiling gently. "Max."

"Max," she nodded in acknowledgment. "Thank you for coming in."

"You're welcome, Ms. Reyes."

"Amber."

"Amber," he said.

"Max?"

He turned back. "Yes?"

"How is your brother, Keith?"

He smiled, relieved the topic had changed. "He's doing great, working as an engineer and planning a wedding during Thanksgiving week."

"That's wonderful. Please give him my regards."

"Will do." Then his brow furrowed. "May I ask a question?"

"Sure. Go for it."

"You're younger than any principal I've ever known. How did you do that?"

She licked her lips, her eyes lowered. Then she looked right at him. "I was always one of those kids who love to learn. I knew I wanted to be an educator and I knew there'd be openings here in Destiny if I could hurry to get my degree. So, in the last two years of high school, I took every advanced placement course I could. Then I got special permission to take online classes from the local junior college while I was still in high school.

"I matriculated at the university right after high school with my General Ed done, got my bachelor's when I was twenty and earned my teaching credential at twenty-one. Then I took a job as a third-grade teacher and started taking night classes toward my master's in admin-istration. I taught for three years while finishing my administrative credential and that's when the job opened here in Destiny. Being prin-cipal here was my dream, so I leapt at it."

"You're telling me I'm in the presence of a genius."

Her expression fell as her face flushed. "See why I don't talk about this much? I'm no genius. I just wanted this enough to work hard for it." She stood, clearly dismissing him. "Thank you for coming in."

"You're welcome," he said, leaving her standing by her desk.

Amber had looked so beautiful just now. He looked at the book in his hand. That visit hadn't gone as expected. Now he had both reading and thinking to do. Walking toward his car, he ordered himself to think about his kids and their difficult adjustment without dwelling too much on their principal.

Chapter Five

Amber tossed a jaunty goodbye wave to Liza as she left the front office—on a Tuesday, in the middle of the school day. A chance to leave school for lunch didn't happen very often, especially a lunch with her cousin, Skye, who had practically grown up as her sister. She checked with her assistant principal to be sure everything was going smoothly, then noted the time so she could return within an hour, or maybe just a little longer.

"This is great." Amber slid into the passenger seat of Skye's compact sedan. "You can drop in on me any time, even in mid-week. No, especially in mid-week. You don't realize what a rare treat this is. I've been trying to get together with Paris, ever since we worked side-by-side at Sunny's reception. The best we could manage was a half-hour chat in the office."

Skye looked impressed. "Then I should thank you for joining me."

"Oh no! Thank you for coming and giving me the excuse." She grinned, and Skye smiled back. "But you don't have to feed me every time you come. Sometimes I can buy, though it will likely be at Joe's Sandwich Shop and not Berman's."

Skye pulled onto the road. "I owe you, girl. After all you did for me those months I was in lock-up and rehab. You don't realize how much it meant that you came to visit me so often. Let me take you out occasionally when I'm in the neighborhood. It's a small way to say thank you."

"You're welcome. Glad I could help. Still, you won't have to treat every time you come to town. You're a starving student, after all."

"Not anymore. Now I'm a successful artist."

"Do tell."

"I'll be scrambling to keep up with all the commissions from the

Tahoe show as well as class projects. Thank goodness some of the commission pieces can give me class credit, too."

"That's wonderful, Skye! I'm so proud of you!"

"Thanks. It's nice to hear people say that after—"

"Forget about the 'after.' We're here now, and this is a great place to be."

Skye nodded in response.

Amber watched out the window as they neared the former grounds of the Children of Rah compound, the place where Skye and her sister, Sunny, were born—the place where they'd grown up under questionable circumstances until Amber's mother carried them away.

They passed the wide entryway to what had been the cult's headquarters, once strewn with makeshift, thrown-together squatters' structures. Now it stood proudly, carefully built up with impressive buildings that featured valley views, well-groomed landscaping, and an understated sign: "Welcome to the Destiny Health Spa."

Amber mused, "I guess the developers couldn't think of a better name for their new money-maker than the one the forty-niners put on the place. The miners thought the gold they found here would be their destiny. These investors are looking for a different kind of fortune."

"Never underestimate what you can earn by pampering people," Skye said. Then she added, "I thought the resort would have opened by now."

"It was supposed to open a couple of weeks ago. I hear the new owners are getting nervous."

Skye shook her head. "Who ever imagined the Children of Rah disaster would become a place where people could go for their health?"

"I know, right?" Amber said. "Given what you and Sunny went through there…" She paused, letting the memories pass. "The spa has had a few technical difficulties. Their grand opening was delayed by some issue with their communications technology, but they'll open by mid-October. We expect to get more new people in Destiny then."

"The town already has several new families, right? Because of the mine?"

"At the start of the school year, we had eight new families with children in elementary grades, and we've added another since."

"All good, contributing families, I hope."

"Exactly. Destiny is growing."

"Who would have thought?"

Amber paused, contemplating privacy laws and what she was allowed to say before she asked, "Do you remember a family named Burnett?"

Skye wrinkled her brow. "It rings a faint bell. Oh, wait! Were those the people who lived next door to your family when Sunny and I first moved in?"

"Right. You remembered."

"I remember the couple. Mr. Burnett picked a flower from his rose garden once and put it in my hair." Skye touched the space over her ear, smiling at the memory. "They had a boy your age and an older son too, right? He was older than Tyler. I was only nine, so he seemed like an adult to me. If I remember right, they sold that place and moved soon after he graduated."

"That's right. They were our neighbors the whole time I was growing up...until they moved. Max is the older son you remember. The younger, Keith, was in my class." She paused, smiling. "We all thought Max was so grown up because he rode a motorcycle to school."

Skye chuckled. "Yeah, I remember."

"He has moved back to Destiny."

"Who? Max?"

"Right. Max Burnett. He has six-year-old twins in our first grade, adorable little people with bright red hair." Amber stopped there. Everything she had said to that point was either public record or evident to anyone who saw the Burnett family. To go beyond that would be a violation of professional ethics.

"Imagine someone growing up here and wanting to come back as an adult." Skye gave Amber a slanted look.

"You're right. There aren't that many of us who go away and choose to return. Who knows? We may see more of that as the town grows larger." They reached the parking lot at Berman's Mesa and were soon seated inside.

"I hope you're looking at a good school year." Skye picked up their conversation where they'd dropped it. "Is it going to be as good as last year? Maybe better?"

Amber grinned. "You said it."

"You always say that this year will be the very best ever for your school."

"I imagine every administrator says that at the start of every year. We all hope for things to get better and better from one year to the next." She sipped from her water glass. "But your turn now. Tell me more about your show in Tahoe. Details. I want details!"

Skye leaned back, her look contented. "It could hardly have gone better. When I first got there, I'd already made all the price stickers for each piece. Lachlan—he's the owner of the gallery—came in while I was setting the pieces out. He shook his head and started tsk-tsking as he went from one piece to the next.

"I said, 'What? Too high?' He said, 'Oh no. With the crowd we expect here, if your prices are this low, they'll think you don't value your work. I suggest you go at least a third higher, maybe half again as much.'

"I thought he was kidding, but he assured me he meant every word, especially on the sculptures and the larger canvases. I gritted my teeth, but I know Lachlan knows his clientele." She paused to take a sip of water.

"So you marked everything up?"

Skye nodded. "Between thirty and forty percent."

"And—?"

"We sold nearly half the pieces the first night. Everything else was sold out before we shut the show down yesterday, and I have four commissions, people who want me to create 'something unique, but with the same theme as...' and then they name the painting or sculpture they wanted but couldn't get because it had already sold."

Amber reached across the table to touch Skye's hand. "May I have the honor of touching the art world's next great discovery?"

Skye laughed as she grasped Amber's hand. "It's not that big a deal. It was a small show in a secluded gallery."

"A very exclusive gallery that caters to a highly select crowd." Amber raised her glass. "If you're in with that group, you're in."

Skye nodded. "I sure hope so." Then she added, "Yeah. It was cool. It felt good."

The conversation ebbed as both women studied their menus. Over the top of hers, Amber also surreptitiously studied her cousin.

"You don't have to do that, you know." Skye lifted her chin.

"Do what?"

"You're checking me over, trying to see if I'm healthy or maybe using again. You've done that for years. I can't say I blame you, but your concern is no longer necessary. I'm clean, Amber, and I fully intend to stay clean."

Amber felt her face warming. "I didn't realize I was doing that, but you're right. It's become a habit. Please don't be offended. You know I'm just concerned."

"I know. Your mom and dad do the same thing. And Summer. My sister makes at least one thorough study of me, head to toe, every time I see her."

"She cares too. We've all been worried. Scared for you, really."

"I know, and I've given you reason." Skye sat up straighter.

Their server arrived, ready to take their order. Amber spoke first. "I'd like the smothered pork cutlet, please. Red sauce."

"Yes, ma'am. Good choice." The server made a note. "And you, miss?" He turned all the charm he could manage toward Skye.

"I'll take the Cobb salad, no cheese or sour cream." Skye gave her menu to the server.

"You've got it. Can I start an appetizer for you while you wait?"

Amber said, "No. I think that's enough." When the server moved out of hearing range, Amber said, "He was flirting with you, you know."

"I know." Skye looked in the direction the young waiter had gone. "He's a cutie, but way too young for me."

"I don't know. He looked fairly close to your age."

Adopting an Indiana Jones drawl, Skye said, "It's not the years, it's the mileage."

Amber nodded. "I get it. Okay, so another question: You're suddenly avoiding dairy?"

"For the moment. I don't know if it will last. My new doctor, the one I'm supposed to see for ADHD thinks dairy might be interfering with my new medication." She waved dismissively. "I agreed to skip the milk products for a month, just to see if it helps."

"Ugh. I don't know how I'd feel about that. No ice cream? No ham and cheese sandwiches? No pizza?" Her voice rose higher with each. "Or can you use non-dairy substitutes?"

"I've tried them all. Cheesy food is better with nothing than with soy cheese. Ew!" She pulled a face. "But there are non-dairy ice cream substitutes that are very good. It's true that no pizza is kind of a bummer, but if it helps me stay off the…" She paused. "…stay off the stuff I'm supposed to stay off of, it's well worth it."

Amber picked up on the cue. Skye never named her drugs of choice. "How's it going for you? The medication, I mean. You look healthy."

"I am healthy, and it's largely your fault. For a long time, you were the only person I knew who still believed in me."

"I'll always believe in you." Amber blinked back tears and placed her hand over Skye's.

"Getting arrested was a well-disguised blessing." Skye gave a little laugh, wiping a few tears of her own. "Going to jail, a tough jail where I couldn't get the stuff that fueled my addiction, helped more than anything I'd tried. By the time the judge let me finish my sentence in rehab, I'd had nothing intoxicating or hallucinatory for weeks. The physical addiction was long past. I only had to banish the emotional and psychological cravings."

"And get some prescription meds to help you deal with the ADHD so you weren't self-medicating on the street."

Skye quirked a half-smile. "Yeah. That, too."

"I'm glad you've come so far."

Their food arrived and they let the conversation drift as they ate.

ALL THAT WEEK, Max watched his children carefully. By the next Friday morning, a week after his last talk with Amber, he realized she was right: Both children were more depressed than they'd let on. The book Amber lent him offered important insights. Now he could clearly see much of what she'd been trying to tell him earlier.

Kate, definitely a pleaser, struggled to do anything and everything that would bring his attention to her in positive ways. Will just wanted the attention, however he could get it, and a deep anger glowed in the embers of his mother's death. He needed to keep a close eye on these two. That brought him to another resolution. He skipped lunch and called the school to make an appointment.

AMBER LOOKED up as Liza ushered Max into her office. "Friday afternoon and here we are again." She stood, shook Max's hand, and waved him toward the chair. They both sat. "Should we make this a standing appointment?"

"I'd really prefer to sit." His lips lifted in amusement.

Amber rolled her eyes.

"Sorry. That was too easy."

"And not worth the trouble." She smiled to soften the sting. "What can I do for you, Max?"

"I've been watching the kids. You're right about both of them, and for the first time, I'm becoming concerned." He struggled with what he was trying to say. "I mean, I've been concerned about them all along. What our family went through was, well, rough. But I thought they were doing okay. Adjusting, you know?" His look begged her understanding.

"Um-hm." She nodded, encouraging him to go on.

"I realize now that I have a long way to go in helping the kids through this adjustment. The book you lent me made a lot of difference. Oh, by the way, I brought it back. I gave it to your secretary."

"Thanks. What did you learn?"

"I realize now that my kids may need professional help." He paused. "Not that I don't appreciate what you're doing, and I know you're a professional at what you do—"

"It's all right, Max." She leaned toward him, letting her body language back up her words. "I know exactly what you're saying, and I agree. In fact, I recommended that at the beginning."

His brow furrowed. "Yes, I guess you did."

"I believe both your children could use the guidance of a professional counselor to help them through this…difficult time."

He dropped his eyes, focusing on his folded hands. "I've always had a…well, I guess a prejudice against therapists. I mean, you hear about people who can't make a move without consulting their therapist, and it always makes me wonder if those folks don't have a mind and will of their own. Often I suspect they don't." He looked up. "Do you know what I'm saying?"

"I do." Amber straightened. "Some people rely too much on therapy. You and I both know we aren't talking about that with Kate and Will. We're talking about finding someone trained in helping children through serious trauma who can help *your* children work through what they've experienced and how they feel about it."

"Exactly. I need a referral. Can you help me find that person?"

Amber reached into her desk drawer and pulled out a file. "I've been doing some research this week, and I've called the offices of several therapists. Sometimes I couldn't get past the office assistant, but often the therapists themselves were willing to speak to me." She looked up quickly. "Of course, I didn't offer any names or specifics, but I told them about our school and that I'm working with children who've recently lost their mother. They usually asked questions, and I was careful not to violate your privacy or to speculate on answers I don't know, but I answered as best I could."

She lifted the top sheet from her file and handed it to Max. "This office was recommended by three other therapists I spoke with. Dr. Miles Schafer specializes in working with traumatized children, and lately his practice has narrowed so he mostly sees children under ten who've been hurt by having parents taken from them under traumatic circumstances, or sometimes by parents willfully abandoning them."

"Both apply here." Max had mumbled it under his breath, but Amber heard him.

She chose not to ask. "I spoke with Dr. Schafer. He'll be happy to see your children."

Max read the page and looked up. Relief and gratitude showed where before there had been only distress. "Thank you. Thanks so much." He reached out a hand.

Amber took it. "You're welcome, Max. I'd like it if you can keep me posted on how the kids are doing."

"Sure. You deserve at least that much." He started for the door and then paused, as if he wished to say more. "The executive officers at the mine have all been invited to a pool party at Reed Orchards. It's tomorrow afternoon. Any chance I'll see you there?"

Amber brightened. "Yes, I'm planning to go. The Reeds' harvest party is a highlight of the year for everyone in Destiny."

"Super. I guess we'll see you there."

Amber nodded.

"Well…thanks again, Ms. Reyes…Amber."

"You're welcome, Max."

She watched him go. Suddenly her office felt very large. And very, very empty.

Chapter Six

The parties at Reed Orchards highlighted Destiny's social calendar, such as it was. The two Reed families celebrated special occasions at the compound in the center of their spreading apple orchards. Amber always enjoyed their casual and homey gatherings, but on this particular Saturday, she dressed with care. Her parents would probably be there, so she chose clothing her dad would find appropriate. She was acutely aware that Max would be there too; aware of how things had shifted between them and changed to something…more positive.

Parents sometimes got carried away when they felt she was criticizing their parenting or saying something negative about their children. Now that Max understood, he seemed fully on board with everything she was trying to do. The change in him had been … nice. Max had become *very* nice.

She picked out a modest swimsuit. As the elementary school principal, she needed to maintain decorum. Though the suit offered good coverage, it also showed her tall, slim shape to full advantage. A light cover-up and sandals completed her ensemble. Pleased with her appearance, she packed her full set of picnic dishes and a pasta salad and grabbed a bottle of sunscreen on her way out. Getting into her car, she wended her way up the mountain road.

AT THE BURNETT HOME, preparations went somewhat differently. Max had double-checked to make certain the invitation included families. Assured that it did, he happily announced his plans to the kids shortly after lunch.

"We get to go swimmin'? Cool!" Will bounced around the kitchen, filling the small space with six-year-old energy. "I'll put my swim shorts on under my regular clothes. Okay, Dad?"

"That'll be fine, Son."

"Yes!" Will did a fist pump and charged down the hall to change.

His excitement should have been contagious, but Kate seemed immune. "Do we have to, Daddy? I don't swim real good."

"It'll be fine, Kate." Max pulled her in, hugging her close. "They'll probably have a place where the water won't even come up to your chest. You and Will can just splash and play and not worry about a thing."

When distress did not fade from her expression, he added, "If the water looks too deep and you don't want to get in, you don't have to, not even a little bit."

Kate's relieved smile brought welcome relief to Max as well. "Go put on your swimsuit under your regular clothes. Then if you decide you want to go in, you can. It's all up to you."

"Thanks, Daddy." Kate strode down the hall with a dignity that belied her young years.

You've got quite the little lady growing up there, Max, he told himself. Too bad she caught her mother's fear of the water. He sighed. The kids would have swimming lessons next summer for sure.

THE PARTY WAS WELL underway when Amber arrived. The Reeds had a pair of refrigerators in the large outdoor kitchen behind their two homes. Amber added her salad to the mix of dishes others had brought. A dozen adults and older kids swam and played in the large pool while another dozen or so relaxed in the sun. A third group had teamed up for a lively game of volleyball on the lawn.

Amber's eyes went quickly to the shallow end of the pool where a group of children played with water toys. She was pleased to see the Burnett twins in the mix, equally pleased to see a barrier float marking the place where the pool floor began to drop, and the water deepened.

"They're having fun." The familiar voice behind her caused Amber to turn. She couldn't help the warm tingle inside as she greeted Max.

"Looks like it," she agreed.

"I was worried about Kate. Her mother was afraid of the water and I think she passed that fear on to our daughter."

"That shallow pool at the end seems to have taken care of the problem."

"I have to keep an eye on Will, though. He wants to try his luck in the deeper water. He keeps slipping under the barrier to see how far he can go."

"Looks like it drops fairly quickly."

"He can get several feet out before he has to start bobbing to keep his head up. Then he usually gets a bit spooked and bobs his way back into the shallow end."

"I've been planning on a good swim before dinner. I'll watch out for him."

"Thanks. I promised to help with the grilling, and the guys are just getting that started, so I appreciate your help."

"No problem." Amber smiled her farewell and walked to the far side of the pool. Wearing her sunglasses, she chanced a peek in Max's direction and caught him looking at her as he was cleaning one of the grills. Suppressing a grin, she decided to have a little fun and impishly took her time lifting her cover-up over her head, stretching her long body to full height. Then she slowly wove her long hair into a tight braid, wrapping the end with a band. Taking off her sunglasses, and slipping them into her bag, she strode to the end of the diving board, lifted her arms, bounced twice, and executed a simple, clean dive. *Well, that was fun,* she thought as she came to the surface

Mindful of her promise to Max, Amber kept Will's red hair in her peripheral vision as she swam several lengths of the pool while other swimmers respectfully cleared a lane. As she completed her fifth lap, she saw Will go under the barrier. She got to him just as he started bouncing to breathe. "Gotcha!" she said, playfully catching his arm as she reached him. "Let's get you back under the barrier where you can keep an eye on Kate." She eased him back into the shallow end.

He ducked his head under the barrier and then whispered, "You want me to keep an eye on Kate?"

Amber whispered back. "She doesn't want to admit it, but you know she's afraid of the water. She needs you to stay close to make sure she's not scared."

"Oh. I didn't think about that."

"It's okay. She'll be fine as long as you stay close." Amber winked, including him in their conspiracy to protect his sister.

Will didn't go under the barrier for the rest of the party. He stayed near Kate until the announcement that the food was ready, and he climbed out when everyone else did.

Amber climbed out and pulled on her cover-up just as her parents arrived. She made a point of introducing her mom and dad to Max and his children. Her parents spoke with Max about his family, sharing memories of when the two families had lived next door. Amber's mother asked Max to catch her up on what was happening with his parents and his brother. Max shared where his parents were living and how the family busily prepared for Keith's upcoming wedding. He finished that description just in time for the host's announcement, "Time to eat!"

Amber took her place in line behind her mom and dad and then eased the two Burnett children in front of her, getting out her own picnic dishes for each of them. As they waited their turn, Will motioned her to lean close. When she did, he whispered, "I did it. I watched out for Kate like you said."

"Yes, I saw. You did a good job."

Amber hid a smile as Will puffed out his little chest.

Her satisfaction in the day only grew when Max pulled her aside later on. "Thanks for keeping an eye on my kids and for seeing that they got food. I meant to use my dishes. I'm sorry you ended up getting yours."

"You were busy serving, and the kids didn't know where your picnic things were. It was no problem. Really."

"Thank you anyway." She noticed he smiled slightly as he added, "You looked great out there in the pool today. You, uh, you swim well."

Aha! So he'd been watching after all. "Thanks."

"Your parents look good too," he said. "They're talking about having us over sometime, just to catch up more on the family."

"That's great," Amber answered. "You'll enjoy my mom's cooking and my dad's grilling and I know they'll be happy to hear more about your family." She let her eyes settle on the children, who helped themselves to more of Mrs. Larsen's cookies.

Max followed her line of sight. In a low voice, he said, "I see Dr. Schafer this coming week. Thanks for setting that up too."

"You're welcome, but I just did a bit of research. You set it up and I'm glad you did."

"I think I'm glad too." Max managed a half-smile. "I'll let you know next week."

Amber chuckled. "You'll be fine. Really. You'll see."

"I hope so."

She gave him a mischievous smile. "You may even find that you like therapy."

His expression soured. "You really know how to hurt a guy."

She laughed again at his exaggerated eye roll as they rounded up a matched set of cute little redheads.

Despite Amber's prediction, Max found himself smiling as he left Dr. Schafer's office. *I like him. He's easy to talk to.* Schafer had been *so* easy to talk to that Max had dumped out much more than he'd ever expected to say. The therapist had been calm even through the worst revelations, like he'd heard it all before. Maybe he had. Maybe he'd heard much worse.

Surprised that the doctor wanted to meet with him alone before seeing the twins, Max went in with a load of skepticism and a rather large chip on his shoulder, but Dr. Schafer easily brushed past all that. The therapist had a gentle approach, like Mr. Rogers. He'd be good with the kids. That thought made Max smile again. The number one requirement for anyone he let into his personal life was that they be good with, and for, his children. He didn't know how to be a father, but he wanted to do it well.

He hadn't aways been like that. He sighed, remembering. He was entirely work-focused when he met Isabel, intent on building a career before he even thought about settling down. Beautiful, smart, spoiled, witty, high maintenance, sought-after Isabel had rocked his world and altered his focus. She insisted on marriage or nothing, leading him to the altar by a ring in his nose. He hadn't seen her coming. He certainly hadn't seen what came next, though that circus of a wedding should have given him a clue. He walked toward his car remembering all the red flags her parents had waved even before the wedding day. He should have seen the signs. If he hadn't been so over-the-moon about Isabel, he probably would have. Idly, he wondered how many awful marriages started out just that way.

He reached his car, started the engine, and turned up the hill, knowing he'd need an arrangement with his bosses so he could make this trip once a week. He appreciated that Dr. Schafer's office was in one of the rich bedroom communities in the foothills, not all the way to the valley. As he calculated it, he could pick up the kids at school, make the drive down the hill, wait while they had their appointment or sit in if the doctor preferred, get them to Mrs. Larsen's and return to the mining office, all within ninety to a hundred minutes. He hoped the VP would be good with that. Corporate had policies for this kind of thing.

As he neared town, his first thought was to drive to the school. He wanted to tell Ms. Reyes—Amber—how well things had gone today. She'd arranged it all. That thought made him grin. He wouldn't have known how to start. She was right about the therapist, too. He checked the time and reluctantly decided he needed to get back to the office, squelching his unhatched plan to report to Ms. Reyes. He chose not to admit, even to himself, that he might be looking for an excuse to see her again.

"THAT'S A GREAT UNICORN, KATE." Amber held up Kate's latest art, giving the little girl the affirmation she sought so hungrily.

"Can I take this one back to class?"

"Yes, you may."

"And me? Can I take my army men back to class?"

Amber looked again at Will's picture. This one had fewer figures, but most of them were down and most of the page was red with the blood of the victor's imaginary enemies. If that was all that concerned her, she'd probably let it go, but considering Will's other pictures gave her pause. "Will, how would you feel if I hung on to this picture and added it to the others in the folder we're keeping?"

Will pouted. "Kate gets to keep her picture."

Amber looked to Will's sister. "Kate honey, how would you feel about letting me keep this one unicorn?"

Kate did not pout. She bubbled. "Oh yes! Let me give it to you. Like a present!"

"Is it okay if I put it in the folder we're saving?"

Less enthusiastically, Kate answered, "Okay."

Amber thanked them both for their visit and ushered them back to class. Then she sat down to review the current drawings together with the others she'd saved. In the three weeks the twins had been coming to her office, Kate's images had grown steadily lighter. Amber's first question was always, "How do you feel right now?" Today Kate had drawn a garden full of yellow daisies under a rainbow. When asked why she felt so happy, Kate said she loved making new friends. Amber smiled with satisfaction. At least something was going well.

She looked back through Kate's file. It had been a week since Kate drew anything sad or mentioned her mother. Amber turned to the other file. Will was a different story. He hadn't mentioned his mother again—not specifically—but the images were dark, becoming even darker. Today's army men showed more blood than usual. Will had even drawn what looked like entrails coming out of one body. The little guy had some artistic talent, though the details he'd chosen to include had become increasingly gruesome.

She put the files back together, adding today's notes from her discussion with the children, and was just setting them inside her cupboard when Liza tapped at her door. "Ms. Reyes?"

"Your timing is excellent, Liza. I was just about to ask you to call Max Burnett, to set up another appointment."

Liza grinned. "I don't think that will be necessary. He's here, waiting to see you."

Amber put the picture file back on her desk. "Show him in."

"Whew." Max blew out a long breath, leaning back in his chair. "I didn't realize…" He felt sheepish as he met Amber's eyes—not only sheepish, but maybe a bit off-balance. Amber was more attractive than he'd remembered, much more attractive with those stunning dark eyes. He forced his thoughts back to the less pleasant subject. "Obviously I didn't realize. Thank you for drawing my attention to this…this problem, and for leading us to Dr. Schafer. We've met with him twice now and he's great with the kids."

"You're welcome. It's my job to notice when something's off with our students and to help them—or get them help—wherever I can."

"I'm sorry I wasn't more receptive…sooner." He reopened the file folders of pictures. "I'd like to take these drawings to Dr. Schafer, if you don't mind."

"Of course. I've made photocopies of these images, so you can take these home if you wish. I can't let my notes go, though. Privacy laws allow me to show them to you, here in the office, but I shouldn't show them to anyone else."

"What if I were to sign a written permission slip allowing you to share your notes with the children's psychologist?"

"That would make it legal, I suppose, but I still wouldn't feel good about sending the notes. They're rather cryptic. When I show them to you, I can explain what they mean, but without me to explain them—"

Max reached forward, touching her hand. "Come with us."

"What?"

"Next Wednesday, when we have our regular appointment and I pick the kids up in front of the school, why don't you come with us? I'll call ahead and let Dr. Schafer know what we have in mind. You can show him this folder and tell him what you've been doing with the art therapy. Then you can share your notes and explain them."

"I can't just pick up and leave in the middle of the school day."

"Surely there are exceptions when you're dealing with a student's welfare." He hoped his pleading expression might help. He watched her face change. *Yes!*

"Student welfare *is* primary..." She pursed her lips, looking thoughtful.

He waited. Even her thoughtful expression was beautiful.

"All right. I'll come with you next Wednesday, but it needs to be a one-time thing."

"Great. Sure." He tried not to babble with relief. "I really appreciate this."

"I'll be ready next Wednesday. Is there anything else?"

Max recognized he was being dismissed. "That's it for now. See you next week."

"Yes, of course." She rose and walked with him to the door. For Liza's sake, she spoke up when she said, "Thank you for coming in, Mr. Burnett."

He gave her a quick wink as he said, "You're welcome, Ms. Reyes."

She watched as he walked into the hall, his walk so easy, so confident. *Be careful here, Amber,* her inner voice warned. *You could find yourself getting in much deeper than you imagine.* The flutter in her heart warned that might already be the case.

THROUGHOUT THE DAYS THAT FOLLOWED, Amber wondered if she'd made a mistake. Getting too involved with this family could certainly come back to bite her. Especially if she spent too much time around that very attractive man. She sighed. Yes, he was single, but he had also given the clear impression that he wasn't looking. And he was lugging a trainload of baggage, what with everything his late ex-wife and her family had put him through. That alone should have steered her away. On the other hand, he was blessed with Will and Kate, and though he didn't always seem to know how to parent them, at least he was trying. That was more than some single parents did. From her place as principal, she'd seen both men and women remarry quickly, just to hand off some of the responsibility of caring for their children.

She had even more reason to wonder about her choice when she received a call the following Monday afternoon. A pushy assistant from Dr. Schafer's office demanded that she "come prepared for her interview," as if the meeting was all about her. Then the woman added, "Be sure to bring any therapy licensure you may have and a bibliography of sources you used when practicing art therapy with the Burnett children."

What? That was ridiculous! "I don't see why that's necessary."

"Bring it with you when you come on Wednesday." The woman clicked off.

Incensed by both the officious attitude and the hang-up, Amber fumed. Then some of the woman's phrases came back to her: "licensure" and "practicing therapy" stood out. The realization was abrupt. Dr. Shafer was preparing to accuse her of practicing without a license. The awareness hit her like a smack with a wet towel. In that moment, she knew she might have more to be concerned about than taking a couple of hours away from the office. An accusation like that wasn't likely to hold—she wasn't charging anyone for therapy—but it could surely mess up her year and cause trouble with the school board.

She consoled herself that all would be okay. She'd had classes and workshops to prepare her as an administrator and this basic level of therapy was included in that preparation. She could easily get a bibliography together. Most of the books were right here in her office. Even as she thought it, she knew she could easily be accused of overreaching with the Burnett children. Was her job in jeopardy? "Liza, can you come in?" She had some scrambling to do.

MAX SAID his goodbyes at the mining office and started toward the school to pick up his children and their attractive principal. His bosses at Río Blanco Mining were understanding of his situation. With their encouragement, he now saved a few hours of computer work to do from home in the evenings after the kids were asleep. Those evening work sessions gave him the freedom to take the time he needed for the therapy appointments.

He'd need that today. He wondered what was going on that the doctor expected this to be a longer session than usual? And he wanted to see Amber alone first? That didn't make sense. Max turned in at the school. There they were, the three of them, Amber and his twins. They looked good together. He felt the corners of his mouth turning up as his heart warmed to the view.

He stopped the car and went around to open the passenger side for Amber and the back seat for Will and Kate. "Everybody, remember your seat belts," he said. "Ms. Reyes, thanks for joining us today." He looked at the materials she carried. That was more than just the picture file and notes. "What's all this?"

Amber's smile was tight. "Dr. Schafer wanted to see several things."

He directed the car out of the lot and back to the highway. "Things like …?"

With her eyes, Amber signaled to the back seat. "Perhaps we can discuss it later?"

"Gotcha." What was it she couldn't say in front of the kids? This kept getting stranger. He picked up speed as they left town. Well, he'd find out soon enough. He focused on the drive.

Chapter Seven

"Thank you, Dr. Schafer." Amber shook the therapist's hand as she left his office, grateful his smile seemed as genuine as hers. That visit hadn't started well, but it had turned out okay. She turned to the expectant faces in the waiting room, immediately struck by the differences in their expressions: curiosity and maybe some concern in Max; eagerness in Kate; something darker—maybe resentment—in Will. "Kate, you're up," Max said, holding the door until the therapist greeted the bubbly little girl. He closed the door behind her.

Amber took the chair next to Max. "That went well," she said, choosing to slide past the parts that did not. She looked around Max to the child sitting to his left. "Dr. Schafer agrees with me about your talent, Will. He said your army men look very realistic."

Will brightened. "Cool. He really said that?"

"He did, and he wants you to tell him more about your drawings in a few minutes."

"Cool," Will said again. He picked up a children's magazine and flipped through it, but he smiled as he turned the pages.

Max touched Amber's hand and mouthed, *Thank you.*

She mouthed back, *You're welcome.*

He looked like he wanted to ask more, but she shook her head, glancing at Will in warning, and picked up a magazine about food and cooking. Max took the hint and went back to an out-of-date issue of *National Geographic*. Minutes later, Will traded places with Kate, who came out gushing about the therapist's responses to her drawings. "He 'specially liked my unicorn."

"That's super, honey." Max looked over Kate's head at Amber. "Kate-love, do you think you could entertain yourself with a magazine for a few minutes while Ms. Reyes and I take a little walk?"

"Do I have to look at a magazine? I wanta play with the Magna Doodle."

Max smiled indulgently as he stood, stroking Kate's coppery hair. "That's great, Katydid. Do you think you can draw a unicorn for me?"

"Sure, Daddy." Her happy grin told Amber a great deal about the girl's improvement.

Max held out his hand. "Ms. Reyes? Walk with me?"

"I'd love to." They stepped into the outside hall together.

"WHAT WAS THAT ALL ABOUT?" Max didn't know whether he was more curious or concerned, but he knew he needed to hear all that had happened.

"The good doctor was on the verge of accusing me of practicing without a license."

"No!" Max winced. *Hypocrite!* his inner voice warned. *Didn't you say pretty much the same thing when she first told you what she wanted to do?* He quieted his internal critic. "How did that go?"

"Everything's fine."

The deep breath she took and released told him she meant it, but also drew his interest in a much different way "Um-hm. Go on."

"He relaxed quite a bit when he realized I'm a trained educator with a fair number of classes and workshops behind me, ones designed to help me recognize symptoms of mental illness or abuse in the kids I teach."

"Mental illness?" That hit Max hard. "Are you saying my kids are crazy? Or abused?"

"Oh please, Max." Amber's happy expression faded. "Nobody is saying that, but even a situational depression—that is, depression that has an obvious cause—even that can be considered a form of mental illness. A very mild form," she added when he opened his mouth to speak. "Ignored, it can become much more serious."

"I see," he said, not entirely pacified. He wondered. Had it really been that bad?

"I gave him the bibliography of my sources about art therapy and

pointed out that as soon as I realized the extent of the children's prob
—" She paused. "When I saw the extent of the children's worries, I
recommended professional help immediately."

"I can testify to that," Max said, his mind still ruminating on the
term *mental illness*.

"It looks like your testimony won't be necessary. Dr. Schafer
thanked me for the referral and treated me like another professional. In
a different profession, to be sure. Still, he ended up with a much more
accepting attitude than when I first went in there."

"That's a relief," Max said, but his thoughts had already gone elsewhere. He looked at his cell phone, checking the time. "He's taking a
lot longer than usual with Will."

The receptionist stepped out. "Mr. Burnett, Dr. Schafer would like
you to see you."

"Oh. Yeah, sure." Max felt anxiety creeping over him as he held the
door for Amber. He nodded to the receptionist, cast a concerned look
at Amber, and tapped on the therapist's door.

His son's face shocked him. Red-rimmed eyes and blotchiness
made it clear Will had been crying. Will stared at the ground as Max
entered the office but looked up at his father with an expression of raw
pain and defiant anger. Max felt his heart jump into overdrive. He
swallowed the lump in his throat. "Will? Dr. Schafer? What's
going on?"

"Have a seat, Mr. Burnett." Dr. Schafer's professional smile didn't
slip. "Will has something he'd like to say to you."

Max sat. This was bad. "What is it, son?"

Will started to speak, but once more looked at the floor.

"It's okay, Will," the therapist prompted. "You can tell your dad.
Go on."

Will licked his lips. "I heard you," he said, his voice barely audible.
He kept his eyes lowered, glancing only occasionally toward Dr.
Schafer.

"You heard me when, Will? What was I saying?"

Will looked up, his eyes challenging his father. His voice escalated
almost to shouting when he said, "When you were talking to Papa and
Grandmamá." I heard you say Mom didn't love us! You said if she

loved us, she wouldn't have left." His voice broke as he added, "She did, Dad! Mom loved me and Kate!" He seemed less sure as he added, "She did, didn't she?"

The look on Will's face almost broke his heart. "Oh, Will. Oh, Son. Come here." He held out his arms. Will hesitated, and then he ran into his father's embrace, sobbing against Max's chest.

Dr. Schafer stood. "I'm going to leave you two alone for a while."

Max barely noticed when the therapist left the room. "Will, I know your mother loved you. I know she did."

"Then why did you say—" He stopped, his face a mask of anguish.

"Sweetheart..." Max held his son against him, stroking his back, kissing his hair. He seldom used such tender endearments with his son, but it seemed important now. "Sweetheart," he said again, "I was very angry that day and I said some things I shouldn't have."

Will's voice was small. "You were angry at Grandmamá and Papa?"

"Yes," he said carefully. His inner voice kicked in. He was still deeply angry, but he couldn't burden Will with that. "I didn't want you and Kate to be frightened, so I didn't tell you about it at the time, but that was after your mother left, before she..." He stopped before that sentence went too far. "Her parents, your Papa and Grandmamá, were trying to take you away from me."

Will crinkled his nose in confusion. "Away? To live with them?"

Max warned himself to be careful how he answered. "They thought you should be living with your mother, not with me."

"Why couldn't we live with Mom?"

Max reminded himself that Will didn't know how much that question hurt him. "Your mom wasn't in a good situation for children," he answered, knowing how lame it sounded and also knowing Will wasn't ready for more specific answers.

"Why not?"

Max thought of all the reasons, especially those he couldn't share with his children. He couldn't tell them that Isabel had become a full-blown heroin addict, that she lived on the street and ate out of garbage cans except when she cleaned up enough to visit her parents and beg for more money. Her parents had never recognized how bad it got, but Max knew. He'd once hired a private investigator to follow her.

For Will's sake, he measured his words. "She didn't have…a place for you and Kate. She didn't have…beds for you." *Or walls or a roof or clean floors…* He tried to cut off the bitter thoughts.

"I know some kids with moms and dads that got divorced." Will's speech became stronger. "They get to live with their moms sometimes and their dads other times."

"We talked about that," Max answered in a gentle voice. "Your Grandmamá and Papa thought it would be better for you to live with them and let your mother visit until she got a nice place of her own."

The truth was Isabel's parents wouldn't listen to reason. They'd bought all her stories about Max's behavior and were determined their grandchildren should never be subjected to his temper and his rants. Isabel even told them her tracks and needle marks came from Max abusing her. He knew they looked like *needle* marks, not Ike other kinds of bruises, but her parents bought every lie no matter how unreasonable. The injustice and betrayal still shook him. He took a deep breath and let it out slowly,

"Papa's a judge, right?"

That problem had complicated matters from the start. "Yes, he is."

"So why didn't he just decide to do that? Mikey said the judge decided where he'd live."

Max knew why. The change happened because Will's mom over-dosed. Police knew how and why she died and reported that to the judge assigned to their case, in a different court where his father-in-law had no influence. "He wanted to do that, but right about then your mom…"

"She died?"

"Right. She died. After that, your grandparents wanted you and Kate to come to live with them all the time."

Will looked into his father's eyes. "All the time? Not see you anymore?"

"That's what they wanted," Max answered. He struggled to remember that the boy needed his grandparents, that he shouldn't say anything that would turn Will against them. "They were just as sad as we were about what happened to your mom. They couldn't have her back, so they wanted you to come and stay with them." They had also tried to make sure that Max would never see his twins again. He swallowed down a sick feeling, remembering how frightened he'd been when he thought they might get away with it.

Will sat up straighter. He spoke louder when he asked, "How come we only get to see them when the lady from the court is there?"

That had happened after Social Services caught the kids' grandmother preparing to leave the state with his children. Sadly, his ex-mom-in-law was as sneaky and manipulative as her daughter. Max took a deep breath. He couldn't tell Will that. "Because those are the rules, buddy. Did you want to visit them at their house?"

"Yeah. I want to go there."

"Why? Is there some special reason?"

Will nodded. "I want to play with Pepper."

The dog! This was about the dog! Max felt limp as the sudden adrenaline rush drained away. "Maybe we can all go see Pepper pretty soon." If Will's grandparents would let him in the door.

"When, Dad?" Hope shown in Will's face.

"Maybe during the Holidays?"

"Like Thanksgiving? Or Christmas?"

"Right. Maybe then." He ruffled Will's hair. "What d'ya think, buddy? Sound good?"

Will nodded. "Do we have to wait that long?"

"I'm afraid so, kiddo. I'll look into it, like at Thanksgiving when we'll be near there for your Uncle Keith's wedding." He'd hate it, but he'd ask.

"Okay. Cool." Will seemed pacified.

"Good. You're feeling okay now?"

"Yeah. Better, anyway."

"Shall we tell Dr. Schafer he can come back?"

"Yeah." Will jumped up. "I'll get 'im." He jogged to the door. "Dr. Schafer! You can come in now!"

Max smiled at his son's enthusiasm.

"Thanks, Will." Dr. Schafer entered but held the door open. "Do you mind if I talk with your dad alone for a few minutes?"

"Nah. That's cool. I'll stay out here with Kate and Ms. Reyes." He waved as he left.

Dr. Schafer sat across from Max. "You remember I told you on the first visit that I record everything that's said in this room?"

"Yeah. Um, yes, I do." Too bad he'd forgotten.

"Let's play back what just happened here." Dr. Schafer reached for a button.

"Uh…" Max balked. His chest tightened and his face began to heat. Checking his watch, he said, "Isn't our time up by now? We've been here longer than usual."

"The appointment after yours canceled and I asked my receptionist to reschedule the appointment after that. We can take all the time we need."

"I don't know if…"

"Don't worry about the fee. Your insurance covers this." He pressed the play button.

"Wait!"

The doctor stopped the playback. "Yes?"

"I'm not worried about the fee, or the insurance. What about Ms. Reyes?"

"I spoke with her while you were in here. She has called her school and everything's set. You can stay as long as you need—we're making some good breakthroughs." He backtracked with a little smile. "That is, until the office closes. I get to go home too."

"Sure." Max realized he couldn't delay much longer. "Okay then. I guess we're ready." He wasn't ready. That conversation had been private, between Max and his son. Max didn't want to share or discuss it, but since he was here…

Dr. Schafer said, "I marked the time. Let me go to that point."

The recording began with sounds of people shuffling and sitting, then Dr. Schafer's voice: "I'm going to leave you two alone for a while."

The panic Max was feeling must have shown on his face.

"It's going to be okay, Max," the doctor said.

Max sat back, dumbstruck, listening.

A few minutes later the conversation ended, and Dr. Schafer turned off the replay. "You handled that well."

"I'm glad you think so. I'm not so certain."

"You're feeling an awful lot of anger that you aren't sharing with your son."

"But—"

"Don't misunderstand me." He gave Max the same encouraging smile he'd used with Will. "It's good that you aren't sharing that with your children, but you probably need to share it with someone. Why don't you tell me what happened with your in-laws?"

Why don't you give me a root canal instead? Max let out a long, calming breath. "I guess we'll have to get around to this sometime. May as well get it over with."

Max started talking, and dumped out the whole, sad story.

Amber checked her watch. They'd been in Schafer's office for more than two hours. When Max picked them up at the school, Amber was concerned about how the appointment would proceed, including how Dr. Schafer viewed her art sessions with the children. But she was pleased to see the children seemed more relaxed after their time with the doctor. Amber was grateful Liza and her assistant principal were holding down the fort back at school. More importantly, she was glad she could be here to help. She glanced at Will and Kate. Whatever had transpired with Dr. Schafer seemed to have had a positive effect on the kids. She could only hope Max came out feeling just as relieved.

The door opened. Amber stood as Max and the doctor exchanged goodbyes and confirmed the next appointment. Max turned to Amber and the children. "Shall we go?"

Amber smiled at the kids. "Come on, you two. Let's put the toys away." Max came out red-eyed. This family's wounds were deeper than she'd recognized. She grinned at Kate as the little girl took her hand. A lump rose in her throat at the trust in the child's face.

Max said, "I think we've earned some ice cream. What d'ya think, kids?"

The children responded eagerly.

Amber stopped herself from commenting that ice cream now would ruin their dinner. "I know a great place for ice cream. It's on our way." Her expression asked the unspoken question, *Is this okay, Max? Or is it a mistake?*

"Sounds good." Max nodded. "You can show us where." He took Will's hand, leading the way toward the car.

"This ice cream shop is really good," Amber said. "They have a sundae called a Tremor. It's big enough for all four of us. Are you guys up for it?" she teased.

Will answered first. "Do I get to pick my own flavor?"

Amber nodded. "It has eight scoops, so each of us can pick *two* flavors."

"Yes!" Will said, pumping his arm.

Max chuckled, ruffling Will's hair again.

Amber tightened her grip on Kate's hand, glad both Max and Will approved her idea. "Come on, Kate. Let's race your dad and Will to the car."

All four of them laughed as they ran across the parking lot.

Chapter Eight

For the rest of the week, Max put in overtime after the kids went to bed. Besides enabling him to get extra work done, it got his mind off his session with Dr. Schafer. On Friday, he left the office early, content with his week's efforts for Río Blanco and the mine and looking forward to some fun with Kate and Will.

Max mentally checked off his to-do list for their outing. He'd been numb for so long, simply surviving from one day to the next. It felt good to get organized, to plan for fun activities with his children beyond the basics of getting by. Maybe they—he and the kids—could finally have a normal life. The thought eased the tightness in his chest.

He took a deep breath. It felt good. He wondered how much his visit with Dr. Schafer—unburdening himself—might have to do with his new level of ease. Dr. Schafer didn't usually work with adults, but he sometimes saw all the individuals in a family when the whole group had been traumatized. The therapist had asked Max to schedule appointments for himself as well as the kids and Max had said no. Maybe he should reconsider?

He was not the kind of guy who went to therapy. At least, he'd never thought he was. He rubbed the back of his neck. He hadn't believed in therapy at all. Considering what Dr. Schafer had done for Kate and Will—and for him, too—he'd begun rethinking that. In the days since their visit to Dr. Schafer's office, he and Will had been getting along better than they had in months. Of course, if it hadn't been for Amber, they would all still be trudging through daily misery and calling it normal.

Amber.

His imagination took off in another direction. Images came flooding back of Amber serving chicken at the wedding reception; fending off the obnoxious drunk; warm and tight but curvy under his arm; speaking of his children with gentle compassion in her eyes; teasing him just a little with that show at the Reeds' swimming party; looking at him with concern as he emerged from Dr. Schafer's office. She was kind, smart, beautiful, and highly desirable, and he had been alone a long time now, since well before Isabel left.

"Maybe I should start dating again," he mumbled aloud. His inner voice scoffed. He had no one he'd like to date except Amber Reyes, and it didn't seem smart to date his kids' principal. Maybe he shouldn't even consider dating again, given what Isabel had put him through. He *was* thinking about it, though. He couldn't seem not to.

FROM HER OFFICE WINDOW, Amber looked out on the parking lot and the covered area where children waited for their after-school rides. She had pushed to change the one-way drive-through to two lanes. Drivers in the outer lane could either pull through to the parking lot without having to wait behind others, or they could make a second orbit to come back in the pick-up lane. She'd also planned and raised the funds for the covered area where several children now waited. It had been a good idea to keep the kids safe and to help prevent any unwanted accidents.

She caught the direction of her thoughts and knew where they'd come from. There'd been some push-back when she was first hired. A few unhappy parents and even a couple of teachers felt Amber was too young and inexperienced to handle the job. Even after a couple of years, she often still felt she had to prove herself. *Relax, Amber,* she told herself. *You are the principal here and no one is fighting that anymore. Have some confidence!*

Looking out again, she noticed Mrs. Larsen pulling up in her van to pick up the kids in her after-school program. Will and Kate weren't there.

Uneasy, she turned her attention back to the letter from the district office—a new policy on reporting excessive truancy—but found she couldn't focus. She glanced out the window again in time to see the

Burnett twins take their place in the waiting area, apparently unaware they had missed their ride.

"Liza," she said as she entered the front office. "I'll be in the front drive-through for a few minutes. If anyone needs me, send them there."

"Gotcha." Liza gave her a thumbs-up.

Amber approached Kate and Will, with a smile on her face, so as not to worry them. "Hi, Kate. Will. Are you waiting for Mrs. Larsen?"

"Nah." Will scraped the toe of his shoe against the sidewalk. "We're waiting for Dad."

"Your father is picking you up today? Is everything okay?"

"We're having a picnic!" Kate giggled, jumping up and down.

"A picnic! That sounds like fun. Have a great time." She turned to go inside.

"Look, here's Dad!" Kate declared, catching Amber's hand.

Amber's heart warmed at the child's inherent trust in her. On impulse, she decided to wait with the kids as Max pulled into the driveway.

"Hello," Max said, getting out of the car. His eyes held a touch of concern. "Is there a problem?"

"Not at all." Amber smiled. "I saw Mrs. Larsen come by. Then when I saw Kate and Will, I thought they had missed their ride. Kate here—" she raised their linked hands, "told me about your picnic. This is a good time for it, before the weather turns cooler." She squeezed Kate's hand and let it go. "Have fun."

Kate grasped her hand again. "Come with us! We can all have a picnic together."

Amber felt her smile weakening and tried to shore it up. Flashing a *help me!* look at Max, she said, "You three need to have family time and I need to get back to the office."

Max stepped in. "Come on, Kate, Will. We have a park waiting for us." He opened the door to the back seat and gestured. Will got in.

Kate pouted. "I want Ms. Reyes to come."

"Honey," Amber said, carefully monitoring her tone. "You'll have lots of fun with your dad and brother."

"You came with us on Wednesday." Kate's defiant look made her position clear.

"That was different." Max stepped in and took Kate's free hand.

"Dr. Schafer wanted to see me on Wednesday because I'm your principal."

Kate tightened her grip. "Daddy, I want Ms. Reyes to come."

Max pulled her toward him, but she didn't break her hold on Amber. "Kate, Ms. Reyes needs to get back to work and we need to get going," he said, his tone firm.

Kate scrunched up her face in a tight, angry pout, her look still defiant, but she complied with her father's order and got into the car, thumping hard on the back seat next to Will.

"Put on your seat belts, both of you." Max closed the door. Dropping his voice, he gestured toward the school. "Can we talk?"

"Sure." Amber took several steps away from the car.

"I could use your help here," he said, speaking quietly. "Kate asks for so little. It's obvious she feels close to you. Is there any chance you can join us?"

"I don't think so, Max."

His disappointment showed. "I guess you need to get back to your office…"

"It isn't that. I often close the office by four o'clock on Fridays and it's almost three-thirty now." She checked her watch. "Correction. It's just after three-thirty. No, Max. This is about your relationship with your daughter. You don't want Kate to think she can get her way by pouting, especially after you've said no." She stopped herself. "I'm sorry. I have no right to correct your parenting. Besides, I don't want to intrude on your family time. That's too precious."

He sighed. "I understand what you're saying and you make a good point. Still, I wish there was a way—" He grinned. "I think maybe there is." He began to explain his plan.

I DON'T KNOW *if this is a good idea.* Amber stood in Joe's Sandwich Shop waiting for the sandwich Max had ordered and paid for an hour earlier. Max had argued there was a way for him to be obeyed that still let Kate have what she, wanted. "If you just happen to show up in the park half an hour or so after we get there …"

Amber thanked Joe for the sandwich. As she left the store, she mumbled aloud, "I don't know how I let him talk me into this." Her inner voice reminded her to be honest with herself. She liked the twins and she found their father highly attractive. She'd said yes to this goofy idea because she wanted the excuse to spend time with them all.

"I'm going to have to do something about this," she murmured. Then Kate called out and Will waved to her. *Maybe tomorrow.* She grinned broadly as she hurried to cross the street.

SHE'S AMAZING. Max stopped the thought almost before it occurred to him. He told himself sharply that he couldn't think that way, that after Isabel, he needed to be immune to attractive women. He couldn't risk subjecting his beautiful children, or himself either, to someone who might hurt them again. He ignored the little voice that said Amber Reyes would never hurt his children.

Watching her with them was almost a message in itself. He watched her dishing up salad for Kate, filling Will's water cup, doing all the little things he didn't even think of. She worked with children all day every day, yet her patience never seemed to run out. He thought of the scene at his house last Saturday morning—Kate sobbing in the bathroom over the sink that wouldn't stop dripping; Will refusing to put down his computer game and clean his room until Max lost it and yelled at him—and wondered how she would handle a morning like that. Would her unflagging patience run thin then?

Max sighed deeply. Thinking of Amber in his home was not a good idea. He studied her, watching how her dark hair gleamed in the sunlight, how her dark brown eyes softened with affection when she told Kate she'd push her on the swings after clean-up. Somehow, without yelling or issuing dire warnings, she had his kids cleaning the table, putting leftovers back into Joe's reusable containers, and packing everything into the picnic bin he'd brought from home. "Okay, let's go play on the swings," she announced, her voice bright.

"I want to go high-high-high!" Kate ran toward the swings.

"I don't wanta swing." Will pouted. "I wanta ride the merry-go-round."

Amber sent Max a look that said *You're the parent here.* He gave a slight nod. "Tell you what," he said to Will. "Ms. Reyes can go push Kate on the swings and I'll push you on the merry-go-round. Sound good?"

"I wanta go fast!" Will, his excitement mirroring his sister's, ran for the merry-go-round.

Amber grinned. "Well-played, Dad." She hurried after Kate.

Over the next hour, Max pushed a merry-go-round and then a swing, stood at the bottom of the slide to watch Kate and then Will come down, and held his breath as both kids swung their way across the monkey bars. Though he stayed involved with the children, he was always aware of where Amber was and what she was doing, how her body moved, how her face brightened when she smiled at Kate and Will.

Max, cut it out. Although he warned himself firmly, he managed to ignore the warning as his eyes followed her, watching her play 'Mother, May I,' giving Will scissor steps and then assigning giant steps to Kate, keeping the game more-or-less even. The name 'mother' rang in his head. The thought came unbidden, *My kids deserve someone like Amber for a mother.* His mouth went dry. He couldn't keep thinking like that! But he couldn't seem to help himself either.

ON FRIDAY EVENINGS, Amber almost always dropped in to visit her parents, at least briefly. She arrived to find another car in their driveway. She entered through the kitchen door to find Sunny and Evan sitting at the table, snapping beans. Seeing her at the door, Sunny stood and came toward her. Evan followed.

"Sunny! Great to see you!" Amber hugged Sunny and then Evan. "So how are the newlyweds? Classes? Work?"

"Everything's great." Evan looked like he meant it. "People warned me Sacramento County would be tougher than Butte, and we do have more serious crime there. This sheriff organizes differently too, and that has taken some getting used to, but the work is familiar. I like it." He patted his stomach. "My only problem is Olivia taught Sunny to be a great cook. I'll have to watch it, or I'll soon fit the out-of-shape cop stereotype."

"Flatterer." Olivia spoke from behind the stove. "Are those beans ready?"

"Yeah. Right here." Evan stepped around the table, fetching the snapped beans.

Amber took a seat. "How about you, Sunny? Classes good?"

"Classes are hard!" Sunny sat beside her. "But I love them! I'm already looking at people I might want on my grad committee. The professors I've spoken with all want to see my work on the mammoth fire that destroyed Paradise, and they're helping me focus my research."

"Sounds promising," Amber agreed.

Evan prompted, "Hey Babe, tell her about your job."

"You're working, too?" Amber asked. "Isn't graduate school a full-time job?"

"I only work part-time in the department office. It's mundane stuff —making copies, sorting mail, that sort of thing—but it puts me in contact with everyone in the department. I'm learning everyone's specialties and interests—"

"— and getting acquainted with personalities and office politics," Evan jumped in.

Sunny nodded. "Yeah. That, too."

Amber nodded. "You find politics everywhere."

"That's what I told her," Evan said. "It's just as well she's figuring it out now, before she puts people together for her grad committee."

"I agree." Olivia said, then looking to Amber, asked, "Will you stay for dinner?"

"Not tonight, thanks. I've already eaten."

"We know." Sunny looked to Evan with a secretive smile. "We saw you in the park. Want to tell us who you were with?"

Olivia looked up. "Amber, you were with someone?"

"A couple of the children from my school," she said. Seeing the looks on their faces, she added, "And their father."

"This father," Olivia said, "he's single?"

"Yes, he is." Scrambling for a new topic, Amber asked, "How long are you two staying?"

Sunny ignored the question. "How long have you two been dating?"

"Oh, we're not dating!"

Sunny chuckled. "Tell yourself that if you like, but you can't fool us. We saw what we saw, didn't we, Evan?"

Evan nodded in agreement. "You two were looking pretty chummy when we drove past."

"You were," Sunny said. "Who is he? What's his name?"

"Really, we're not dating." She looked from one face to another. Even her mother looked skeptical. She sighed. "His name is Max Burnett. His children are Kate and Will."

Sunny asked, "Will and Kate, like the royals?"

"Yes, named for them."

Olivia said, "And he's Max Burnett, as in the same family that used to live next door."

Sunny said, "No kidding."

"It's the same Max Burnett," Amber answered.

Sunny said, "The kids look the same age. They're twins?"

"Right."

"Cute kids," Evan said.

Sunny smiled. "All that red hair …"

"Oh no!" Sunny put her hand to her mouth. "You know what I just thought of? Mom, remember the guy who used to run that downtown gift shop? The one where Joe's is now?"

"Oh, yes. I haven't thought of him in years. He moved away after he sold the place. Mr. Chapman, wasn't it?"

"Right," Sunny said. "Amber, remember how he used to tease us? He used to say if we didn't watch ourselves…"

Amber nodded. "He said if we weren't good, he'd beat us like a red-headed stepchild." Then she realized what Sunny was thinking.

Sunny pushed on. "If you marry this guy, then his kids will be…" Olivia and Evan joined her as she finished, "…your red-headed stepchildren!" Sunny looked very pleased with herself. She and Evan did a high five.

Amber groaned, shaking her head. "I can't believe you said that. I told you, we aren't dating."

"Whatever you have to tell yourself," Sunny said again.

Amber stood. "If you two will be around, I'll stop by again this weekend. Until then, I need to get out of here. You people are all crazy."

"And you are dating again," Sunny said. "No matter what you tell yourself!"

Amber heard her mother muttering to herself, "It's probably time to have the Burnetts over."

Chapter Nine

Alone in his bed that night, Max struggled with conflicting thoughts. He couldn't stop thinking about Amber Reyes, but he had to. Didn't he? Or did he? Things seemed to be going well.

No, he couldn't risk getting involved again. He and his kids had been through too much. Max rolled onto his back and gazed at the ceiling. He thought of what had happened with Will at the therapist's office, and how he'd broken down and sobbed like a baby. Only now was he coming to recognize how much pain, how many issues he still had to deal with. What was fair about involving Amber in that?

Amber is already involved, his inner voice reminded him, also reminding that Amber was the one who had started him with therapy and even helped him find the therapist. If it hadn't been for her, he wouldn't know what Will had overheard or why he was so angry. That made Amber part of his healing.

Schafer had pointed out some of Max's comments, ones that showed him being skeptical of all women. Negative experience with Isabel and her mother had made him mildly misogynistic. He needed to get over that without relying on a woman to help with healing.

"She can't be part of it," he murmured aloud. Max flipped his pillow to the cool side and lay back. What if he and Will and Kate came to depend on Amber and she ditched them the way Isabel had?

But what if Amber taught them all how to trust again? Max groaned and pulled the pillow over his head. "I've got to get some sleep," he mumbled, trying to still the dueling thoughts. Sometime later, exhausted by his inner turmoil, he finally came to a decision. He would cool things with Amber Reyes—avoid meeting with her except at the school, and then only for school-type purposes.

The last vision he had in his head before falling asleep was

Amber's long dark hair and velvety brown eyes. Avoiding her might be more difficult than he imagined.

Alone in her bed that night, Amber struggled with herself. She liked Max, maybe liked him too much, and she was crazy about his kids. She knew she shouldn't be, hadn't any right to be. She had promised herself she would never be a cliché stepmother."

But she knew that not all blended families had issues and not all stepmothers were sad or caught in the middle. And anyway, her situation was different, wasn't it? The kids had been without a mother for a while now, maybe longer than she knew, due to Isabel's drug addiction, and Max's children needed a mom. Was she the right woman for the job? And what about Max? She was already falling for him, but he didn't seem to return her feelings.

She groaned and rolled to her side, pulling the covers up to her chin. "I have to get some sleep," she said aloud, ordering her mind to be still. A while later she came to a decision. She'd cool things with the Burnett family. No more going with them to therapy. No more picnics in the park. She'd see the children at school, but she'd only be their principal and not imagine anything more. Maybe she'd better cut down the art therapy in the office as well. As for Max, she'd talk to him only regarding matters pertaining to his children at school.

Her eyes growing heavy, she finally fell asleep. Her last image was of Max's teasing grin and gleaming dark eyes.

Destiny's first snow of the year fell in mid-October. It was light, no more than an inch, and it melted quickly, but it was snow. Tradition at Destiny Elementary allowed the children to go outside for a few minutes to watch the year's first snowfall. Since the school day was almost over when the snow began, Amber dismissed classes ten minutes early, her announcement encouraging the children to stay under the eaves or on the covered walkways while they waited for pick-up.

"Come on, Liza," she said to her secretary. "Let's go look at the snow."

Liza stood. "I was hoping you'd say that." The two walked out to the front waiting area. Three minutes later, Amber felt a small hand in hers and looked down to find Kate Burnett at her side, looking at her with such a hopeful, adoring expression that Amber simply couldn't pull away. *I'll wait with her until Mrs. Larsen comes.* She squeezed Kate's hand. "Did you have snow where you lived before?"

"No. Mommy didn't like snow, but Daddy took us to the snow once." The little girl stared in fascination as large, dry flakes floated to the earth.

Amber squeezed Kate's hand again. How long had it been since she'd held this little hand? Two weeks? She'd stopped the art therapy just as she'd resolved. It was for the best—besides, Dr. Schafer was doing such a good job with the children. Amber was thrilled by their progress; they'd almost caught up with others in their grade. It was evident to their teachers and to Amber that both Kate and Will were happier, better adjusted, and more engaged at school. They were both such bright kids. She smiled inwardly. Will and Kate were as bright as their coppery hair. It was so easy to love them... Amber stopped. Where had that thought come from?

But she knew where it came from. She was already overly involved with Max's kids, not to mention falling for their father. She almost groaned aloud.

Mrs. Larsen pulled her van up to the curb. "Your ride's here." Amber let go of Kate's hand. She looked around. "Where's Will?"

"Will had to go to the washroom. We aren't going with Mrs. Larsen today," Kate said, taking Amber's hand again.

Amber felt a small tremor of worry. "Oh? Why not?"

Kate's expression said she should already know the answer. "It's Wednesday, Miss Reyes. This is our day to visit Dr. Schafer. We're waiting for Daddy."

Before she finished her sentence, Amber saw Max's car approaching. "Of course," she answered, freeing her hand again. Too aware of how vulnerable the moment had made her and knowing she couldn't see Max when she felt like this, she said, "I need to get back to the office, Kate. You have a good visit with Dr. Schafer." She started to turn.

"Miss Reyes?"

"Yes, Kate?"

"Don't you like us anymore?"

"What?" Amber saw the sadness in Kate's eyes and her heart broke. The last thing she wanted was to hurt these kids. "You know I like you, sweetie." She crouched down and tucked a red curl behind Kate's ear. "I just have to get some office work done." She smiled as she straightened. "Have a good afternoon, okay?" Moments before Max reached the pick-up area, Amber turned and practically ran to her office, inwardly condemning herself as a lily-livered coward.

MAX ADDED another bag of candy to his grocery cart. Halloween was only days away, and he expected he'd get trick-or-treaters; he just didn't know how many.

He thought back over the afternoon he and the kids had spent with Enrique and Olivia Reyes the past weekend. He'd been surprised to realize they hadn't invited Amber. In fact, they seemed to have kept his invitation a secret from their daughter. Though Olivia asked many questions about his parents and his brother, their lives now and what they were doing, Enrique seemed focused on finding out how Max felt about Amber. Enrique had even arranged an informal, one-on-one interview, asking directly what Max intended toward Amber and being very clear about not wanting to see his daughter hurt.

Max had answered as honestly as he could, letting Enrique know that he and Amber were not seeing each other socially now, that as far as he was concerned, Amber was his children's principal, and that was that. Enrique's look alone had told Max he didn't quite believe that, but Max didn't know what else he could say. He'd packed up his kids and left soon after Olivia served dessert. The interlude had got him thinking more about Amber, though, and he wondered if he'd been too hasty when he cut her off.

He checked his watch. The birthday party that was keeping his kids occupied should be over soon. He needed to finish his shopping, get home, and hide the candy before he picked them up. Always eager to please him, Kate would leave the bags alone if he told her to. Will, who had both a sweet tooth and a contrary streak, might not. He decided to make do with what he had. It could take a while to check out and he didn't want to make the kids wait. He pushed his cart toward the end of the aisle.

Amber came around the corner. "Oh!"

Max's heart rate picked up and he grinned. "Well, hello."

"Hello." Amber seemed to recover from her surprise and slipped into that professional tone she'd been using since their picnic in the park.

He said, "It's been a while …"

"Yes," she answered. She looked around. "Where are the kids?"

"Birthday party."

"Jacob Nguyen. I remember."

He glanced around. "The store is busy every Saturday morning, but this seems busier than usual."

"It could be the health spa is bringing in traffic. They're having their VIP open house this weekend. They'll start receiving guests in another week."

"Yes, that could explain it."

They stood side by side, carts almost touching. After a few moments of awkward silence, Amber pointed down the aisle. "Halloween candy. I'd better stock up." She moved her cart to pass his.

"Yeah. Me too. Say, how much will I need?" He gestured toward his cart. "Is that enough? Or should I buy more?"

Amber looked thoughtful. "I can't say for sure. I'll need more than that since every kid in town comes to the principal's house." She offered an uneasy smile. "I don't know about you, though. Where are you living? Is it right in town?"

That startled Max. Amber didn't know where he lived? "We're leasing the Nowak place," he began. "It's been standing empty since

Lech's grandmother died. Because he's living with a foster family until he graduates, it would have stayed empty, if Lech hadn't put it up for rent. We have the option to buy after Lech turns eighteen and can sign, but I'm looking around, just in case he decides to keep the place." Realizing he'd begun to babble, he stopped himself. "But you didn't need to know all that, did you?" He shifted uneasily and lamely finished his thought, "We're a little out of town."

"You're less likely to get many kids, then." She gestured toward her cart.

"Yes," he said, moving out of her way. "That makes sense."

With a small nod, Amber went around him and moved down the aisle.

Max steered toward checkout. He couldn't picture that exchange being any more awkward. He checked out as quickly as possible, but as he drove away, he pondered. There had to be a better approach than this. He began to anticipate another rough night.

Two days later, on Monday afternoon, Amber was finishing up some paperwork before she left for the day. Trouble was, she wasn't getting much work done due to obsessing over the awkward scene in the grocery store. Max seemed to have come to the same conclusion she had—that spending time together was a bad idea. He hadn't shown the least bit of interest since that impromptu picnic and was obviously avoiding her just as she was avoiding him. But that didn't make a lot of sense. Destiny was too small a town, and they were bound to run into each other frequently. Amber resigned herself to more awkward moments in the very near future.

Liza interrupted her thoughts. "Excuse me, Ms. Reyes. Mr. Burnett is here to see you."

Trying not to show her surprise, she said, "Show him in."

Max entered immediately. "Hi. Do you have a minute?"

"Sure." She waved toward a chair. "Have a seat."

"Thanks," he said. "I've been thinking…" He hesitated, biting his lip.

This moment was becoming as awkward as their grocery store encounter. "Yes?"

"Well, I think we need to talk about it."

"Uh, about what, exactly?"

Max rubbed the back of his neck. "About what happened in the grocery store and running into each other from time to time…you know, because we live in such a small town and you're the principal at my kids' school, and…" Max cleared his throat.

"And what, Max?"

"And…well…why we're not dating," he blurted. "Yeah…I think that's it," he said as though he'd just figured it out. "I think we need to talk about why we're not dating."

Amber's heart rate picked up and she squirmed in her chair.

Taking that as encouragement, Max went on. "Look, I'm attracted to you and I think you're attracted to me too, that is, if I'm reading the signals correctly…"

Amber nodded, not trusting herself to speak.

"So we've got these feelings that are drawing us toward each other, and I think we need to talk about what's keeping us apart."

Amber nodded again, but this time she found her voice. "That makes sense."

Max said, "You start. Why is it that you think we shouldn't date?"

Why did he think it was okay to lay the situation out there and then dump the burden on her? She gathered her thoughts. "There is the matter of me being the principal at your kids' school."

"Okay." Max paused, weighing the thought. "That's a good place to start. I've been thinking about that one. You know my kids went to Jacob Nguyen's party…"

"Yes…"

"There's only one first-grade class in Destiny. Mrs. Nguyen teaches that class, so that means she's Jacob's teacher."

Amber could feel her brow drawing together. "Yes. What's your point?"

"If you had moved to Destiny with a husband and a couple of elementary-aged kids, your kids would be in your school, right?"

"Right. I guess I see your point."

"You know the parents and sometimes the grandparents of all the kids in your school. It only makes sense that you could find yourself dating the father of one or more of those kids. That is, unless you only date guys who are childless, which, come to think of it, might be a smart move on your part…" he said, his voice trailing off. He shifted in his seat, his face flushed.

She decided to let him off the hook. "I understand. My being the principal isn't a good enough reason. Your turn. Why do you think we shouldn't date?"

"My biggest reason has been cowardice. Pure, plain, simple cowardice." His sheepish grin made her smile back. "Let's just say my marriage was…difficult."

Amber cleared her throat. "I know your wife died, and you've hinted that things weren't good before that."

"We divorced almost a year before she died. It was…bad. Very bad."

Max certainly had a lot to offer in a relationship; definitely not the kind of man who should be single forever, but she could see he'd been badly hurt. "I know that kind of split can make a person …hesitant to get involved again."

"Hesitant? I've been terrified!" He took a breath. "But I'm still a young man, and I don't want to be single forever. Being around you has encouraged me, has made me want to date again."

Amber had to suppress a shiver. She'd just been thinking the same thing. "I guess you're starting to feel brave?"

"Brave enough to ask you to dinner this Friday."

So much for her resolutions. "Another picnic in the park? I know the kids will enjoy that."

He shook his head. "No kids this time. I've found a trustworthy babysitter, the teenage daughter of one of the guys I work with at the mine, Luisa Salvador. I'll see if she can watch the kids this Friday."

"The Salvadors are a good family, and I know Luisa. Will and Kate will like her."

"What do you say? A real date, just you and me? I thought maybe Berman's Mesa."

Berman's? For a first date? He must be eager to impress. "That sounds great. I'd love to."

He stood. "Okay then. I'll pick you up at your place at, say, six-thirty?"

"Six-thirty is good."

"Good." He started toward the door. "Oh. You'll have to tell me where your place is."

Amber couldn't help grinning. Max looked so adorable, all flustered and sweet like that. She reached for one of her school business cards and began writing on the back. "Here. I'll give you my cell number. Send me a text and I'll text back the address."

"Okay, great. Well…see you Friday, then."

"Yes, definitely."

"Right. And Amber?"

"Yes, Max?"

"Let's stop this awkward tiptoeing around each other, okay?"

She grinned. "You've got it. See you. Oh, and Max?"

"Yes?"

"This isn't the kind of conversation I typically have at my place of business. Let's draw a line between the professional and the personal, okay?"

He looked around. "Yeah, I get that. Well, see you." He left, closing the door behind him.

Amber sat in her office, listening as the school quieted and Liza left for the day. What had happened to her good resolutions? She sighed, happy to let them go. She slipped on her winter coat, grabbed her purse, and grinned as she locked the front office. Sunny and Evan were right. She was dating again. She smiled all the way to her car.

Chapter Ten

Max drove his children home from their counseling appointment. Dr. Schafer had seen him alone for part of their time. It was all good. Schafer saw progress in both kids. He was wrong about Will, though. His son was not the angry child the counselor saw. Not *that* angry, anyway. Max's inner voice argued that the therapist—actually, both Dr. Schafer and Amber—had been right about the children so far, even when he denied it. Was it possible Will was still that angry?

He shrugged the thought away, deliberately turning toward his upcoming date with Amber. He had been divorced for more than two years and widowed, if he could call it that, for more than half that time. Until now, there had been no one, and maybe it was time. On the other hand, there was some question of his judgment. He couldn't have been more wrong about Isabel. Was Amber another mistake?

His inner voice slammed that argument hard: *Amber is nothing like Isabel. Besides, you aren't marrying her this Friday. It's a date. You're getting to know each other.*

Max blew out a breath, realizing he needed to relax. Noticing the ice cream parlor at the end of the block, he called to the back seat, "Who's up for ice cream?"

Hearing the predictable, enthusiastic cheers, he turned into his kids' new favorite place, the one Amber Reyes picked.

His inner voice reminded him this was another good reason for dating Amber. Everything she'd said and done so far had had a positive impact on Will and Kate…and him, for that matter.

Max grinned to himself as he helped the kids out of the car. He couldn't argue with logic, now could he?

～

AMBER HAD NEVER SEEN Berman's Mesa so crowded. Max even had trouble finding space in the parking lot. "I'm glad you made a reservation," she said as they walked toward the door. "I doubt we'd get in otherwise."

"Is it always like this?"

"Never, at least not in my experience."

Max held the door for Amber as she stepped inside. "Maybe this all has to do with the health spa? They finally had their grand opening last weekend."

"I heard someone suggesting they put off the opening on purpose just to build interest."

"Possible, I suppose, but it doesn't seem likely," she replied. "There's no shortage of interest in the spa; people have been talking about it for months."

The host greeted them. Max gave his name, and they were led to a quiet corner of the main dining room, next to the outside window. "Good view from here," Max observed as they sat and picked up their menus. They chatted as they chose their meals, but to Max, the conversation seemed stiff and artificial. They needed to talk about something meaningful, but it couldn't always be about the kids. He smiled at Amber and said, "We promised we weren't going to let this get awkward."

"True," she said with a wry grin. "Although we can't always talk about Kate and Will."

Max answered with a tight smile, stunned that she'd echoed his thoughts.

Amber's grin turned impish. "What do you remember about living next door to my family all those years ago?"

Over the next few minutes, they both recalled that the Burnetts had moved away from Destiny a short while after Amber's cousins came to live with the Reyes family. "I think I remember their arrival," Max said, "but we had the house for sale then. We moved a few weeks later."

"You never got to know Sunny or Skye."

"No. I just saw them around. I didn't run in the same circles as they did, anyway." He shook his head. "The age difference…" He rolled his eyes. "You know."

"Yes, I know." Amber's smile was gentle. "Those few years make a great difference when you're a kid."

"Not so much now."

"No, not so much." She set down her menu. "I used to think you were so cool and grown up, especially when you rode around on that motorcycle."

He laughed. "I hope you're about to tell me that you had a crazy-mad crush on me."

She laughed. "Sorry. You were too far out of my age range. I remember looking at Keith a few times, but he never seemed to be looking back."

"Just as well. Keith went through some difficult times in high school. I don't know for sure, but I think he may have been acting out at our parents for moving him away from his friends. He found some new ones that weren't the best kind of influence."

"That certainly can happen. He's doing okay now, though?"

"Yeah, he's doing great. Sometime early in his junior year, he realized that college would be a good way to get out of the house. Turns out scholarship applications are a very civilizing influence for some kids."

"Good to know." The smile in Amber's eyes told him she agreed.

The server arrived to take their order. When she left, Max found the awkwardness gone. He and Amber spoke easily about people they both knew. By the time their food arrived, they were chatting about Halloween.

"We know it's a risk," Amber said, "but the faculty discussed it and we've decided to let the children wear their costumes to school on Halloween. The rule is no masks and no toy weapons, not even pretend light sabers. Also nothing with obscene or coarse words."

"Costumes." Max could feel himself sinking. "I haven't even thought about costumes."

Amber chuckled. "You thought of candy, but not costumes?"

Max grimaced. Maybe he wasn't as good at this single-parent gig as he'd hoped. "I'm afraid that's right. Do you have any ideas?"

"Actually, I might. With their beautiful hair, and especially given Will's cute curls, they'd make a great Raggedy Ann and Andy."

"Raggedy Ann?" Max blanked.

"You don't know Raggedy Ann and Andy?"

Max searched his memory. "I don't think so."

"Then your education has been sadly neglected." She got out her phone and did a quick Google search. "Here they are."

"Ah! I see why you think that would work for my kids."

"I have some ideas about how to dress them, too. Can you bring them to my place tomorrow afternoon?"

"Yeah. Sure. And thanks! I always feel like I'm playing catch-up when it comes to being a single parent. How do other people do it?"

"I've never been a parent, of course, but I suspect most parents feel like they're playing catch-up, even the ones who have a partner working with them. Parenting is a huge job under any circumstances. It's also one of the most important you can do, since you're shaping the lives of the next generation."

"I hadn't thought of it that way. I just always think of how much Kate and Will both mean to me."

Amber touched his hand. "That's the most important part. Kids are pretty resilient. They can overcome the little mistakes we may make as parents or educators, so long as they know we care about them."

"Thanks." He took her hand. Her dark eyes were luminous in the candle-lit ambiance of the restaurant. "That means a lot."

They finished their dinner, and both declined dessert, opting for a coffee instead. As they walked back to the car, Max said, "It's early yet. If you don't mind, I'd rather not take you straight home." He shrugged. "There isn't much to do in Destiny, though, not at this hour."

"The spa is still doing grand opening tours and I think they go 'til after ten on the weekends. Are you interested in seeing what they've done there?"

"Sure. Let's see what the spa has to offer."

As they followed the tour guide through the various buildings, Amber took a trip of her own, a walk down memory lane. Her mother had never let her come along when she visited Aunt Donna in the Children of Rah compound. Amber had seen the buildings from the road, and she'd heard her cousins' stories of what happened here, although she suspected she didn't know the worst.

"I'm glad this tree is still here," she said as their tour passed from one building to another. "Sunny and Skye have both told me about swinging from this tree. It was one of their better memories."

"You must be mistaken," the guide said. "There was nothing here before the spa was built. This land was unoccupied."

Max flashed her a look. Amber responded. "I know that's the official story. If you do a little research, you'll find there was a cult compound here for several years. They called themselves the Children of Rah. They put together some rough buildings that would never have met building codes and they squatted on this property for some twelve or thirteen years."

"You must be mistaken," the guide said.

"I assure you, I'm not mistaken. You can research it online," Amber said. "It made the Sacramento papers when the owner showed up and wanted to sell his property, but the cult claimed squatters' rights and sued to stay."

"I never heard of that."

Amber gestured around. "My aunt was involved in the cult and my cousins were born here."

"I'm sure that's not true."

"I'm certain it is," Amber said firmly. Then, voice shaking, she changed the subject. "What's on the rest of the tour?"

Half an hour later, Max drove Amber up the road toward her home. "You okay?"

"Yeah." She let out a frustrated sigh that suggested otherwise. "It bothers me that nobody recognizes that time. It's like my cousins' childhood years have been erased."

"But they haven't," Max said. "You remember, they remember, all of the people who lived in Destiny during that time remember."

"You lived in Destiny then. Do you remember?"

Max looked thoughtful. "I can't say I remember much, but I remember the slapped-together buildings we could see from the road, and I know some of the guys from school liked to hang out around the compound, hoping to see the women come out naked."

Amber nodded. "Yeah. I knew that was going on. The cult members were generally careful to wear coverings when they came outside. By choosing not to offend the sensibilities of their neighbors up the road, they were able to hang out here longer than they might have otherwise."

"They were a nudist colony, right?"

"That was part of their story. Mostly they were into drugs—lots of drugs—and fairly free..." She gave Max a wary look, wondering how to say what she was thinking.

"Fairly free...uh, coupling?" he asked.

"Well said." She nodded. "Both Sunny and Skye have birth certificates that list their fathers as unknown. Instead, their mother wrote 'Rah, the Sun God.' The fact is, without DNA testing, nobody knows, but it's clear Skye and Sunny had different dads."

"I remember meeting the bride at the reception. When someone pointed out her sister, I was pretty sure I was seeing the wrong person."

"A very pretty girl with darker skin and curly black hair? Looks a lot like Meghan Markle?"

"Yes. Exactly."

"That's Skye. Both the girls have had trouble adjusting to the healthy world outside the cult, but Skye's transition has been harder."

"I can imagine being a child in a place like that would be...difficult. Did your cousins get counseling? You know, the kind of help you recommended for my kids?"

"No, they didn't. They undoubtedly needed it, but my dad had an even more negative response to the idea than you did. Besides, it took some time before my folks were officially the legal guardians, so their insurance didn't cover my cousins. The cost was too much for them to pay out of pocket."

Max nodded in understanding. "I'm glad you talked me into it, and I'm glad my insurance is covering most of the bill because yes, it's expensive. It's worth it, though."

That brought them to the topic they'd been avoiding all evening and they let themselves talk freely about how both children were adjusting. The conversation lasted longer than the drive, so they sat in his car outside her home, talking about the most recent visits in Dr. Schafer's office and how concerned the therapist was about Will's ongoing anger. "He says it's normal, but we can't let it go on."

"I imagine it could be normal in a situation like you describe. You mentioned you'd separated from your wife some time before she… passed away. Do you want to talk about that?"

Max leaned back, physically withdrawing. "Not yet. Maybe when we know each other better…"

"I understand. Well, I think it's time for me to go in."

He nodded. "I'll walk you in." He came around to open her door and walked with his hand at her back as they went up her front walk. She unlocked the door, leaving it slightly open as she turned to him. "Thank you, Max. It's been a lovely evening."

"We should do this again."

"Yes. That would be nice. In the meantime, I'll see you and Will and Kate here tomorrow to work on Halloween costumes."

"You've got it." An awkward moment ensued as neither seemed to know what to do next.

Amber took control. She rose on tiptoe, placing a quick kiss on Max's cheek. "Good night, Max. See you tomorrow."

He touched the place she'd kissed. "Yeah. See you tomorrow."

She went inside and closed the door but watched through her front window as he drove away.

MAX PAID THE BABYSITTER, and she called her parents for a ride home. He had worked that out with the Salvadors in advance, since he didn't feel he could leave his sleeping children while he drove Luisa. "Thank you," he said to Luisa as her dad pulled into the driveway. "Okay if I call you to sit with the kids again sometime?"

"Sure. I'd like that. You have great kids." Luisa waved as she left.

It pleased him that Luisa was willing to come back. He wanted to see Amber again. They'd had a few rough patches this evening, but that was to be expected on a first date. Not to mention it had been so long since he'd dated at all. Still, it had gone well enough, hadn't it? He was sure glad Amber was willing to help with the kids' costumes tomorrow. It scared him how much there was for a parent think about.

As he got ready for bed, his mind kept drifting back to Amber. She was different when not acting in the role of principal or counselor. She'd been more relaxed, fun—just a beautiful woman out for a nice dinner. He remembered the way she looked in the glow of the candle on their table, and how her eyes had flashed as she stood up to the tour guide at the health spa. Amber was a beautiful, intelligent woman, and a good person. She'd never be the spoiled pet Isabel was. She was also amazingly dedicated to her job. She had worked hard to become principal at the elementary school, and she cared about the kids. She certainly cared about Will and Kate. He blew out a breath as he settled into bed. He'd find it very easy to fall for her.

You already are falling for her, his inner voice chimed in.

Max smiled as his eyes grew heavy with sleep. His last thought was of Amber's velvety-dark eyes and warm smile.

Chapter Eleven

"There," Amber said aloud, looking around at the items she'd gathered. "I think I'm ready." She'd spent the morning gathering material and other items she'd need for the kids' costumes, grateful her mother had taught her sewing basics years ago, grateful too for the red-and-white striped socks she'd purchased for a "Where's Waldo?" game at school. She'd bought one pair for their chosen Waldo and another for back-up, in case something happened to the first. Both pairs were too big for the Burnett twins, but with some elastic sewn into the tops, they'd do the job.

Amber's mother had been wonderful, jumping on board with enthusiasm. "I like those kids," she told Amber. "I want to help." Digging into her fabric stores, Olivia had made a checked shirt for Will and a loose dress for Kate while Amber worked on Will's short blue pants and a matching apron for Kate. The look might not be perfect, but everyone would recognize Raggedy Ann and Andy—that is, everyone who recognized the dolls at all. How had Max grown up without ever hearing of Raggedy Ann and Andy? Amber set the colorful costumes on the dining room table.

Stepping into the kitchen, she made a pitcher of lemonade and put it in the fridge to keep cold. Then she set out a plate of whole grain crackers, cheese, and some carrot sticks for the kids. She was rapidly becoming involved with this family. Maybe too involved?

Stop worrying and enjoy spending time with them, her inner voice scolded.

She sighed as she bit into a carrot stick and stilled her negative thoughts.

～

"Okay, kids, time to head out!" Max had spent the morning trying to psych up the kids, getting them excited about their Halloween costumes.

Kate was all in. "Raggedy Ann and Andy are so cute!" She practically bubbled.

Did everyone recognize these characters but him? "How do you know about Raggedy Ann and Andy, honey?"

"Oh, Daddy. *Everybody* knows about them." Kate hurried to put on her heavy black shoes, the ones Amber had suggested to go with the costume. So much for family solidarity.

"What do you think, Will?"

Will wore only one shoe. He threw the other one, hitting the couch just under the seat cushion. "I think it's stupid. Who wants to look like a stupid doll?"

"Stop that, Will." Kate stood in front of her brother, hands on hips. "You're just being mean because it's Ms. Reyes who's helping us."

"She's our principal. She's not supposed to be messing with stuff like our Halloween costumes." Will's pout could have won awards, if anyone gave awards for pouting.

"Enough, Will." Max put his hand on the boy's shoulder. "Get your shoes on and get ready to go. We should be grateful Ms. Reyes is willing to help."

Will's mouth tightened until his lips disappeared. "You just say that 'cause you want to hang out with her."

Max felt his temper rising. "Will, I said that's enough. Get your shoes on now."

Will seemed to understand he had pushed far enough. His face a mask of anger, he grumbled as he put on his shoes.

Maybe Dr. Schafer was right about Will. "Okay, kids. Let's go." He held the door open while Kate bounced out to the car and Will dragged behind, grumbling under his breath.

"I can hear you, son," Max said as he locked the front door. "You need to behave yourself the whole time we're at Ms. Reyes' house. Understand?"

"Yeah."

"Will?"

"I mean yessir."

"Thank you." Minutes later, he put eager energy into his voice as he stopped the car at Amber's curb. "We're here, guys! Let's go try on those costumes."

"I DON'T THINK I've ever seen a cuter Raggedy Ann or Andy." Amber walked around the children, examining from every angle. She and her mother had guessed the sizes surprisingly close, just a little large. "We may have to take in those shorts some more, Will—

The boy turned on her. "Why can't you just leave me alone? Why can't you leave all of us alone?"

"Will!" Max stepped forward. "You need to apologize. Now."

"I don't wanta 'pologize!" Anger colored his features. "And I don't wanta be a stupid doll!" He ran from the room, slamming the door behind him.

Reality hit Amber hard. No one had asked the children what they wanted to be for Halloween. She knew better than to do that, but she'd forged ahead anyway, not taking the kids' wishes into consideration in her eagerness to help their dad.

Max looked to Amber with an unspoken apology. "I need to go after him. I'm sorry about this, Amber."

"It's okay, Max. Will has a point so go easy, okay? Kate and I will wait here. We'll be fine, won't we, Kate?" She smiled reassuringly.

Kate's eyes were wide. "Is Will gonna be okay?"

"Of course, sweetheart." Amber stroked her hair. "He just needs time to adjust. Your daddy will help him." She hoped that was all it would take. Will was a very angry child.

For the next twenty minutes, or perhaps a little longer, Amber kept Kate busy with costume alterations. In a gentle and patient tone, she showed Kate how to hold the fabric in place while she sewed a button on more securely. Amber smiled at Kate in encouragement, but inside she worried about Will and Max. She almost sighed in relief when the front door finally opened.

"Will has something he wants to say to you, Ms. Reyes." Max pushed a frowning Will forward.

Amber knelt to his level. "What would you like to tell me, Will?"

"I'm sorry I was rude." Will spoke the words, but they were barely audible, and he kept his eyes on the floor. "It's nice of you to help us with our costumes."

"Thank you, Will. It's kind of you to say so." She smiled as she took his hand in hers. "If you'll let me work on your costume, it will fit better when you wear it next week." She took a deep breath. "Or, if you prefer, you can pick something different that you'd like to be for Halloween and I'll see what I can do."

"It's okay. I can wear the doll costume." Subdued but defiant, Will took little care as he removed each piece of the costume, dropping them in the middle of Amber's kitchen floor. The fitted shorts and shirt he'd worn underneath were thin for the weather outdoors, but that didn't seem to discourage him. "Can we play outside now?"

"Yes," Max said. "Just stay close. We'll be ready to go in a little while."

"Okay." Will all but ran for the door.

"Is he gonna be all right?" Kate asked, as she trudged behind him.

"He'll be fine," Max assured her. "Stay close, okay?"

"Okay, Daddy." She waved and closed the door behind her.

"There's my Kate, the people pleaser."

Amber noted the phrase Max used to describe his daughter. Dr. Schafer must have made the same determination she had. "You know Will is right. We never consulted the kids about what costumes they'd like. I think there's still time to change that."

"No need," Max said. "Maybe we should have asked, and I'll know better in the future, but for now, I've talked Will into this costume, and it's good to leave well enough alone."

"Okay," Amber answered. Then she asked, "How are they doing, Max?"

"Better."

"Better enough?"

"I don't know." He rubbed the back of his neck in a gesture of total frustration. "I can never tell what's really going on with them. I think they're doing just fine and then something like this comes up…" He left the sentence hanging.

Amber gestured toward a chair. "Can you sit for a minute?"

"Yeah, but not for long. We've got plenty of regular Saturday chores to take care of."

She started work on Raggedy Andy's shorts. "May I ask how you settled him down?"

Max looked ashamed. "I failed the parent test."

"You're going to have to explain that."

"I told him that if he behaves himself all the way through Halloween, I'll get him the puppy he's been begging for."

"Oh."

"Yeah. Oh indeed. I gave in to basic bribery, your ultimate cop-out in parenting. I wanted so much for him to settle down."

"Can you handle a puppy?"

Max let out an exasperated huff. "I suppose. I feel so overwhelmed with the kids and the new job in a place that isn't completely new to me but is different enough to feel new."

Amber nodded her understanding.

"Anyway, I'd been thinking for a while that, if we get permission to fence the back yard in the place we're renting, I might let Will have a dog. Now I have to hope Lech Nowak will give his permission."

"I'm sure he will."

"Even if he doesn't, I'm committed now. I told Will we might not get the puppy until after the first of the year. That gives me a little time to get things together."

"What kind of dog will you be looking for? Does Will have a specific breed in mind?"

"My in-laws…well, my ex-in-laws, that is, the kids' grandparents… they have a beagle they call Pepper. Will's crazy about him."

"Beagles are good dogs, and they're supposed to be very good with kids."

"Yeah. I guess we'll be looking for a beagle. If we want to get one around the first of the year, I imagine we'll be looking at litters born right around now." Max shook himself as if the idea had suddenly become too real.

Amber finished tightening the elastic in the costume shorts. "You really don't feel ready for this, do you?"

"Not at all."

She put her hand on his shoulder. "It'll be okay, Max. You're going to be just fine."

"I appreciate your faith in me, but…"

"I have an idea about Halloween, if you don't mind. It might make things easier."

"Yeah?"

"Why don't you take the kids out early? Cover some of the blocks where the homes are close together. Then, when the kids start getting tired, come here. We'll let Raggedy Ann and Andy hand out candy while we grown-ups unwind. Sound good?"

"Yeah. That sounds good."

Amber folded the kids' costumes and placed them in a paper bag. "Here you go." She smiled, handing him the bag. "I guess I'll see you on Halloween, if not before."

"Sounds good," he said again, taking the bag. "Thanks, Amber. I don't know how we'd have gotten through Halloween without your help. I appreciate it."

"How have you managed before?"

"My mom came up for a week and helped the kids get ready. I worked long hours, so I didn't even take the kids out. Mom did." He looked into her eyes and for a moment neither of them said anything. "I still have a lot to learn about being a parent."

"But you love them, and you're making the effort. That's a great start."

Max leaned in and Amber waited for his kiss, but at the last moment, his lips brushed her cheek.

"Thanks again," he said softly. "See you soon."

"Right." She swallowed her disappointment. "See you soon." She watched out the window as he rounded up his children.

"Come on, kiddos! We've got stuff to do," he told them.

Kate, ever the pleaser, ran to climb in. Amber watched as Will dragged behind. She'd won him over once at the pool party, but he had fallen back into his earlier position of distrust. She'd have her work cut out for her to win over again.

Aha! her inner voice teased. *You're already thinking long-term.*

Amber smiled and blew out a breath. "I guess I am," she said aloud. "Yes, I guess I am."

∾

MAX FUMBLED with the bits and parts of the costumes, trying to help the kids dress for school on Halloween morning.

"Not like that, Daddy." Kate pulled her lips together in a look of distress—or was it disgust? However he described it, he'd seen that look on a number of female faces.

"Why don't you show me how it goes?" He winked at his daughter, who quickly took over, sorting the parts of her own costume and her brother's in perfect order.

"Wow! You've got it perfect." Were women born with it? He guessed there must be a how-to-wear-things gene on that second X chromosome. Meanwhile, his son looked as dazed and confused as Max felt. "Come on, Will. Let's get you dressed."

"Yeah. Like I wanta be some stupid doll," Will grumbled in a voice that was barely audible.

"Enough, Will. Come on and get dressed. You don't want to be late for school." Max held the costume pants so Will could step into them.

"They're too loose, Dad. They're gonna fall off!"

"They won't fall off. Miss Reyes fixed them, and you've also got these straps that go up over your shoulders to keep them on. Besides, even if they did fall off, you've got your biking shorts underneath."

"Why can't I just wear my biking shorts?"

"Because that's not a Halloween costume." Max tried to keep his voice even and his temper in check. He remembered what Dr. Schafer had said at their appointment the day before: "It's difficult to tell whether he's more resentful of the costume because he's afraid other boys will make fun of him or because it was Ms. Reyes's idea."

"He's resentful of her?" Max could hardly have been more shocked. "Why?"

"He thinks she's trying to replace his mother."

"Oh. I never thought—"

"Is she, Max?" Dr. Schafer had been straightforward with the question. "Or are you maybe? Are you and Amber Reyes becoming a couple?"

"We went out to dinner together once. And she helped with the kids' costumes. That's it, though."

"That isn't all there is to it. She came with you to your first appointment."

"True. But you were the one who asked her to come."

"Yes, but she was already involved with the children. You and Amber: are you interested in taking it further?" Dr. Schafer looked every inch the stereotypical therapist as he leaned back in his chair, his legs crossed, his note tablet in hand, his glasses slipping down his nose.

Max felt like telling Schafer to mind his own business, but then remembered he had made his family's happiness the therapist's business. "I like her. Until I met Amber, I hadn't been on a date since... well, not since I dated Isabel before we got married."

"Does Will have reason to think she might be intruding into the family you have now?"

"I don't know, but that could explain why he always seems so angry when we're around her."

"Exactly. You need to do some thinking. Perhaps you and Ms. Reyes should discuss it."

"Yeah, maybe we should." Max wondered how he could raise that topic, and why he couldn't just tell Will to behave himself.

Dr. Schafer must have guessed Max's thoughts. "He's only six years old, Max. He doesn't understand anything about what happened to his mother, and he doesn't like the way his family has changed. He wants to focus the blame for that somewhere. That's a pretty typical response for a boy his age."

"I guess," Max answered. "What do I need to do?"

"Talk to Ms. Reyes. Decide what you want from your relationship down the road. If you are moving forward with it, take it slowly. Give Will time to adjust, and make sure you spend some time just with you and the children or you and Will alone, not always with Amber present. It isn't just about her replacing his mother, you know. He's afraid that if you come to care too much for her, she'll replace him in your affection, and you'll forget about him."

Max's jaw almost dropped. "How could he even think that?"

"Maybe he isn't thinking it consciously, but it's the fear at the bottom of his anger. He feels his mother abandoned him for something she wanted more. Now he's afraid the same thing could happen with his dad."

"Whew." Max blew out a long breath. From a kid's perspective, that made sense. No wonder Will was so angry. No wonder Kate worked so hard to keep her father happy. "They both need to know I would never leave them; that no matter what happens, I'll always be there."

Dr. Schafer nodded, looking pleased. "That's the essence of it, yes. Their world turned upside down when their mother left the house and then when she passed away, it only added to their pain and confusion." He cleared his throat. "They need to know you're not leaving, not for any reason. That's why Amber Reyes represents a threat, especially to Will. In their minds, if you care too much about her, she could replace them in your affection, maybe even cause you to leave."

"Never." Max stared daggers at Dr. Schafer. "That will never happen. Even if I should happen to fall in love and want to marry again—with Amber Reyes or with anybody else—I'll always be my children's father. I'll always love them and take care of them."

"Well said, Max." Dr. Schafer beamed approval. "Now you just have to get both Will and Kate to believe that. Even if you tell them what you just told me, they may not believe you. At least not at first. But those children need to believe it; they need to feel it down to their bones."

"How can I make them feel that way?"

"Give it time. Let both children see you putting them first. Often."

"Okay, I'll work on that."

Max had left Dr. Schafer's office wiser, and much more concerned, than he'd been before. He didn't know what to say to Amber or how to put Schafer's formula to work, but he knew he needed to figure it out, and he knew he needed to talk with Amber. Soon.

Kate's bouncing around the kitchen in excitement brought his mind back to the present. Max fastened the red bow tie on Will's costume and stepped back. "You two look awesome! Come on. Let's get you to school." Maybe he could make the opportunity to chat with Amber while the kids passed out candy at her house this evening. At least, they could make a start.

Chapter Twelve

Amber waved as a trio of trick-or-treaters left her porch. "You look great!" she called after them. "Very scary." Her exaggerated look of fear made the vampires giggle. She wondered when Max would arrive, and then cut off the thought as she saw his car.

He'd barely turned off the ignition when Kate burst out from the back seat. "We got lots and lots of candy, Ms. Reyes! Everybody likes the Raggedy Ann and Andy costumes."

"Everybody? I'm so glad." Amber accepted Kate's huge hug.

Will was slower to get out of the car, and he didn't approach Amber for a hug, but he smiled as he walked up.

"How was it, Will? Did everybody like your costume, too?"

"Not everybody," Will said. "A couple of the older boys—you know, Peter and Kaiden in the third grade—they teased me about wearing a doll costume, but lots of the girls said it was cute." His shy grin barely showed his broad dimples.

"That wasn't so bad, was it?" Amber suppressed a smile as a blush colored Will's cheeks even more rosy.

"Nah. It was okay."

"Hey, you two," Max called, taking two bags of candy out of the trunk. "Are you ready to take over distributing Halloween candy to other ghosts and ghoulies?"

"I am!" Kate jumped forward, reaching for the plastic jack-o-lantern that held Amber's candy supply.

"You too, Will?" Max held out a second bag for his son. "You can take the back-up bag."

"Yeah. Okay." Will looked at his father and straightened, a half-smile on his face. "I mean yes, sir."

"Thatta boy. Looks like you have a pirate or two coming up the walk with some ghosts right behind."

"Let me!" Kate jumped forward.

Max watched from behind his children as they managed the next two groups. "Looks like they have it well in hand," he said to Amber. "Can we talk?"

"Sure. I made Mexican hot chocolate. Come on into the kitchen."

"Yum. I smell the chocolate and something else." He sniffed. "Cinnamon?"

"That's right." As she led the way, Amber wondered what direction this talk might take. "Here," she said, taking a chair and gesturing toward another. "What do you have in mind?"

"So THAT's what Dr. Schafer thinks is happening," Max finished. He watched Amber's face carefully, looking for her reaction.

"It makes sense," she said, her expression thoughtful. "They feel their mother abandoned them. Did she?"

Max wondered how much to tell Amber. "I'm pretty close-mouthed about the details," he said carefully, "but I think you have a right, maybe even a need, to hear at least some of it. Just…" He looked in the direction of his children. "Now's probably not a good time."

"Okay. I get that." Amber nodded. "We won't talk in present company. Is there another time that works better?"

"Maybe tomorrow evening? I think I can ask Luisa to watch the kids again."

"We'll plan on it. Send me a text when you have it arranged."

"Okay. Maybe we can go to dinner again—"

She shook her head. "You don't want to be in a public place when you talk about this."

"You're right. I hadn't thought that far. Then I don't—"

"I'll cook," she said, smiling sweetly. "I'm actually a pretty good cook. Now and then I like an excuse to prepare something nice. You like Mexican food?"

"Sure do."

"Great. I'll make some family favorites. We'll plan for six o'clock. If that doesn't work, you can text me another time, or if Luisa can't make it tomorrow, we can plan for another day. Work for you?"

"Yeah, that's great. Thanks for making this so easy."

"No problem. We'll plan for tomorrow, then. Want some marshmallows for your chocolate?"

"Sure. Why not?" He sat back, grinning, letting Amber spoil him and thinking he could get used to this.

THE SCHOOL always struggled the day after Halloween. Amber looked forward to the years when Halloween landed on a Friday or a Saturday, so the kids could get over their sugar buzz before their next school day. That wasn't happening this year.

She watched as the first, second, and third graders played musical chairs in the multi-purpose room. Knowing that quiet, concentrated learning activities would only set them up for failure, the faculty always planned for what they called "active learning" on the day after Halloween, or the last day before Christmas, or other days during the year when sit-down learning was not going to happen.

"Nicely done," she said to Mrs. Nguyen, who supervised the activity. "What's next?"

"Miss Sanchez brought a half-dozen Twister games. She'll call the directions in Spanish so the kids will be learning right and left, hand and foot, and a series of colors while they play."

"Excellent. That helps us justify it as a learning activity."

Mrs. Nguyen nodded. "Yes, that's what we both thought. Uh-oh."

Amber looked in the same direction and saw Will Burnett being bumped off a chair, landing on the wood floor.

"Not fair!" Will yelled.

"Looks like I'd better—" Amber started in Will's direction.

Much to her surprise, the boy who had taken the chair said, "You're right. You were in the chair first." He stood up, offering Will his hand.

Will gave the boy, a third-grader named Mark Sullivan, a suspicious look, but he accepted his hand and let the boy help him to his feet. "I'm out," Mark said, and stepped to the side to stand with the others who had already been eliminated.

"Wow." Mrs. Nguyen looked pleasantly surprised. "I never expected to see that." She walked to the sideline to praise Mark for doing the right thing.

Amber watched with a warm sense of contentment. Maybe some of the school's lessons on respecting the rights of others were sinking in. The music started and stopped again. This time the chairs were filled before Will reached one. Amber waited for the outburst, but it never came.

"I'm out," Will said. He went to stand beside Mark and the game went on without incident.

Mrs. Nguyen raised an eyebrow in a look that said, *We're making progress*. Amber nodded. Will was coming around. She'd plan to mention this to Max when she saw him.

A text from Max later that morning confirmed their dinner plans. She had a batch of Anasazi beans simmering in her slow cooker. She'd also taken a batch of pork *tamales* out to thaw and compiled the ingredients for *chiles rellenos*—well, everything but the fresh green chiles. She'd pick those up at Gale's Produce Market on the way home, along with ingredients for a simple green salad. She'd been cooking for one for a while now, and she found it pleasurable to cook for others. When her inner voice asked if her real aim was cooking for Max, she chose to ignore it.

Chapter Thirteen

Max sat at the kitchen table, watching Amber as she put the finishing touches on the salad and began cooking the *rellenos*. She reminded him of a professional chef, the kind you see on TV shows, whipping up something delicious and chatting at the same time. She did that with such ease, truly an amazing person. Not to mention beautiful…

Max reminded himself to keep his thoughts on her words. Amber was saying something about the activities at the school that morning, something about Will.

"You would have been so proud of Will," Amber said, finishing her story. "I was proud of him and of Mark, the third-grader too. I think they've become…well, friends."

"That's great. Will told me about playing musical chairs. He didn't say anything about getting bumped or about the boy helping him up."

"Maybe he decided it was no biggie."

"I hope so. That would be good progress."

They kept the conversation light throughout dinner. Amber talked about the school's active learning day, the Spanish-language Twister game with Miss Sanchez, and other general topics that avoided anything intense or personal. Max stuck with the non-proprietary information he could share about the mine, and the facts and numbers included in public press releases. He added, "I like what I do, and I'm glad I don't have to go to the mine every day, but sometimes I miss getting down and dirty with the team doing the real work."

"You worked in the mine?" Amber's surprise was obvious.

"Not this one, but yeah. When I was finishing school. It's how I paid for my last couple of years." He shrugged. "Better pay than washing dishes, and I liked the adventure of it."

"Aha!" Amber winked. "That explains your physique."

Max chuckled and rubbed the back of his neck, feeling the heat flush his face. "Uh, thanks?"

"You're welcome. Those of us who look at you get the benefit." Her flirtatious smile warmed him even more.

When they finished eating, Amber cleared the table. "I have flan for dessert, if you'd like it now, or we can hold it for later."

Max decided it was now or never. Time to suck it up and tell Amber what happened—at least the essence of it. "Let's save dessert for later." He gestured toward the couch. "Shall we get comfortable?"

She nodded. "Yes. Let's."

Max couldn't help noticing how nervous Amber looked as they walked to the couch. Her edginess mirrored his own. Amber sat near him, but not close enough for him to slip his arm around her shoulders, although Max thought that might help them open up to each other. The warmth of her smile made his heart do a backflip.

"You were going to tell me what happened with your wife," Amber prompted.

"Yeah. I guess I'm trying to decide where to start."

She offered another smile. "It's your story. Start wherever you feel comfortable."

Max decided it was best if he gave her the whole thing, especially if there was a chance for the two of them in the future. "Isabel sparkled," he began. "She was one of those people you hear about who is at the center of everything fun or imaginative. She was beautiful and intelligent and full of energy, and she loved a good party. She blew me away. Right from the first time I saw her, I was…I don't know how to say it."

"Enraptured? Enthralled?" Amber's expression was unreadable.

"Yeah, something like that. I could hardly believe it when she turned her attention to me. I thought I had to be the luckiest man on earth."

Amber nodded. "A man should feel that way when he's in love."

"That's what I thought too. I was so…enraptured, was it? Was that the term you used?"

She nodded.

"I was so enraptured that I didn't see the problems, the cracks in that perfect façade."

Amber leaned back against the couch. "Go on."

"Even before the wedding, those cracks started showing up, like the way she had to have everything exactly as she'd imagined it. She was a Bridezilla, demanding that the roses be *ivory*, not white, the ribbons four inches wide, not three."

"Her parents were paying for the wedding, right?"

He nodded.

"They went along with all that?"

"Isabel was their only child. They'd spent a lifetime spoiling her and why would it have been any different for her wedding? Besides, her dad is a superior court judge in the county where they live, so they had people they wanted to impress, friends and political supporters. They were all for whatever Isabel wanted. I was the only one who balked at some of her choices. When she told me about the bow tie I was supposed to wear, I told her I never wear bow ties. You should have seen her face!"

"A tantrum, was it?"

"Oh no. Tantrums were beneath Isabel. She'd lift her chin with an imperious look, stare down her nose at the offender, and say, 'You will wear the bow tie exactly as I told you.'"

"I gather you wore the bow tie?"

"Yeah, I did. I felt ridiculous, but I wore it." He cleared his throat. "Fast forward three years. I'd been doing things her way for the most part. That was how I kept the peace. I was working on building my career at Río Blanco, and I wanted some time to focus on moving up in the company, but Isabel had decided it was time to have a baby."

"And Isabel always got her way."

"You're catching on." He swallowed. "Of course, I ended up agreeing. During the engagement, we'd agreed on two children and we both thought it would be great if we had a son and a daughter. I assumed we'd make a baby and find out later if we were getting a girl or a boy. You know, parenthood the way it's been done for millennia."

"Um-hm."

"Isabel informed me that she only wanted to be pregnant once. We would therefore do *in vitro* and pick one male and one female embryo, implanting them so she could have boy-girl twins and 'get it over with.'"

Amber bit her lip before asking, "I gather you weren't crazy about that?"

"I hated it. I told her I wanted to have babies the old-fashioned way. She put her foot down. I reminded her that her plan would cost a fortune and we didn't have that kind of money. She said she'd already talked to 'Daddy' and he would be happy to pay." Max shook his head.

"And that's the story of how you got Will and Kate," Amber said softly.

"Exactly."

"Are you okay? Do you want to keep talking?"

He licked his lips. "Actually, I'm almost there." Max knew the next part of his story would be the most difficult. He closed his eyes as he said, "That was when things got...weird."

"Weird how?" Amber said, shifting a pillow to her lap.

Max paused for a moment realizing that Amber seemed...upset. But he couldn't tell if it was because of Isabel's manipulation or his own inability to stand up to her. Maybe both.

"The *in vitro* was successful," Max went on. "Because the doctors were working with a woman who could have conceived easily without medical intervention, the implantation worked the first time. Within a couple of months, Isabel was pregnant."

"That must have made her happy."

Max shook his head. "She hated it. I don't know how many times I heard her say, 'This is rotten. This is miserable. I don't know how other women put up with it.'"

Amber looked sympathetic. "Perhaps she was having a difficult pregnancy."

"Not so. Her obstetrician said it was one of the easiest she'd ever seen and given that Isabel was carrying twins, she should be pleased at how easy it was."

"But Isabel didn't buy that?"

"Isabel gave her doctor that imperious look and declared she was miserable, and the doctor must come up with something to help her. Making a very long, awful story short, she demanded painkillers. By the time she delivered, she was addicted to narcotics."

Amber clutched the pillow close to her chest. "It's a blessing the twins turned out healthy."

"That's what I thought." He cleared his throat. "By then, I was completely irrelevant. Isabel and her mother ran the whole pregnancy. Isabel even stayed with her mother the last two months while I lived in our apartment alone. Everything had to be Isabel's way, and her mother was the only person who could baby her as she wished."

"That must have been hard for you," Amber whispered.

"It was horrible. I couldn't help wondering what I'd gotten myself into. But then the twins were born—caesarean section, of course, with Isabel deadened with a spinal block so she could observe while the babies were delivered without having to go through labor. She also arranged with her doctor to have her tubes tied before she was closed up again."

"You didn't want that."

"Not at all. I had agreed to two, but I wanted to keep the option open in case we changed our minds. Isabel made the decision without me and had the procedure despite my objection."

"That must have been difficult."

"It was, but it was what Isabel wanted, so of course, everyone else was all for it."

Amber set the pillow aside and reached for his hand. "I'm so sorry, Max. That must have really hurt."

"Thank you. Isabel gave birth in the easiest way she could imagine and then behaved as though she'd suffered the worst experience ever. She complained about the pain and kept insisting on heavier opiates—"

"You said she was addicted even before the birth. What kind of doctor would do that?"

"One who didn't want trouble with her dad, I guess. I don't know exactly what happened because I was never included in medical visits or decisions." He drew in a breath and went on with his story. "So

Isabel was already addicted, but things didn't really get out of hand until she was recovering from the surgery."

"They say the opiates can be bad for the babies," Amber said. "They transfer through breast milk."

"Oh, Isabel didn't breastfeed. She was adamant it would have ruined her perfect figure; it was also beneath her dignity. Turns out Isabel wanted to have children. She just didn't want to *have* them."

Amber wrinkled her forehead. "Can you explain, please?"

"During the pregnancy, she and her mother planned for an *au pair*, also a night nurse. They had bottles and formula all set up and a nursery in her parents' home."

"Your wife didn't bring your babies home to you?"

"Not for the first four months. When I objected, her dad said he didn't see what my problem was since he was paying for all of it. Isabel and her mother were in lockstep on every decision, so there was no room for a mere husband and father to step in."

"I hear the bitterness in your voice. I'm sorry it was so rough." Amber squeezed his hand.

"I'm the one who's sorry. I promised myself I wouldn't let the old bitterness show."

"It must be hard not to."

"Apparently." He smiled, trying to calm himself and reassure her. "When I realized I wasn't going to be with my children except under the watchful and disapproving eyes of my mother-in-law, I considered just walking away, especially when Isabel made it clear that she was staying at her mother's home while she 'adjusted' to being a mother and I wasn't welcome."

"So, you were left on your own."

"Yeah, under the circumstances, I wondered whether I'd get to be a father at all."

"What happened?"

"The kids. I'd seen them a few times, but I'd hardly been allowed to touch or hold them. One day when the babies were about two weeks old, I dropped in at my in-laws' place when Isabel and her mother were out. The judge wasn't home, so it was just me and the *au pair*. She didn't see any reason why I couldn't go in and spend time with my babies."

"So you did."

"Yeah, I did. I at least wanted to study what the combination of my genes and Isabel's had produced. Kate was sleeping when I walked up beside her crib. I reached down and touched her hand. She grasped my finger. Then she opened her eyes and looked at me, just looked at me." Max felt emotion swell in his throat. He swallowed it down. "Her eyes were so clear, so deep and so wise. She looked at me with perfect trust, almost as if she understood who I was and knew I'd take care of her. I fell in love then and there. I stood and let her hold my finger until she went back to sleep, maybe fifteen minutes."

"It was Kate who won you over."

"Not just Kate. When I left her crib, I stopped by Will's. He was awake, but not fussing at all. It was as if he'd been waiting for me to come to him too, to let him have his turn. I touched his hand and he took my finger. Then he looked at me, just as Kate had done."

"That's very sweet, almost as if your twins were telling you something."

"They were. I swear there was real communication in the way both looked straight into my eyes. It was almost as though they were telling me that they trusted me to see they were cared for, no matter what their mother and grandparents had planned for them. Before I left that room, I promised them both that I would love them and care for them, that I'd see to it they had the best lives I could give them—not with money, because the judge and his wife had that covered, but with all the love I had in me."

"You stayed in the marriage even when it had already gone bad, and you stayed for the children…Did you also stay for Isabel? Did you still have feelings for her?"

"Definitely not Isabel, and I'm sorry if that sounds cold. By then I realized Isabel didn't care about me at all. The babies and I were all possessions she could show off, like fashion accessories. She wanted to have a husband and children the way her friends had husbands and children. What she didn't want was to take time out of her busy social life for the three of us. The babies and I were on our own."

"If she wanted a husband and family—for whatever reason—why did she leave?"

"That was all in the *how*, in the *way* she abandoned us. She had already left me emotionally, although I hadn't yet grasped that fully. I soon came to wonder if she'd ever loved me at all, and it seemed clear she had no love for the babies. She acted perfectly happy to stay with her parents and leave the children with hired help. For a while, I put up with it, not thinking I had any option.

"One day, when the babies were almost four months old, I staged a palace coup. I went to their house with a small trailer and a couple of buddies. I deliberately picked a time when Isabel and her mother planned to have a massage, so I knew they wouldn't be there. It was during the workday, so the judge wasn't home either. I told the *au pair* I was taking my babies home. Then my buddies and I loaded up everything and did exactly that."

Amber's eyes widened, but she also grinned. "I'm guessing that didn't go over well."

"The *au pair* told me later that Isabel had a complete meltdown and her mother was almost as bad."

"Then how did—"

"It was the judge. That was the one time he took my side. I don't know why. Maybe he'd just gotten tired of having crying newborns in his house, or maybe he was sick of his wife being completely consumed by Isabel. I'm not sure what motivated him, but he told the women that it was time Isabel went back to her husband and we put our own family together."

"The *au pair* came with them?"

"At first, I argued against it. Then I realized Isabel wasn't going to care for the babies on her own. She didn't even know how. We kept the *au pair*—her name was Cynthia—until the kids were potty-trained. I couldn't have afforded it, but the judge paid for it. It may have been his way of making certain Isabel didn't move herself and the babies back in again."

"Was that how she abandoned the babies? Just leaving them for the nanny to raise?"

"Remember I mentioned an opiate addiction?"

"She didn't get help for that?"

"No, and because of who she was, the family doctors didn't question it when she asked for more. She told them she had pain and they believed her. After a while, she was seeing three or four different doctors, supposedly for one complaint or another, and getting prescriptions from all of them. When that wasn't enough, she started buying it on the street."

"I'm guessing you tried to intervene?"

"Amber, I didn't know about the problem. I realize how crazy that sounds, but Isabel spent so many evenings and nights out and I was at work all day... She managed a heavy opioid habit without my ever seeing it or recognizing what was happening."

"Did her parents know?"

"I'm sure her mother did, but her mother bought in to every argument Isabel ever made. When she said she was in pain and needed relief, her mother said, 'Oh, my poor child. What can I do to help?' After a few months, my mother-in-law was going to various doctors complaining of pain and getting drugs for herself that she handed off to her daughter."

"My goodness. Talk about an unhealthy relationship..."

"You don't know the half of it. I'll spare you the details, but it was Isabel's addiction that took her. When the twins were a few weeks short of three, Kate developed a fever. It was evening, the nanny had the night off and Isabel was out, so I was home alone with the babies. I went digging for a thermometer and found a huge bottle of oxycontin —that is, I found a huge bottle, but it was practically empty.

"I did what I had to for Kate and got her settled, and then I went hunting. I dug into all kinds of places that I didn't usually go like Isabel's lingerie drawers and her jewelry box. I pulled all the shoe boxes out of her closet and went through them. When she finally got home, I'd found all kinds of things I never imagined were in my house, including syringes, needles, even rubber bands that she'd use to tie off her arm and pump up a vein."

Amber's eyes filled with tears.

"There was other stuff too. I didn't even recognize what it was, but I found out later it was crystal meth."

"Max, I'm so sorry," Amber said, her voice husky. "Did you confront her?"

"You know I did."

"And?"

"And she lied. This bottle was for her friend, and that one was for her mother, even had her mom's name on it. She was just holding these drugs for other people. I told her that wouldn't wash, that I knew she was lying. I asked how long she'd been using, and she kept insisting she didn't use. It was all surreal, certainly not a conversation I ever expected to have."

"How did you—"

"I gathered up everything I'd found and put it into my briefcase. I sometimes carried sensitive materials for the mining company, so I had a locking briefcase that could only be opened with a very specific combination that Isabel didn't know.

"By then Isabel had gone hours without a hit and she was getting desperate. She stopped pretending she wasn't using and began begging me to give her a little bit of something. I told her no. She took off in her car and went to her mother. I guess her mom must have had something there. She didn't come back that night and she wasn't home the next morning when I got up to get ready for work. The twins weren't fully potty-trained, and Cynthia was still with us, so I left her in charge and went to work."

Max was heartened when Amber reached for his hand again. "That couldn't have been the end of it."

"It was just the start of a new chapter in our book of misery. During my lunch hour, I took the stuff in my briefcase to the judge's chambers and showed him what was going on."

"Did he support you in that, too?"

"You'd think so, wouldn't you? He told me he'd been aware of his daughter's habit for some time. He said things like, 'The poor girl. The way you terrorize her, it's no wonder she needs chemical help.'"

"No!" Amber looked horrified.

"Apparently she'd been laying the groundwork in case she ever needed to defend her drug habit. Since before the babies were born, she'd been telling her parents how unreasonable I was and how I made impossible demands. When her dad started noticing the bruises—you know, the tracks from where she was using the needles—she claimed I was grabbing her and pushing her around, abusing her physically as well as verbally and emotionally. Needle tracks look like tracks, not like other kinds of bruises, and I'm sure the judge knew that, but he'd bought her argument completely. That day, when I took the paraphernalia to the judge's chambers, he threatened to have me arrested if he ever saw bruises on his daughter again."

"You told him the truth about those bruises?"

"I tried. He had the bailiff throw me out. After that, the war was on. To protect their little girl, my in-laws had her move back into their home. They said they were taking the babies as well, but I wouldn't allow it. I arranged to take them to a day care program just across the county line. Before the in-laws could discover where it was, I went to court with the evidence I had of my wife's drug addiction and got an injunction keeping her away from our babies."

"The judge fought it, of course."

"He did, and because of who he was, he got people to listen to him, but then Cynthia and several of the sitters we'd hired came forward to testify about Isabel's drug use. Isabel went to drug court. With a nod to my father-in-law, the judge there gave her probation, but he agreed she shouldn't be around the twins until a medical doctor certified her clean and sober."

"Did she try to bribe a doctor into doing that?"

"She wasn't able to just then. Soon after, she filed for divorce on the grounds of physical and mental cruelty. She also tried to claim I was abusing the kids and she sued for full parental custody. I was able to argue, even in front of one of my father-in-law's colleagues, that she hadn't been certified sober by any medical doctor and that, until she was clean, she was the greatest risk our children faced. My in-laws were beside themselves when I won custody and Isabel got only supervised visits.

"We were divorced, but Isabel and her parents were still constantly in our lives, sometimes showing up during the day, hoping they could take the children from a preschool or a sitter. They even took us back to court. For more than a year, I spent everything I had on lawyers and legal fees. Even had to borrow some."

Amber leaned forward, her hand moving up his arm to his shoulder. "I'm so sorry you went through that. But she finally left you...when?"

"When she took an overdose. She died."

Chapter Fourteen

Amber felt emotion tightening her throat. "I was afraid you were going to say that. I mean, I knew she passed away, but to have died from an overdose? That must have been so difficult—for you and the children."

"They were barely five years old. They didn't understand it at all. My in-laws tried to have me barred from Isabel's funeral, and I considered not going. Then I talked with my parents and with the kids' pediatrician. They told me the twins should be allowed to attend the funeral. They felt that, even at their tender age, it was better to give them a sense of closure than to just let their mother disappear. We all knew they wouldn't understand, not fully, but we agreed the kids deserved to know. I went to the funeral so I could take them."

"That's where Will's picture of his mother in a coffin came from."

"Yes. My father-in-law came up while the children and I stood by the coffin. In harsh, hushed tones, he demanded that I leave. He said I was inflicting psychological abuse on my children and he was going to see that the kids were taken from me.

"We left then, but I went straight to the kids' pediatrician and got a statement and a promise that she would testify in court should that become necessary. My in-laws have been trying to find ways to take the kids ever since. My mother-in-law was limited to court-supervised visits, or visits with only me present, after she tried to kidnap the kids and take them out of state."

"Oh Max, I'm so sorry you and the kids had to go through that! I hope that was the worst."

He shook his head. "No, actually, the worst was when they accused me of murder."

"No! Oh, Max!" Amber moved in closer and laid her hand on his leg.

"Isabel's mother bought into the lies one-hundred percent," he went on in a shaky voice. "She argued that Isabel needed the drugs because she was in real pain due to being abused at home. Of course, the irony of that was that Isabel was hardly ever home. Her mother went to the police and told them she was a witness to how careful her daughter always was, how she only used medications prescribed by her doctors and used them only in the prescribed ways and amounts."

"They bought that?"

"She said that since Isabel was so careful, she would never have taken such a large overdose voluntarily, that I must have forced the dose on her with the intent to kill."

Amber felt sick, anger combined with a debilitating sense of horror. Her first instinct was to wrap her arms around Max and hold him close, but she didn't want him to think she acted from pity. She sat back and grabbed the couch cushion instead, holding tight to it. "Please tell me no one believed her."

"I don't think anyone at the police department believed it, but they checked it out anyway. Due diligence, you know?"

"Yes, I understand."

"The investigation came to nothing, but for a few days—" he choked out the words, glancing away from her. Silence stretched between them as Max composed himself.

Amber stroked his hand and arm again. "Maybe it will help if I tell you a little of my own story."

"Your story?"

"You know about my Aunt Donna, right?"

"The Children of Rah."

"Right. It was a drug cult, at least to a large degree. Donna Reyes, a.k.a. Dawn Ray, used heavily and neglected her daughters as a result. That's why Sunny and Skye came to live with us. My parents also fought for custody. And sadly, a few years after the cult broke up, Aunt Donna was found dead in a doorway with a needle in her arm."

"Much the way Isabel died."

"Yes, as I understand it. You see, I have some idea of what it's like to lose someone to addiction, even though that death wasn't as close to me as yours was to you. That isn't the only experience, either."

He gave her a sharp look. "You know another drug addict?"

Amber's thoughts went to Skye and her struggles over the years, how Skye's past self-destructive behavior had not only impacted Skye's own life, but the entire family. "Let's just say that I've seen more than I wish I had," Amber said.

Max gave a slight frown. "Forgive me for being blunt, Amber, but knowing an aunt who overdosed isn't quite the same—"

"I'm not claiming I can fully understand what you went through. I just want you to know I can sympathize. I know the havoc drugs can wreak on a family."

"Okay, I get that." He let out a long, frustrated sigh. "I'm sorry for my reaction. Some things I will never understand. For one, Isabel was never much of a mother and never really wanted to have kids, but even under those circumstances, how could she choose drugs over her own babies?"

"You know it isn't like that, Max. It isn't a conscious choice at all. Addiction really is a disease—"

"Oh, come on!" He slammed his hand into the couch. "You don't buy all that nonsense!"

"It isn't nonsense, Max. When you are able to step away from your pain a little more, I can show you some good-quality medical evidence of why addiction is a disease and how it takes over the survival mechanisms of the brain. It isn't—"

"Not interested." He pulled away, his features set.

"Really—"

He turned on her, his face reddening, his expression severe. "What about the lying? What about everything she was hiding from me, not just now and then, but every day for years? What about that?"

Amber fortified herself with a deep breath. "I know you still carry anger and hurt about Isabel, but you're directing your anger at me right now—"

"You're trying to defend her actions. What she did was…" He seemed to be hunting for the right words.

"Despicable? Disgusting? Unacceptable?"

He crossed his arms over his chest. "Yeah. All that."

"Please understand. I'm not defending her. I'm just trying to explain that addiction does things to people, makes them behave differently than they'd ever consider if they weren't caught in the throes of a deadly—"

"Stop!" Max stood. Amber could see his hands tightening into fists. "I don't want to hear any more about how she had a disease and she couldn't help it, yada, yada. You say you're not defending her, but that's exactly what you're doing. I—"

"Max! Please listen. I'm not trying to make excuses for her—"

"Yes, you are, and it's time for you to stop talking and listen to me for a change." Max's face was flushed and the look in his eyes was mixed pain and rage.

Amber answered meekly, "All right."

"She put me and the kids through hell. Even before the drugs, Isabel was a manipulative, spoiled brat."

"I'm sorry, Max." She reached toward him.

He pulled away. "I think I should go." Max grabbed his jacket and slipped it on as he walked toward the door. "Thank you for dinner and…for listening," he said over his shoulder. "I'll see you later."

She followed him to the door. "Please don't leave angry."

He turned to face her again. "I just—"

She kissed him. She hadn't planned their first real kiss to be this way, but she needed him to understand. Stiffly at first, he accepted the kiss, almost without responding. She kissed him again and this time he fell into it as if quenching a thirst only she could fill—his arms pulling her toward him, his mouth enjoying hers.

When they finally separated, Amber panted for breath. "Whew."

"Yeah." He scrubbed his hands through his hair, his breathing as ragged as hers. "Listen, Amber…" He looked into her eyes. "I guess it's obvious I've got some…some stuff to work on. I'll call you, okay?"

"Sure. We'll talk soon."

He opened the door. "Good night." He hesitated, as if uncertain what to do next.

"Get some rest. I will too. We can talk again when we're both feeling better."

"Yeah. That should help." He gave her a slight smile, then turned and left.

"Huh, *that* sure went well," she murmured aloud and prepared to spend another late evening alone.

MAX TOSSED and turned in bed all night. And the next night too. In fact, the whole week went wonky. He just kept rehearsing his last talk with Amber.

What had begun as a great evening for them had turned into—well, something else. They'd had a fine conversation throughout dinner. When Amber told him about Will's good behavior during the games at school, Max's heart had swelled. It felt good. He was proud of his son, but when Amber said how proud she was of Will, it made Max feel like something had shifted. It felt like they were a couple sharing their day, talking about their kids. It felt like he had a partner, someone he could rely on and confide in and share in the responsibilities of raising Kate and Will. Even while he was sharing his story about Isabel, Amber was supportive, she held his hand, and her beautiful eyes showed caring and concern.

Then it all went off the rails. He knew he'd overreacted, and he felt like a jerk because of it, but he couldn't understand why people always wanted to make excuses for those who chose a pill or a needle over the people in their lives, and he couldn't begin to grasp why intelligent, apparently sane people could swallow the whole disease argument. Maybe they'd never been hurt by someone else's addiction. Or maybe they just needed to rationalize their way out of the pain. Maybe that's what Amber was trying to do when she started in about her aunt who died. But that wasn't the only problem. Why did she have to try to fix everything? Couldn't she have just listened while he poured out his pain?

But man, that kiss had been unforgettable.

His workday over, he shoved a few more papers into his briefcase and waved to the two remaining coworkers still in the office. Glancing at his watch, he realized he'd be late picking up the twins at Mrs. Larsen's house. Then he remembered he hadn't planned anything for dinner. Maybe he should stop off at Joe's and pick up some sandwiches? He silently cursed his situation. He wasn't keeping up very well with the single working parent routine. How did other people do it? He'd heard some buzz about online groups where people in the same boat gave each other survival tips. It was probably a load of whining and complaining, but it couldn't hurt to check it out. Maybe he'd even find it helpful.

His churning thoughts turned to his upcoming appointment with Dr. Schafer. Maybe he could talk with Schafer about the single parent crush he felt. Hearing his own thoughts brought him up short. When had he started relying on a therapist to work through things?

If he wanted to be completely honest, he'd relied quite a bit on Amber lately, on talking things through with her. He thought again about their last talk. That brought his thoughts looping back to the way she'd defended Isabel's behavior. That had not been what he wanted to hear. He wanted to know that the woman he'd just bared his soul to was on his side, not his late ex-wife's. He blew out a breath. He hadn't seen or talked to Amber since that evening. Four long days and he was still holding a grudge. But these negative thoughts weren't doing him any good. Besides, Amber had a soft heart, so of course she would feel badly about Isabel's death. And she'd lost her aunt under similar circumstances...

He missed her, missed her a lot. He promised himself he'd call Amber as soon as he got the kids something to eat and had them doing homework. That settled, he realized he felt better. He was smiling when he knocked on Mrs. Larsen's door.

FOUR DAYS. Max hadn't called in four days. He must be furious. Amber closed the front office for the day and double-checked the locks on the door to the school as she left. She knew she'd pushed it with her talk about the disease of addiction. She'd been hoping to help him understand so he could let go of the pain. She sighed, wondering what Isabel must have been feeling.

Not everyone is like Skye, her inner voice reminded her. *Some addicts are just lousy people.*

Amber rolled her eyes. Well, it might be too late for a course correction now. She'd let that genie out of the bottle and he was not going back in. Maybe she and Max would get past this or maybe they'd come to the end.

She swallowed the lump in her throat and pulled her car into her garage, feeling more dejected than she had in some time. She hadn't realized how much she'd come to depend on seeing Max. Way too much, really. If she wasn't careful, she could fall in love with him…

I think the train has left the station on that one, her inner voice shot back.

"How was your day?" Max asked the obligatory parent question as he pulled away from the Larsen home. He tried to listen, to really hear the kids as Will gave his customary "okay" reply and Kate babbled about an art project and a new goldfish and something with math.

"Sounds like a good day, Katydid." He grinned at her over the seat. She grinned back.

"Hey, guys." He tried to put enthusiasm into his voice. "What do you think about sandwiches for dinner? I thought we might stop by Joe's on the way home, get some sandwiches, some side dishes, make it kind of a picnic at our kitchen table. Sound good?"

Will said, "Yeah," and went back to playing with an action figure he kept in the car.

"Hey Daddy?" Kate brightened. "Can we get a sandwich for Ms. Reyes too? You know, like when we had the picnic in the park?"

"I don't know, honey. We haven't arranged anything with her."

"I bet she'd love it!" Kate practically bounced on her booster chair. "You already know what kind of sandwich she likes, and I remember which salads she was eating."

"You do?" Max couldn't keep the surprise from showing. It had been weeks since they'd had that picnic, and Kate still remembered the salads Amber liked? His little girl might already be more involved than he'd realized.

"She didn't touch the pasta, but she took some potato salad and she really loved the fruit."

"Okay, good to know. We can get some of those salads even if we're not eating with Ms. Reyes. I know you like them too."

"But we can ask her, can't we? Maybe she'd like to have an inside picnic."

Amber probably wouldn't mind not needing to cook tonight. It might be worth a try. "Tell you what. We'll pick out sandwiches for the three of us and something for her too and we'll buy the salads we all like. I'll call Ms. Reyes and see if we can drop by her house so she can join us. Sound good?"

"Sounds great!" Kate lit up like a Roman candle.

"Will?" He looked back at his son.

"Yeah. Okay, I guess."

Will was making progress, but he still had his sullen moments. "We're here," Max said, stopping at the curb next to Joe's. "Let's go get the makings of an indoor picnic."

Kate tumbled out as soon as he opened her door. Will dragged along behind her. Max prepared to issue an invitation, and maybe eat some crow, if necessary.

Chapter Fifteen

A mber stood in her pantry, examining the ingredients on her shelves. She had already perused the offerings in the refrigerator. A few items needed to be used soon, but nothing seemed in danger of spoiling immediately. On the other hand, nothing seemed to call her name, either. Maybe she wasn't hungry, or maybe discouragement over a broken relationship had dampened her appetite.

"Maybe I'll go grab something at Joe's," she murmured aloud. But she didn't really want to go out. She sighed and lifted a box of cold cereal from the pantry shelf. It was a fallback she couldn't use very often, not if she wanted to stay healthy, but maybe just for tonight.

She set the box on her table and added a bowl and spoon. She had just opened the refrigerator and was reaching for the milk when her cell phone rang. Annoyed that her guilty indulgence had been interrupted, she answered. "Max?" she said as soon as she saw his name. She heard his suggestion and put away the cereal. Minutes later, she went to the door and looked out through the peep hole. Her heart rate shifted into high gear as she opened to the Burnett family. "Hi. Please come in."

Kate practically bounced into the house. "We got your favorite sandwich, Ms. Reyes, and I know you like the fruit salad, and we didn't get any pasta this time and—"

"Slow down, honey," Max said, cutting off the flow. "Ms. Reyes, we decided for our dinner tonight, we want to have a picnic in our kitchen. Would you like to join us for an indoor picnic at our house?"

Amber cleared her throat. She'd been thinking about her answer since she'd answered Max's call. "Yes, I'd like that very much."

"Yay!" Kate jumped up and down, clapping her hands.

Amber added, "I don't see any reason why we need to travel, though. I mean, you're already here, the food is here, and I have a kitchen table too. In fact, I have all the makings for fresh lemonade to go with it. Sound good?"

Max looked to his children. "What do you think? Will it be just as good to have our picnic at Ms. Reyes's house instead of ours?"

"Yes! Yes!" Kate said, hopping up and down again.

"Will? She'll make fresh lemonade." Max gave his son a hopeful look.

Will raised a shoulder in a half-shrug. "Okay."

"Okay then!" Max said. "Ms. Reyes, what can we do to help set up?"

"You can unwrap the food you brought and set it on the table. Kate, if I hand you some plates, can you set them out?"

"Yeah, sure." She held her hands out and eagerly waited for the plates.

"Will, you can take the napkins you see here on the counter and put one at each place. Will you do that?"

"Yeah, I guess." He shuffled toward the napkins.

With her guests all busy, Amber set about making the lemonade. She kept a container of sugar syrup in her fridge for just this purpose, along with a quart of juice she had squeezed from fresh lemons over the weekend. All she had to do was mix them in the proper proportions and pour the result over ice, add water, and stir. With her hands busy, she let her thoughts roam. Was this Max's way of smoothing things over without having to talk about it? If it was, it was working rather nicely.

She carried the pitcher of lemonade to the table. "Ooh, good job, Kate, and Will, and Max too. It looks like we're ready to go. Let me just get us some glasses…" She grabbed four water glasses and returned to the table. Happier than she'd felt in days, she took her seat at the table.

November slipped by and life seemed to work itself into a comfortable routine. Olivia and Enrique invited the Burnetts twice more and had Amber join them both times. To reciprocate, Amber cooked for her parents and Max's family at her home.

Kate and Will were doing well in therapy, Will's behavior at school and home was improving, and they were both catching up in school. They were particularly enthusiastic about the first Thanksgiving and learning about the pilgrims and the Native Americans. They came home one day with construction paper turkeys cut out from their handprints and lists of what they were thankful for. Max got choked up reading them. *I'm thankful for Daddy* made it on both their lists. Kate had also written she was thankful for Ms. Reyes, and Will wrote he was thankful for family dinners and Ms. Reyes' lemonade. Amber considered that progress.

Workers at the mine struck a particularly rich vein, and the decision-makers at the mining company promised a tidy Christmas bonus, which certainly added to Max's positive outlook. Once or twice a week, Max and the kids ate with Amber or invited her to join them for a crisp day in the park, and Max and Amber went out almost every weekend.

Max loved spending time with Amber, but they continued to tiptoe around the elephant in the room, carefully giving it space. They avoided talking about Isabel and drug addiction. Other topics also went unaddressed, perhaps the most notable being where their relationship was headed. Max was well aware when Amber dropped small hints, here and there, creating an opening for him to talk about his intentions, but he couldn't go there. At least not yet. Everything was going so well; he didn't want to muck it up.

On the Saturday before Thanksgiving, they sat across a table at Broadway Louie's Kosher Mexican. The server had taken their order, and Max listened while Amber spoke of new software the school district insisted its administrators learn. When they'd said everything they had to share about software, he asked, "Amber, have I told you about the coming weekend?"

"You mean Thanksgiving?" She paused as if giving the topic some thought. "A little. I know you're leaving town."

"The kids and I need to go to So-Cal. We'll have Thanksgiving dinner with my parents—they haven't seen the kids since we moved here—and Keith's wedding is the Saturday after."

"I know you mentioned that."

"Also, Isabel's parents have a court-mandated visit scheduled with the kids on Wednesday evening. It will be awkward, since there's no one appointed by the court available at that time, so I'll be taking the kids myself. It's supposed to be a three-hour visit and I have no doubt I'll be miserable the entire time."

"Why did they schedule it then, when no one from the court was available?"

He shook his head. "I don't know, but I suspect the usual folks were all on vacation this week and my ex-mother-in-law insists on seeing her grandchildren while they're in town. Maybe she hoped to intimidate me so I wouldn't show up and she could try to snatch the kids again."

She laid a comforting hand over his. "I'm sorry it's so tough."

"Really, my ex-father-in-law isn't so bad. It's the other half of the equation..." He shrugged. "It is what it is, and I doubt I'll ever be able to change it." He took her hand. "But I have a reason for telling you all this. I'll need your cooperation in a couple of ways."

She straightened. "I'm listening."

"First, I'll need to take the twins out of school from about midday on Tuesday. There's a big dinner with our family and the bride's family at noon Wednesday and we'll need to leave early to be sure we get there on time."

"No problem," she answered. Then she dropped her voice to a whisper and crooked her finger at him. "Don't tell anyone I said this. I'm supposed to be very strict about the kids never missing a single day unless they're sick. Just between us, it won't be a problem." She winked.

"Good." He winked back. "Now...about the other thing?"

"I'm still listening."

"I want to tell them about us. That is, I want to tell my family that you and I are seeing each other and that...well, that I like you a lot, that I maybe even see a future for us. Together." He saw a pretty blush color Amber's cheek and felt his own face warming. "I'm telling you this tonight because I thought I should say it to you before I say it to them, and because I need to know that it's okay with you for me to say it to them." He held his breath as he waited for her to respond.

Amber began to blink rapidly, and her lips began to tremble. Finally, she smiled. Not just any smile. A bright, beautiful, beaming smile.

"Yes! I mean, yes, you can tell them we're seeing each other."

"You're not crying, are you?"

"Just happy tears, Max." She squeezed his hand. "Thank you for saying that. I…I like you too, and I agree that we could…maybe…have a future. Together."

He took a deep, relieved breath. "I'm glad you feel the same way."

Her smile brightened even more, and it was his turn to blink rapidly.

The server arrived with their food. As he picked up his fork, Max said, "I thought about asking you to come with us." He cleared his throat. "You could renew your acquaintance with my family and see Keith again. Also, it would be kind of like taking a date home to meet my parents, given it's been so long since we lived next door to your family."

She raised her eyebrows. "Are you ready for that? Taking me home to meet the family?"

"I am." He set his fork down. "How about you? I didn't ask because I knew we'd have to leave early and I guessed that meant you couldn't come—"

"You're right about that, I'm afraid."

He took her hand. "Amber, if you could come? Would you want to meet my family?"

She used her free hand to cover their linked ones. "Max, if I could come, I'd want very much to meet your family again, maybe even to meet the monsters-in-law."

He chuckled. "Thanks. I'll remember that when I'm counting the minutes during my visit with them next week."

"No problem. Glad I could help."

They chatted as they enjoyed their dinner. Amber detailed her own Thanksgiving plans—*rellenos* and turkey *tamales* with her family while Max described what he knew of the wedding plans. "They're keeping it simple. Brynn—that's the bride—says it's the marriage that's important, not the one day of the wedding."

Amber nodded. "Sunny said the same thing. She wanted us to keep the wedding simple."

"Sunny and Evan? That was a great wedding, really nice."

"You were there, weren't you? I mean, I know you were at the park, but at the wedding?"

"Um-hm. One of the guys from the office had an invitation for himself and his wife. She was sick and he didn't want to go alone, so he asked me along. I felt awkward about it, since I was new in town, but he knew I'd lived here before. He thought maybe I'd meet some old friends."

"Did you?"

"I found a few people I remembered from before and even one or two who remembered me, though I couldn't recall who they were."

"Like me," she teased.

"Yeah, like you." He grinned. He paused, and then repeated, "It was good, though, the wedding. It was nice."

"I'll take that as a compliment."

"I know you were in it."

"I was maid of honor. I ended up with most of the planning. It didn't help that Sunny and Evan decided to get married just three weeks before."

"No kidding!"

"No kidding. They realized they wanted to be married and they didn't want to wait. So, we put together a wedding in three weeks."

"You put together a *nice* wedding in three weeks," he corrected. "Well done."

"Thanks. Because Sunny wasn't picky, it was easier than you might imagine."

"I get that." Max licked his lips. "The way Isabel approached our wedding should have been a major red flag for me. I get that now. Wish I'd understood it better then."

"Water under the bridge," Amber said, lifting her water glass. "Let's toast to water under the bridge and moving on."

Max touched his water glass to hers. "I'll drink to that."

Late Tuesday evening, Amber received a text. Max and his children had arrived safely at his parents' home. He ended with:

I like Keith's fiancée very much. I miss you.

She replied:

I miss you too, Max. Have a great holiday and I'll see you soon.

She put her phone away.

She found her thoughts drifting. For the first time in many years, maybe ever, she realized she was not looking forward to being with her family, not the way she usually did. She wished she'd gone with Max instead, and that told her much about her growing commitment.

Her inner voice asked the difficult question: *Are you ready for this?*

Yes! She answered.

As she started preparing for bed, her inner voice teased, *You don't think you're going to fall sleep, do you?*

"Shut up," she said aloud. "Just shut up."

To her relief, she heard no answer.

Chapter Sixteen

M ax looked at the clock on the mantel. It rested just under the full-length portrait of Isabel in the home of his former in-laws. There she stood in her debutante gown, glorious coppery hair tumbling around her shoulders. The image tugged at his heart, reminding him of the sparkling young woman he'd once loved.

The clock brought him back to where he was now. Twenty minutes. They had only been there twenty minutes and already he longed to strangle Lovenia. The criticism from his ex-mother-in-law had begun even before he brought the children through her door. The first thing she said was, "You brought the children in *those* jackets? Are they warm enough?"

That was only the beginning of her assault. "Look at Will. The knees in those pants are wearing out. He looks like a homeless child." "Do you always let Kate wear jeans? She looks like a boy." "What are you feeding these children? Will is as thin as a garter snake." Max had to pause after that one to wonder what Lovenia knew about garter snakes, or any snakes at all. The insults seemed more grating when spoken in her overdone Georgia-peach accent.

"Kate, who braids your hair? Your part is so uneven…" "Will, are you okay in public school? I know you aren't getting the attention you're used to…" "Really, Max, can't you afford decent shirts for these children…?" She was incessant.

Max glanced at the clock again. Thirty minutes down. That left two and one-half hours to go. He wondered if he could manage this. His inner voice suggested, *Think of how disappointed Amber would be if you went to prison for murder.* He couldn't help the chuckle.

"You find something funny, Max? You were always a little unfocused. Are you wool-gathering again?"

His grin was genuine when he answered, "No, Lovenia. I'm

wondering what would happen if you hurt your throat and couldn't speak. It's possible you'd explode."

"Well, I never!" She turned to her husband. "Dennison, did you hear—"

"Yes, Lovenia. I did. Max, may I speak to you alone for a moment?"

Max kept his tone pleasant. "Not if it means leaving the children with her."

"We'll just step to this side of the room. You'll be able to see them."

"All right then." Max prepared himself for a different kind of assault.

What Dennison said was not what he expected. "I want to apologize for my wife. She can be—" He paused, as if searching for a word that could describe her behavior without getting him in trouble, should Max ever repeat it.

Max chose to let him off the hook. "Yes, she can."

Dennison gave him a relieved smile. "Please try to understand. Isabel was her life. She's been lost since our daughter..." He stopped, apparently unable to continue.

"I'm sure that's true," Max said, keeping his voice low. "It doesn't excuse the way she enabled Isabel's addiction. Or tried to kidnap my kids. Or accused me of—"

"You're right. It doesn't." The judge sighed. "And frankly, life with her hasn't been the same." He stopped, shook his head. "I've said too much already. I just want you to know that I don't blame you for what happened with Isabel. Lovenia spoiled our daughter terribly and I was always too busy with work to notice what was happening until...until it was too late." He sighed again. "I realize now that Isabel was an addict, that she inflicted on herself the hurt she suffered. Lovenia will never accept that. Please just try to put up with her." He offered his hand.

"I will." Max grasped Dennison's hand. "Thank you for saying that. It makes everything so much easier."

"I should have said something months ago."

"What changed your mind?

"One of the officers who found Isabel. He appeared in my courtroom on another case and asked if he could speak to me. He wanted to say how sorry he was about what happened. He told me about the many times he'd seen Isabel drunk or high, obviously in trouble, and issued warnings instead of taking her in, all because of me, because of who I am. He acted as though I already knew the whole story, assuming I did. Then he apologized again, saying he knew he'd been an enabler. He didn't know he was telling me a story only you had shared before. I realized he was telling the truth. It stung something awful, but I couldn't deny it any longer."

"How long ago was that?"

"A few months, shortly after you and the kids moved to the mountains." Dennison nodded in the direction of his wife and the children, and the two men walked that way. Louder, the judge said, "Will, Kate, your grandmamá had the cook prepare some special cookies just for you. Come on in the kitchen and you can each have one."

Lovenia spoke immediately. "Dennison, I was saving those for later."

"Sorry, my love," he said, although Max thought he didn't sound sorry. "I didn't realize. Well, too late now. Come on, children. Max, why don't you come, too? We have plenty of cookies."

"I don't want a cookie," Max said, but he wasn't about to ignore the lifeline he'd been thrown. "I'd love to come with you though." The four of them went into the kitchen, leaving Lovenia standing alone in the living room. Max heard her disgusted sigh as they walked away. Moments later, she followed. He glanced at the kitchen clock. Two hours and twelve minutes to go.

AMBER LOOKED up from the pie she was making and glanced at her kitchen clock. Max and the kids should be back from their visit with the crazy in-laws. She checked her phone. Again. She'd expected to hear from him before this, at least a text. Just then her cell phone rang. Looking at the caller ID, she sighed in relief. "Max?"

"Hi."

"It's done?"

"Yeah. Thank goodness." She heard his deep sigh.

"Was it as bad as you expected?" She sat, getting comfortable.

"Yes and no. She was as horrible as ever, but *he* apologized. Quietly, of course. He didn't want to deal with the fallout if she heard him siding with me, and I don't blame him. But yeah, he apologized. That made it easier."

She felt herself relaxing. "I'm so glad. Then you know you have an ally when you have to go back there again."

"I hope I won't have to go back there again. Better for the court-appointed child advocate to deal with her. Lovenia will find fewer insulting things to say to an officer of the court."

"Her name is Lovenia? I don't think you ever mentioned that."

"Yeah. She's Lovenia. He's Dennison."

"Their names are as pretentious as…" She stopped, unable to come up with a comparison.

"As the rest of their lives?"

She could hear the amusement in his voice but controlled her amused grin. "You said it. I didn't. And she insisted the kids call her Grandmamá. Is she French?"

"No, just pretentious."

Amber could almost hear him smile. "I've never met Isabel's grandparents, but I'm betting Lovenia was raised very much the same way as Isabel. It probably wasn't as bad with Dennison. He has his mother's maiden name. It's a tradition, or so they tell me, among Southern families."

They talked for nearly an hour. Max extolled the virtues of his brother's fiancée and praised her family, who he said seemed like good people. Amber offered supportive comments and told him about her family's plans for the holiday. "I'm almost ready to bake the pecan pie," she told him. "You should be here to taste it. I make a great pecan pie."

"That's one of my favorites." He paused. "I told them about us. My family, I mean. After I got home from the in-law visit from Hades, I found Mom and Dad and Keith all sitting together in the living room, and I mentioned that I'm seeing someone."

She took a deep breath. "How did that go?"

"They all said they're happy for me, and, of course, they want to meet you."

"Maybe we can arrange that later."

"I hope so. I'd like that."

The conversation went on for a while, but Amber had already heard all she needed. *I'll be able to sleep tonight,* she told herself as she put the pie into the oven. Max had survived the monsters-in-law and had told his family they were dating. And they were supportive! Suddenly she felt tempted to dance around the kitchen, congratulating herself. No one was watching. Why not?

She put on music to back up her happy dance in case someone came to the door.

THE TWINS TUMBLED out of bed early on Thanksgiving morning waking Max, who slept near the kids in the same room of his parents' home. "Happy Thanksgiving, Dad!" Kate said as she climbed up next to him, pulling most of the covers off him in the process.

"Yeah. Happy Thanksgiving." Will sat next to his dad's head.

"Happy Thanksgiving, kids." Max enveloped them both in a huge hug, almost ready to forgive them for the wake-up. "Will, you look happy this morning. Is there something special going on? Besides Thanksgiving, I mean."

Will lifted a shoulder in a typical Will response. "I'm just glad we already saw Papa and Grandmamá and we don't have to go back there again." He lay down, snuggling against Max. Kate climbed over him to snuggle on the other side.

Max agreed, but he hadn't expected Will to feel that way. "You know the court will want you to see them again every now and then."

"Yeah." Will scooted up, putting his head on his dad's shoulder. "But not for a little while, 'specially since we live in Destiny now."

"That's true. Not for a little while." Enjoying a rare moment of perfect contentment, Max lay still, taking pleasure in the love and closeness of his children.

Seemingly out of the blue, Kate said, "I miss Ms. Reyes."

Max almost answered, *So do I, baby.* Instead, he said, "She couldn't come."

"I know," Kate said. "We had to leave early and she had to be at the school."

"You got it. That's why she didn't come. She wanted to."

"Yeah," Will said. "She told me that."

"Really? When was that?"

"When we were getting out of class early. She came to say goodbye."

Max controlled the inner celebration, saying only, "That's great."

"Yeah, I guess." Will's enthusiasm was underwhelming, but he snuggled closer.

Max lay still, basking in the moment and the knowledge that his son, like his daughter, might be coming to accept Amber in their lives.

The moment didn't last. A pounding on the bedroom door was accompanied by his brother's voice. "Hey, sleepyheads! Mom says breakfast is almost ready."

"Okay," Max answered. "We'll be down in a few." He looked into the faces of his beautiful children and noticed, not for the first time, how much they looked like their mother. The thought came that his children got the best of all Isabel had to offer. What he said was, "Well, guys, who's first in the bathroom?"

"Amber honey, slice that cheese a little finer. Sunny, will you check the *tamales*, please. You may need to turn down the heat." Olivia Reyes buzzed around her kitchen, the queen bee directing the hive as the women prepared the family's traditional dinner.

"Thanks for putting the *tamales* together early, Auntie," Sunny said. "Evan had a couple of things to take care of this morning and I couldn't have got here much sooner."

"It isn't like the old days when we all lived together." Olivia set down the green chili she was stuffing. "Don't misunderstand me, girls. I'm glad you have your own lives and you're getting on with them, but sometimes I miss those days."

"Me too." Amber caught her mom in a quick hug. She loved being here with the family but knew she wouldn't do a happy dance like last night's in her Mom's kitchen.

"Me three." Sunny snuggled them both from the other side.

"Okay, girls. Enough with the mushy stuff. We have hungry people to feed." They all went back to work.

Amber said, "I'm sorry Skye couldn't make it. I'd like to see her."

"Actually, I've been saving that news for a surprise." Olivia looked pleased. "Skye should be here by dinner time, and she's bringing someone." She raised her eyebrows.

A man? Amber was about to ask, but Sunny beat her to it.

"Is this someone male? Like a boyfriend?"

"He is," Olivia confirmed as she went back to stuffing. "Skye says he's an engineer. I couldn't imagine how she met an engineer, but she said—"

"Let me guess," Amber interrupted. "She met him at an AA meeting."

"Almost right." Olivia nodded. "It was Narcotics Anonymous, NA not AA." She paused before adding, "I'm not sure how I feel about that."

"I'm told it's pretty common," Sunny said. "People who are in recovery, especially in the beginning, often spend a lot of time in twelve-step meetings. It makes sense that she'd meet people there, people who have a lot in common with her. Recovering addicts understand one another's challenges."

"Yes, I suppose so. Amber, will you hand me that casserole dish? I need a place to put these extra *rellenos* before we dip and fry them."

Amber brought the casserole. "It might be good for her to be with someone who understands what she's dealing with, what she's been through. People who've never experienced addiction often have little sympathy for the disease." Max currently fit that pattern.

"That's true." In a clear change of subject, Olivia sent Amber to see if the men, deeply engrossed in the first football game of the day, might need fresh drinks or snacks. The women catered to the men at Thanksgiving, partly because they expected male help in the kitchen at other times, and especially at the outdoor grill.

Amber took off her apron as she left the room. She couldn't speak for anyone else, but she hoped Skye had found a good guy. She deserved to be happy.

Amber stepped into the family room to find her dad and brother-in-law arguing with the ref over a decision that went against their team. She wisely waited for a commercial break before asking about refreshments.

"Mom, you outdid yourself this time." Max pushed back from the table, happily filled, and not just with turkey. He sighed, thinking, *This is how a family should be.* He glanced around the room. This furniture was meant to be used, not admired. The décor made people feel welcome, not envious. This home was warm, inviting, so different from the place his in-laws lived. Amber would fit in well here.

Keith and his fiancée joined them just as they finished eating, having already eaten one Thanksgiving dinner with her family. "I told Brynn she should watch how my mother does it," Keith explained.

"Hey!" Brynn gave him a playful slug.

Keith quickly added, "Then I saw her family's Thanksgiving dinner and realized she doesn't need lessons."

"Thank you. Apology accepted." Brynn reached for the casserole in front of her. "Anyone want more candied yams? I have leftovers."

"I've already eaten way too much," Keith said. Others at the table agreed.

Kate asked, "May I please be excused?"

"Me too." Will chimed in.

"Yes, you may. Come on, family. Let's clear the table." Max stood and started stacking plates. Others joined him.

As Max carried a stack into the kitchen, he thought again of Amber. Isabel had left him broken, nothing but damaged goods. After her, he didn't know whether he could ever open up to a woman again. Amber had sneaked into his life, and he was grateful. But when his inner voice asked if he'd be willing to commit, he avoided an answer.

∽

"WILL DINNER BE READY SOON?" Enrique asked as he entered the kitchen from the family room, Evan trailing behind him. "You've got hungry men here."

"It's ready now." Olivia looked at the clock. "I've been holding it for a little while longer, waiting for Skye and her friend—"

The door opened and Skye came in carrying a pie. "Hi, everyone. Sorry I'm late."

"Where's—" Olivia began.

Skye cut her off. "I'm here by myself. Are we ready to eat?"

Looking at Skye's face, hearing her voice, Amber knew better than to ask what happened. The rest of the family saw the same signals.

Olivia said, "Take your places, folks. Amber, Sunny, will you help me bring in the food?" The new pie was brought to the kitchen, the rest of the food to the table, and the family's Thanksgiving dinner began. Good food and happy company soon banished the tension that arrived with Skye.

An hour later, when everyone had eaten their fill and the men were doing clean-up, Amber found Skye in the hallway, reading a text message and grumbling under her breath.

"You okay?" Amber asked.

Skye jerked around. "Oh! You startled me."

"Let me ask it again. Skye, are you okay?"

"Yeah." She let out a long breath. "Angry and frustrated, but okay."

"Want to tell me what happened?"

"The jerk." She struggled to compose herself. "I went to pick him up and he was high, really high. When I asked him about it, he denied it, but it was obvious. He finally broke down and admitted he'd used 'a little.' He said he couldn't handle meeting my family sober. He needed some 'help.'" She spat out the final word.

"I'm sorry, honey." Amber reached to give her a hug.

Skye stepped away. "Please don't try to make me feel better. Not yet. I'm still dealing with a load of righteous wrath."

Amber smiled. "I can understand that. I'm guessing you told him to take a walk?"

"I just now blocked his number." Skye pursed her lips. "You know what bugs me most?"

"No. What?"

"I'll have to find a new NA meeting. If I go where Ryan can find me, he'll never leave me alone."

"He probably knows where you live."

"Yeah." Skye set her phone down. "I've told him to stay away, that I'll get a restraining order if he comes around."

"Whoa. Do you think that's necessary?"

"I don't know. I know I don't want to deal with him. Getting high before Thanksgiving with my family?" She growled. "That one is a deal-breaker. A rotten, cowardly, weak-kneed deal-breaker."

Amber suppressed a smile. "I see you're getting over your righteous wrath."

Skye grimaced. "Just like you're getting over your sarcasm." She glared at Amber with an exaggerated frown but ended it with a small smile.

"You've come so far, honey. You've been sober for how long now? Almost a year?"

"More than a year. It's just under thirteen months since I was arrested. Then jail, then rehab."

Amber reached for her again. "I'm so proud of you." This time, Skye accepted her hug.

"It's hard." Skye teared up. "It's really hard."

"I know, but you're doing it. You're doing so well."

This time it was Skye who hugged her.

Chapter Seventeen

I n the kitchen of his parents' home, Max helped his mother clean up. The family had just eaten a traditional lunch of Thanksgiving leftovers, keeping it light before the wedding rehearsal, which would be followed by the rehearsal dinner. Max worked silently, putting away the remaining turkey and pie.

"You're quiet today." His mother looked concerned. "Just digesting?"

"Yeah, I guess." Most of what he was processing now wasn't the meal. He was thinking of what had happened with the kids' other grandparents. He broke off the thought, recognizing it could take time to work through everything that had happened there. "You created another great Thanksgiving, Mom."

"Then why do you look so glum?" She set down the large platter she'd been drying.

"That visit was rough."

"With Isabel's parents?"

Max felt his face tightening as he thought of the poison in Lovenia's words. The poison in Lovenia. "Her mother is one bitter, angry woman."

"—who has turned all that anger on you," Linda Burnett added. She pulled out a chair. "Here, Son. Sit." She took a chair across from his.

Max sat, waiting for what his mother would say.

Linda sat forward. "What kinds of things was she saying?"

"Just the usual: the kids are skinny, their clothes aren't good enough, they're unhappy, maybe unhealthy, I'm not taking good care of them." He paused. "Dennison surprised me. He actually apologized."

Her eyebrows went up. "He took your side?"

"Not where she could hear it. The man isn't suicidal."

She responded with a smile. "He said it to you, though."

"Yeah, he did. He made excuses for her. You know, all about how Isabel was her world." Max made a gruff sound. "Like that makes it okay."

His mother lifted a shoulder. "He still has to live with her."

Max chortled. "Yeah. I guess."

"Max?" The concerned look on her face deepened. "Was any of the anger about the way you are...uh, moving on?"

"You mean dating again?"

"I'm talking about what you told us, about Amber Reyes. You wouldn't have mentioned her if you weren't getting fairly...serious. Maybe they're afraid of losing their grandchildren even more if you someday choose to remarry, to give Kate and Will another set of grandparents."

Max felt his head snap up. He and Amber hadn't used the M-word, not yet. But they were talking long-term, weren't they? And didn't that imply—

His mom interrupted his thoughts. "Max? Did you tell them? Or did they maybe find out another way? Did the kids let it slip? What I'm asking is, do they know you're dating?"

"No. That is, I don't think so. I didn't say anything, and I was there whenever the kids were, so I'd have heard if they did. I'm pretty sure no one said anything."

"Well. That's good."

"Yeah, I guess. It isn't any of their business anyway." Then another thought occurred. "Mom? Are you saying something more than I think you are?"

Linda looked thoughtful. "Aren't you worried that maybe this is just a rebound? That maybe you aren't ready to get serious?"

This was not the conversation Max had expected. "Mom? I thought you'd be pleased to see me dating again. You said you were."

"Dating, yes. Something casual, you know. Seeing different women, getting back into the rhythm of the social scene." She reached across the table and patted his hand. "Not getting serious. Not yet, Max. You've been hurt very badly, and it hasn't been long since Isabel—"

"A year, Mom. More than a year since she died and well over that since she left us."

"Yes, well… It's been long enough that you should be getting out there again, but casual dating, son, not thinking of marriage. And Amber Reyes? She's so much younger—"

He snorted. "You're thinking of the little kid who used to live next door. Many years have passed, Mom. Amber grew up. She got older, just like the rest of us."

"How much older?" Linda's look of concern deepened. "Isn't she years younger?"

He shrugged that off. "A few years. She's Keith's age. We haven't noticed differences, except now and then when we listen to oldies." He grinned.

"Then there's the fact that she's your children's principal—"

"Amber mentioned that too…at first. I'll tell you the same thing I told her. It's Destiny, a very small town with a limited number of eligible singles. If I date anyone who lives there, it's the kids' principal, or their teacher, or the woman who keeps an eye on them after school, or someone else we all know." Realizing what he'd said, he quickly added, "Not that I'd date their teacher or their after-school babysitter, since they're both married. But you get the point. In a town that size where everyone knows everyone, I'll have some additional connections to anyone I see socially."

"What happens when …I mean if, you break up?"

"Mom!"

"You know what I mean. What happens with the children if you and their principal stop seeing each other?"

Max respected his mother too much to lose his temper, but he might have to bite his tongue. "Then I go back to being my kids' single father who isn't dating anyone and she goes back to being their concerned principal who is not dating their dad. And why did you say *when* and then correct yourself?"

Exhaling on a long sigh, Linda sat forward. "I'm worried, Max. You were so badly hurt by Isabel and her family. I'm worried you're jumping into a relationship because you're lonely. I'm worried this woman…wait. I don't mean to imply that she's going to turn out like

Isabel." She paused, cleared her throat. "Amber Reyes is quite a few years younger than you, and she may be jumping too quickly into a relationship because she sees others her age pairing up, and she's worried about her chances. Maybe she hears her biological clock ticking and wants to have a baby before she gets older. Have you considered that?"

"That she may want to have a child? Or that she might be hearing the clock? And which is she anyway: too young or too old?" This didn't seem like his mom at all.

"Maybe she'll want more than one baby. Are you ready to consider more children? What about Kate and Will? How do they feel about this?"

"Kate loves her. She'd start calling Amber Mom right now if I let her."

"And Will?"

"He's not as eager, but then again, he's the one who's had the most trouble with...with everything. I only recently found out—" He cut himself off, realizing he didn't want to tell his mother this story. Learning what Will had heard would only hurt her.

"Found out what?" Linda waited.

Max chose to minimize the damage. "Found out how badly hurt Will was."

"You mean *is*. That child needs healing."

"We all need healing, Mom—"

"Don't you think it would be best to get that healing done before you bring a new person into the mix?"

Time to end this. He stood. "Mom, I love you. You've been a rock through this whole thing with Isabel. I can never tell you how much I appreciate all you've done. But now, I'll invite you to please butt out."

"Max!"

"I mean it, Mother."

Linda sat back, her eyes wide.

Max realized he might have gone too far. "Mom, please listen. I moved back to Destiny the first chance I got. I expected there'd be little opportunity for a social life there, but I remembered how the community pulls together, how I always felt at home when we lived there, like

I could turn to anyone and they'd be there for me. I wanted that same feeling for the kids, and when I saw that the mining company I worked for planned to open operations in Destiny, well—" He paused.

"It seemed providential," his mother supplied.

"I don't know about providence," Max said, "but it sure looked like a good idea. Finding Amber Reyes was a surprise, a very nice surprise. At first, I thought she was too young—too young to be the kids' principal and way too young to date. But it sort of just…happened, and when it did, it felt good. It felt right." He looked at her, his expression begging her to hear what was unsaid, to understand the emotion behind it.

Linda Burnett bit her lip.

Max saw both her frustration with him and the hurt feelings she was trying to hide. He also saw the moment when she chose to back down, to let things stand and not make them any worse. "I see," she said. "I just want you to take care. I don't want to see you hurt again."

He put both arms around his mother, hugging her close. "Thanks, Mom. I've always known you were there for me."

Slowly relaxing her stiffness, Linda Burnett returned the embrace.

In the kitchen of her own small home, Amber rolled out sugar cookie dough. Beside her, Sunny sprayed a cookie sheet while, on the other side, Paris turned on the oven and set the temperature. The house smelled of vanilla and sugar. Amber breathed it in. "This is fun," she said. "It's been a while since we did something like this."

"If you mean baking, yes." Paris looked up. "Is it three-fifty? Or three-twenty-five?"

"It's three-fifty for this recipe, and yes, I meant baking. I guess we did have a project together when we did Sunny's wedding."

"You betcha." Sunny set the cookie sheet next to Amber. "You did a great job of it, too."

"Still I'm glad you were both hanging around this weekend. It's fun to get together like this, and I'm always grateful for company in the kitchen."

"You're the one who volunteered to bring refreshments to the town meeting." Paris gave Amber a knowing smirk. "Not that volunteering cookies isn't just like you."

"It's the final discussion about Christmas decorations. They'll be deciding whether or not to do a live Nativity in the park and how to organize the decorating downtown."

"Isn't it getting a little late for that?" Paris asked.

Amber answered, "Yeah. The town usually has details organized months ahead of the holiday. Everything got put off this year because two new and highly vocal members of the town council have been sparring over how best to use Christmas to bring in new business."

"You do have lots of new people coming up to look at the town lately." Sunny started cutting out stars to go with Amber's Christmas trees. "Do you expect any push-back on the idea of a Nativity?" Seeing the looks on her friends' faces, she added, "You know what I mean. Other communities are getting complaints about public entities supporting religious holidays."

"Not in Destiny." Paris started cutting the dough into the shape of Christmas stockings.

"No, not in Destiny," Amber said. "Even the families who aren't Christian don't complain. They understand it's a national holiday and everyone gets time off even if they don't share the religion. They've been very supportive." She chuckled, "Mr. Abbas from the grocery store said he likes seeing what we do for Christmas. He said, 'The only people who get bothered by Christmas are the atheists who want everyone to believe, or not believe, just as they do.'"

"Whew!" Paris grimaced. "That's pretty plain."

"It's what he said. He likes the way the community comes together to organize."

Sunny nodded. "That sounds like Destiny."

"Of course," Amber added, "Mr. Abbas also told me he likes the extra sales he gets from living in Christmas Town." She waited while the other women chuckled. "People here are generally supportive. No one complained when Mrs. Nguyen's sister showed up at the farmers' market with a Buddhist shrine in her booth, either."

"Live and let live." Paris sprayed a second cookie sheet and began laying out Christmas stockings. All three worked quietly for a time.

"Okay," Paris said, putting the loaded cookie sheet aside. "Enough small talk. Amber, tell us about you and Max."

Sunny raised an eyebrow. "You and Max? Have I missed something?"

"Maybe you weren't listening when I mentioned it to the family. I haven't made it a secret that Max and I are dating."

"But...wait. Is it serious? I haven't been here to watch this develop."

"That's true." Amber put the first cookie sheet into the oven and set the timer. "To answer your question, yes: I think we are getting serious."

Sunny whistled. "Whoa. I didn't realize... Amber, are you in love with him?"

Amber was glad she wasn't holding a tray full of cookies. "Holy Hannah, girl. Way to get right to the point."

"Well," Paris said, "are you?"

"I think... I think maybe... I mean, I could be falling—"

"You are! You're in love. Huh." Paris looked at Sunny with an expression that said, *How about that?*

"I didn't say—"

"But you might as well have," Sunny said. "It's written all over your face."

"Sunny, I—"

Brushing off the denial, Sunny asked, "And the kids? Are you falling for them, too?"

Amber saw no point in denying. "Yes, I believe I'm falling for Max, and I've been crazy about the kids for a long time. Who wouldn't be? They're adorable."

Sunny fought a grin when she said, "These are the same kids we were talking about earlier, right? You're thinking of making them your red-headed stepchildren?" Sunny giggled.

Paris pursed her lips. "Okay, ladies. What am I missing?"

Sunny explained, and Paris chuckled, too. She quickly sobered. "Amber, are you sure you aren't hurrying into this?"

"What? I thought you'd be happy. You've been encouraging me to date Max!"

"I encouraged you to date him, I know, but I expected it would be casual, that you'd work out the kinks with Max. You know, get back up on that dating horse that threw you, or however the saying goes. I don't really see you two ending up together."

Amber bridled. "Why not?"

Sunny stepped in. "He's so much older..."

"Not that much. Paris and Greg are as far apart. Almost anyway."

"True," Paris said. "That's true, Sunny."

Sunny bit her lip. "Okay, cards on the table. What really concerns me is the kids, I mean you and the kids. When we were little, you were the one who carried home stray kittens and baby birds that fell from the nest. You wanted to mother everybody and every little lost creature you found. Remember that fawn you carried home?"

Amber shuddered. "Please, let's not talk about the fawn."

"Your dad always said the doe took it back." Sunny took out the first batch of cookies and put the second tray in the oven.

"I hope she did. I suspect Dad said that to make me feel better. Anyway, your point?"

"My point," Sunny said, "is you might not really be falling in love, either with the children or with Max. The part of you that wants to mother all motherless things might be taking over. You see a couple of cute children who have no mom and you start believing—"

"Okay. I've heard enough." Amber, who had been using a spatula to move cookies onto a cooling rack, dropped the spatula on the counter, letting it clatter. "We're back to baking cookies, ladies. No more on my love life." She swallowed the sudden anger that tightened her throat.

"Amber—" Sunny began.

"I mean it." Angry tears backed her words.

"I'm sorry." Her face a mask of apology, Sunny laid a hand on Amber's arm. "You know I'm just concerned. I want everything to go well for you." When Amber didn't reply, Sunny said, "You know that, don't you?"

Amber nodded. Finding her voice, she added, "Let's not talk about it anymore, okay?"

"Yeah. I got that." Sunny started lifting cookies onto the cooling rack. She and Paris exchanged a look.

Amber saw it, but let it go for the sake of future peace. She forced pep into her voice as she said, "Come on, girls. Let's get some cookies made."

Chapter Eighteen

On Saturday evening, Amber sent a quick text asking Max how things were going. Max called and reported on Keith's wedding, which he said had gone well with the newlyweds now off on their honeymoon. Amber told Max about the community meeting. "Mom and I will be helping with costumes for the living Nativity."

"Sounds like you," Max said. "I'll look forward to seeing that."

They talked again Sunday evening, Max checking in to let Amber know they were home and safe and the kids were tucked into bed. "I'll have some catching up to do after the long weekend," he said. "I won't have much time this week, but how about dinner on Friday?"

"I'll count on it," she answered. They said a quick good night so he could get some rest. Later, Amber lay awake, thinking about Max and rehearsing the things Sunny had said about Amber's penchant for rescuing motherless creatures. Was it possible Sunny had a point?

But Amber had loved those kids almost since she met them. She'd noticed right away how unhappy the children were, but she hadn't known they were motherless…

She stopped the thought, aware she tended to overthink. But had she thought enough about the relationship with Max? About her relationships with Will and Kate? There was so much healing to be done. Was she just complicating things? Then again, relationships were always complicated and most men in her general age group carried emotional baggage of some kind. Amber glanced at the clock. Almost two. She had to be at school in six hours. Time to get some sleep. She slammed her fist into her pillow, rolled over, and gave sleep another try.

~

MAX DRAGGED through the next couple of days, increasingly focusing his attention on Wednesday afternoon's appointment with Dr. Schafer. On Tuesday, he called the office to ask if they could plan to extend their time. Maybe Schafer could help him navigate the stuff with Isabel's mother...and his own mom as well. He wanted to write off that conversation in the kitchen, but he couldn't help recognizing that his mother sometimes knew him better than he knew himself. She'd tried to warn him about Isabel and he'd waved her off then. Maybe he should consider... But no, he couldn't deal with that now. He'd wait and let Dr. Schafer help him through it.

He rolled his eyes at his own thoughts. A few months ago, he'd hated the idea of seeing a therapist, of even having his kids see one. Now here he was becoming dependent on Schafer's advice. He conjured an image of Amber during those first meetings in her office. She'd been right all along—about therapy, about his kids, about every-thing. He jumped as his phone rang. The receptionist called back to tell him Dr. Schafer's schedule had cleared, and Max's appointment had been extended.

AMBER GAZED out the window as Max picked up his kids from school. It was Wednesday afternoon and time for their regular therapy appointment. She smiled as Kate jumped into the back seat, Will drag-ging reluctantly behind. It all looked like business as usual. But if that were true, if everything was business as usual, why was she so uneasy about this week? She didn't usually stare out the window at them.

She tried to think it through. Her unease likely stemmed from her talk with Paris and Sunny. They'd both known her most of her life, and they wanted what was best for her. Maybe she should consider whether they had a point. Before she could talk herself out of it, she called Dr. Schafer and asked if she could make an appointment for herself. "I know he doesn't usually see adults," she told the reception-ist, "but it relates to the Burnett children. Will you ask him for me?" Minutes later, pleased that he could see her on Friday when the school had a half-day and she could sneak away more easily, she finally relaxed and focused on her work.

"I DON'T WANT to listen, but she's my mom, you know?" Max and the therapist had already discussed Will's improvements, but also his slow adjustment overall. Having explained the conversations with both mothers, his and Isabel's, Max now approached Dr. Schafer about his conflicted emotions.

"You aren't at all conflicted about Isabel's mother." Dr. Schafer made it a statement.

"Not at all," Max agreed. "She's a spoiled child who raised a spoiled child. She doesn't want to accept her part in what happened to Isabel, so she's shoving it off on the easiest target she can find—me."

Dr. Schafer nodded approval. "You're seeing that situation quite clearly. Now, about your own mother…"

"She shocked me. When I talked with her and dad and Keith, she was fully supportive. She seemed pleased that I was dating. I thought she was glad I'd found someone, that I could even think about getting serious after…well, you know. Then to come out of the blue…" He shrugged. "It threw me. I don't know what to think."

Dr. Schafer leaned back in his chair, legs crossed, adopting the posture and expression Max had seen in movies and TV shows. "Why do you think it bothered you?" Dr. Schafer asked.

Trying not to give in to the frustration of having the therapist answer his question with a question, Max considered. "I guess the shock of it mostly, and the fact that it seemed such a reversal from her earlier responses."

"What about the content of what she said? Is it possible you are concerned that you could be rushing into a relationship? Or that your attraction to Amber is a rebound, based more on being lonely than on compatibility?"

"No! That is, I don't think so." Max rubbed the back of his neck. "Then I see my reaction to a simple question like that and I have to wonder. Doc, what's going on with me?"

"I'm not going to answer that, Max. Not yet. Let's start with something more basic. Why do you think you reacted sharply? Where does that instant defensiveness come from?"

Max sighed. He had a great deal more to consider by the time he left the therapist's office.

~

"I HAVE to wonder if maybe they're right," Amber told Dr. Schafer as they sat in his office. "Sunny has known me almost my whole life, and Paris for most of it."

"Then you think perhaps you and Max are rushing into—"

"Not me so much," Amber clarified. "I'm a twenty-six-year-old single professional woman. I'm ready for a serious relationship, but I'm starting to wonder if Max is. That is, I suspect he might need more time to deal with the fallout from his ex-wife, from Isabel's selfishness, her betrayal, his own doubts about his judgment because he married her. Not to mention the issues he has now with his in-laws and especially regarding his children."

Dr. Schafer didn't respond, so Amber went on.

"Our personal relationship began because I wanted to talk to him about his kids. Kate is still trying to win approval by being a pleaser. Will is doing much better, but he carries so much anger and resentment…" Realizing she was rambling and that she had a death grip on both arms of her chair, Amber shook out her hands and took a deep breath, letting it out slowly.

"I notice you're gripping that chair like a lifeline."

"It's Isabel," Amber said. "Don't get me wrong. I know addiction is a disease. I keep telling Max he needs to understand. At the same time, I see what her decisions have done to her children, especially to Will, and I almost wish I had her standing here so I could tell her off. Big time." She blew out another breath.

"Your anger is reasonable." Dr. Schafer put down his pencil. "But right now, it's not helping you. What are you going to do with it?"

"Good question. The only option I have is to keep it to myself. Max has enough anger of his own. He doesn't need to hear mine."

Dr. Schafer tapped his pen against his chin. "I wonder if that's the right approach. You say you've been trying to encourage him to understand Isabel, but that doesn't seem to be working. Maybe it would help both you and Max if he knew you also feel anger toward Isabel, and that yours is protective of him and his family."

She nodded. "Huh. Maybe you're right."

Dr. Schafer stood. "Amber, you need to give some thought to everything we've discussed today." He added a stern look when he said, "Don't obsess. You do have that tendency to overthink."

She almost snorted.

Schafer walked toward the door, clearly ending their session. "Do think about it, though. See if you can sort through your emotions, figure out where they're coming from, and decide the best approach to using them."

She shook her head. "I think I'm stuck on the idea you suggested earlier that I'm using this anger as an obstacle to a future with Max."

"And you're surprised by this?"

"Anger is negative, something to eliminate, not to use."

Dr. Schafer shook his head. "Emotions aren't good or bad, they're just emotions. When you figure out how to use them productively, you're developing a healthier approach toward life." He wished Amber a safe drive and said to call when she wanted to talk again.

As she drove away, Amber wondered whether she felt better or worse. Had Schafer given her any answers? Or only more questions to keep her awake at night?

TWO HOURS LATER, Amber sat across from Max at Broadway Louie's. They'd caught each other up on recent events. With their orders in and a lull in the conversation, Amber saw an opening. "I saw Dr. Schafer today."

"You did?" Max sat straighter.

"People I care about have been asking questions about our relationship: Are we hurrying into it? Am I sure I'm not a rebound? Am I applying my tendency to mother the motherless a little too directly when it comes to Will and Kate?" She paused, straightening her knife and fork.

"Are you?" Max's posture stiffened even more.

Amber heard what he hadn't said. She took Max's hand. "I don't believe I am," she answered, her voice husky with emotion.

Max looked down briefly. Then he looked her in the eyes and entwined his fingers with hers. "My mom asked me many of the same questions."

"Really? Your mother? She doesn't know me, but she's working against me?" Amber couldn't keep the hurt from breaking through.

Max shook his head. "I don't think so. The more I run the conversation in my head, the more I think Mom is just making sure I'm ready to move on, that I'm not still too damaged by the mess with Isabel to make a go of trying again."

"Frankly, that's been my biggest concern."

His brow furrowed. "You doubted me?"

"Not you, Max, but I've been wondering if you've had enough time to heal. You went through a very bad time…"

"I agree."

"I saw Dr. Schafer this week too, and we talked about many of the same things."

She licked her lips. "And?"

"And since then, I've had a couple of realizations." He took a deep breath. "First, I realized that I've been grouping the problems with Isabel and Lovenia and holding that emotion against other women in my life, unfortunately including you."

Amber sat back, stung. "That hardly seems fair."

"It isn't, and consciously recognizing that means I've been able to acknowledge how unreasonable and unfair it is, so I can let it go."

"Then I guess that's good." Amber shifted uncomfortably in her chair. "Were there other realizations besides that one."

"Just one that I consider important. I realized I'm in love with you."

"Oh." Amber's eyes filled with tears. "That's good… since I love you too."

"You do?"

Amber couldn't tell whether he seemed more happy or surprised.

"Yes, Max. I love you too. I've suspected it for a while. Then when you were away, I missed you... and I knew."

"That's... well, it's great. It's wonderful!" The wonder showed on his face as he picked up her hand and placed a gentle kiss on her fingers.

She leaned toward him. "I think so too, that it's wonderful."

"I'm... so glad."

The server came and went, leaving their food on the table without disturbing their moment. Max and Amber sat silently, letting their eyes do their talking.

Later that evening, in front of a crackling fire in Amber's living room, they talked through many of their questions, fears, and emotions. Amber's heart danced when Max took her hand, gazed into her eyes, and said, "I believe we should start talking about marriage."

"Max? Are you proposing? Already?"

"Call this a preparatory step. Let's get the abstractions out of the way."

"Abstractions? What abstractions?"

"Like for instance, how do you feel about a family? Would you like us to have a child of our own? Maybe more than one?"

Amber smirked. "I don't consider that an abstraction, Max. Babies are quite real."

"Tell me about it." Seeing her expression, he quickly changed his approach. "So? Do you want to have a baby or babies?"

"Yes. I'd like to have at least one. Maybe after we have one baby, we can talk about having more. How do you feel about that?"

"I hadn't thought about it until my mother asked, but I told you I was upset when Isabel was sterilized without my consent. I think I'd like to have at least one more."

"Good! Then that 'abstraction' is taken care of."

They talked about other things including attending couples therapy with Dr. Schafer, if he was open to it. They would tentatively plan toward a wedding in the summer, maybe shortly after school let out for the year.

"I'm going to have to work at winning over Will." Amber stroked

Max's hand. An idea occurred. "Are you still thinking about getting a puppy?"

"I promised him. We've heard back from Lech Nowak—you know, our teenage landlord—and he says it's okay if I fence that one open stretch in the back, and it's okay if we have a dog. That ends my last excuse for why I haven't done it yet."

"What if I'm the one who does it?"

"Huh? You want to build the fence—"

She snapped her fingers. "Keep up, Max. What if I'm the one who gives Will a puppy? Maybe as my Christmas gift?"

"Oh." He sat back against the sofa. "I hadn't considered that. An AKC beagle puppy can be expen—"

She put her fingers over his lips, cutting him off. "Don't even say it. I can afford a puppy, and I think it might be the answer to help break down the walls between your son and me. The only problem I can see is…if I get Will a puppy, what can I get Kate that will seem at all like parity?" Her eyes danced with mischief. "Does your yard have room for a pony?"

He groaned. "Please tell me you're kidding."

She nodded. "Yes. Absolutely, I am."

"That's a relief."

"But do think about what I can get for Kate that will seem even handed and fair."

"Will do." He looked at his watch. "I didn't realize how late it's getting. I'll have Luisa in trouble for sure."

"I don't have a number for Luisa, but I have her mom's number in my phone, so—"

"You do?"

"Luisa's mom is on the Nativity committee with me. I'll text her and let her know what's happening and that you'll be home soon."

"That's a deal." Max stood. Picking up his coat, he started for the door. Amber followed.

If the time was not already so late, their kiss might have lasted longer. As it was, it ended sooner than either would have liked. Max said, "We made some important strides tonight."

"And some important decisions."

He nodded. "Yes, we did." He started to turn but looked back. "What do you say we take the kids down the hill tomorrow evening, maybe get a pizza?"

"I'd love it."

"Great. I'll call you."

Amber watched as Max drove away. Remembering her promise, she sent a text to Luisa's mother. She set down her phone and thought of Dr. Schafer. Maybe she and Max had both needed to confront their doubts. Now the question was where they'd go from here. She banked the fire and prepared for bed, confident she'd sleep tonight.

Chapter Nineteen

A t the pizza parlor the next evening, Will was more upbeat than Max had seen him in some time. When their assault on the pizza ended, Max dug in his pocket, producing quarters for the video games in the side room.

Will eagerly grabbed the quarters. "Hurry, Kate! I'll beat you at race cars."

"You probably will." Kate moved somewhat more slowly as she followed. "You usually win that one. I'll beat you at Foosball, though."

Will called over his shoulder, "You can try!"

Max watched them go with obvious pride. "She probably *will* beat him at Foosball. She usually does."

"You have a couple of great kids, Max, and I believe Will's more relaxed than usual."

"I agree. I wonder what's changed?"

"Maybe he senses the difference in the energy between us." She paused when she saw Max's skeptical expression. "I'm not trying to get all New Age on you, but I am serious. We've been tentative around each other, often on eggshells, tiptoeing, avoiding difficult topics. He's probably sensed the lack of certainty. Now that we've mellowed some, clarified how we feel—"

"I see what you mean." He watched the children, thoughtfully studying the ease between them. "Maybe you're right. When Will seemed so negative about you, I wondered—"

"Me too. Maybe the fact that you are more certain has helped him feel more certain."

He nodded. "Could be." He put his arm around her. "Yes, it definitely could be."

∾

IT WAS ONLY after the children fell asleep that evening and Amber and Max sit down in front of his crackling hearth, that she felt brave enough to bring up another topic. "When I talked with Dr. Schafer yesterday, I shared with him is how very angry I still feel with your late ex-wife."

"You? I thought you were all about cutting her slack because of her addiction."

"That's the way I came across, I know, and I'm sorry for that. I do hope that one day we can talk about addiction again and the psychological side of it." She saw his expression turn stormy and realized she was venturing back into chancy territory, but she pressed on. "I'm only bringing this up because my cousin Skye is a recovering addict," she said in a tentative voice.

"I'm sorry, I had no idea." Max said, his expression softening.

"I didn't want to go into it before when you were telling me about Isabel, because, well, Skye is recently out of jail and sober and I think this time, she's going to stay sober. I told you about Skye's mother Dawn, but I didn't feel it was my place to talk about Skye before this, and I don't want you to think I was making excuses for Isabel. I haven't experienced what you have, but I do know how addiction impacts the entire family. It's wreaked havoc with ours."

"I'm sorry. I shouldn't have reacted the way I did." Max brushed his hands through his hair. "I know there are a lot of good people out there who end up in bad situations."

"Yes," she said softly. "There are. One day I'll tell you more about my lovely cousin Skye. But what I wanted to say is that addiction or no, a person is still responsible for the collateral damage, for the harm they cause to others. When I think about how much Isabel hurt you and how badly she hurt those beautiful kids, especially Will, I get furious, completely furious." Embarrassed to find her fingers tightening into fists, Amber stopped herself.

He stared in apparent surprise. "You really are, aren't you? Angry, I mean. I don't think I've ever seen you like this."

"I seldom feel like this." She made a conscious effort to relax. "Dr. Schafer asked me what I wanted to do with this emotion. I said I don't think there's much I *can* do, since I can't tell Isabel off." She gave Max a sideways look from the corner of her eye. "I can't slap the living daylights out of her, either."

Max jerked his head back in surprise. "You? You'd do that? Actual violence?"

She bit her lip. "Probably not, but it's satisfying to imagine it."

He laughed. "You're adorable, you know that?"

Now she was the one to look skeptical. "I'm adorable when enraged?"

"You're adorable all the time, and I love that you care enough about the kids and me to feel that kind of anger toward someone who hurt us. I feared you were Saint Amber, so far above human emotions that an ordinary mortal such as myself could never live up to your standard."

"Max, that wasn't what I meant."

"I know that. At least part of what I said is teasing." He leaned down, tenderly kissing her. Then he grinned. "I like you better as a human."

"Max, let me finish."

He listened as she talked, and when she finished, he kissed her again.

Amber knew they still had more to talk about, but she could save that for later. She let herself sink into his kiss.

For Amber, the time between building paper turkeys from handprints and creating reindeer tree ornaments out of candy canes and pipe cleaners always seemed too short. She'd made it a rule to have her shopping done before Thanksgiving so she could spend the last harried month baking, making candy, taking plates of goodies to neighbors, and attending school and community events, along with the occasional friends' party or evening of caroling.

The Daughters of Destiny finished their last pre-Christmas concert a week before the holidays. They sang carols and favorite Christmas songs at the annual festival in Bedford Falls, did impromptu concerts in the park in Destiny, and caroled around town in the evenings, making a point to tell friends and family about the big pre-Superbowl party at the Reed compound in the new year.

The living Nativity shone brightly with a few new robes and head-dresses for the three kings, all made by Amber and Olivia. Even the weather cooperated by delaying snow until Christmas Eve, when a light, snowy blanket made the town sparkle. It was as lovely a Christmas as Amber could remember.

By prior agreement, Max and his kids spent Christmas morning at home, just the three of them, while Amber celebrated at her parents' home with Mexican hot chocolate, *buñuelos*, and gingerbread pigs called *marranitos*. Sunny and Evan came up from the valley and brought Skye with them. The family filled the house with happy memories of Christmases past. Amber enjoyed the morning, but made her excuses fairly early, since she and Max planned to meet at her home at one o'clock.

Around twelve-thirty, Max announced to his children, "This is just the start of Christmas. Ms. Reyes has some special gifts for you at her house. Let's get you dressed and head out."

"Cool!" Kate jumped up, running from the room.

Will looked at his father. "What kind of presents?" Max, who had watched his son carefully through the gift opening, knew Will was disappointed that he hadn't yet seen a dog.

"You'll like it." Max gave Will a wink.

"I hope so," Will said, "'cause I kinda wanta play with my stomp rocket and my space blaster. Can we set up the terrarium when we get home?"

"Sure," Max said, though he doubted Will would focus on the terrarium after he saw Amber's gift. Will went to his room to get dressed and Max texted Amber:

Are you ready for us?

A message came back quickly:

Soon as you can get here. Love you.

Max grinned at the way she ended her text. He sent back:

Love you too. See you soon.

"Come on, kiddos! Let's get moving!" he called down the hallway.

AMBER MADE another quick sweep of the living room. She had Mexican hot chocolate, rich with cinnamon, simmering in the kitchen next to a pot of spiced cider. Frosted sugar cookies and *marranitos* rested side-by-side on a covered tray. The whole house smelled of vanilla, cinnamon, chocolate, the log on the fire, and Christmas. Most important were the two special boxes under the tree. She added a log to the fire and stepped back, pleased with her efforts. She knew Will and Kate would both love what she had for them. Max? Maybe not so much. He'd agreed reluctantly so far, but she hoped to bring him around.

She shook out the tension in her hands and took a couple of deep breaths. She thought about double-checking the warm drinks and started toward the kitchen to do just that when she heard a car pull into the driveway, followed by the shutting of three car doors. She put on her Santa hat and went to the door just as the bell rang.

"Merry Christmas!" She threw the door open and bent down to wrap Will and Kate in a bear hug as they came inside.

"Don't I get a hug, too?" Max made a face, doing his best to look left out and forlorn.

"You bet you do!" Amber's hug came with an eager kiss.

"Ew." Will made gagging noises.

"Don't knock it 'til you've tried it, kid." Max winked at his son.

Will responded with more gagging sounds. Kate grinned.

Amber brought out small children's chairs the kids had used before, setting them at some distance from the tree to cut down on the risk of blowing the surprise. She sat on the couch, Max taking a place beside her. "Was Santa good to you two?"

"We got a terrarium!" Kate said. "I got a unicorn! And art supplies! And a bead-stringing set."

"How about you, Will?"

"I didn't get what I really wanted," Will said, "but I did get some cool stuff, like a stomp rocket and a remote-controlled car that can run up the wall."

"Up the wall? Really?"

"It does," Max confirmed. "I don't know where my mom and dad found it."

"The presents from my other grandparents haven't come yet, so maybe I'll still get what I want." Will gave his father a reproachful look.

"Maybe you'll get something you like here," Amber said. "Are you ready to open your presents?"

"Yeah, I—"

The puppy stole the moment, whining and scratching at the inside of the box. Will's eyes went wide. He looked at his father. "Dad?"

"Don't look at me, Will. Ms. Reyes got you that present."

"Can I open it now?" He looked to Amber.

"Yes, but I think you'd better hurry!" The puppy's efforts were causing the lid to lift.

Seconds later, Will held a beagle puppy that earnestly licked his face. "You got it for me! You really got it for me!"

"Yes, she did," Max said, careful to make sure Amber got the credit.

"Your dad helped by saying you wanted a boy puppy. We bought other stuff for it, too. There's puppy food in the spare bedroom, along with a doghouse and a leash and a few other things you might need."

The party went on hold while everyone watched Will with his puppy. Kate sat down next to him. "Can I hold it?"

"He's my puppy!" Will said. Then, softening his voice, "But you can hold him for a minute."

"Thanks." Kate took the puppy; he eagerly began washing her face with his tongue.

"Don't you want to open your present?" Max nodded toward the other box.

"I bet I didn't get a puppy," Kate said, "but I'm glad Will got his dog."

"No, you didn't get a puppy," Amber said, "but I think you'll like your present."

"Okay," Kate said. She crawled across to the other box, sat beside it, and lifted the lid. Her eyes grew as large as Will's. "A kitten? You got me a kitten?" Within seconds, it was in her arms, held against Kate's neck, rubbing against her face and purring.

"She's so beautiful!" Kate held the kitten in front of her, stroking her calico coat. "Look at all the colors!"

"She is pretty, isn't she?" Amber gave Max a questioning look, her eyes asking, *What do you think now, Max?* Persuading him about the kitten had taken much more effort than talking him into the puppy.

"Kate's happy," he said. "That's what matters." His contented grin let her know he was okay with the choice.

"We have things for the kitten in the other room, too," Amber said. "Your dad will help you get the food and other items home today."

Max asked, "Will, what are you going to call your puppy?" The conversation detoured into names for puppies and kittens while Amber brought cookies and warm drinks to the dining room table, prepping the snack for everyone.

An hour later, Will had decided his dog would be named Scoopy. Who knew why?

Kate asked, "Ms. Reyes, what do you call those Japanese fish with the bright-colored spots?"

When Amber told her, Kate beamed and announced she would name her kitten Koi.

Both children were so absorbed in their gifts that they barely tasted the snack. When they did, Max found Will feeding a *marranito* to the puppy under the table. "Son, you can't do that," he explained. "Scoopy needs to eat puppy food. People food can make him sick."

"Oh. I didn't know." Will looked uncertain but burst into tears when the puppy began throwing up the rich cookie.

"Don't cry," Max said, ruffling Will's hair. "I'm sure he'll be okay. Just don't give him anymore, okay?"

"Okay, Dad." Will nodded earnestly.

"Would you like to open your gift now?" She handed Max a small box.

"Uh, I didn't bring—"

"Don't worry about that. Just open this before I die of suspense."

"I wouldn't want anyone to die." Max lifted the lid from the small box. "Amber, this is... more than you should have done." He took the watch out of the package and put it on. "I usually use my cell phone for time checks, but this has a compass, a barometer, and... I'll have to

179

look at it carefully to see what all these gizmos are. Hey, it's a fitness watch too, isn't it?" He beamed at her. "Thank you so much!" He kissed her thoroughly while Will made more gagging noises. "I'll get your gift to you soon."

"No worries." Amber leaned against him, smiling her contentment.

Minutes later, Amber helped Max load the doghouse, cat bed, food bowls, and other pet accessories into the trunk of his car. "It's a good thing that doghouse isn't any bigger," she said as she helped him tie down the trunk lid.

"It's temporary," Max answered. "Will and I will build a bigger house in the backyard once we get this little guy off to a good start."

"I'm glad you were okay with this." Amber locked her arm through his as the kids piled into the back seat, each carrying a small, weary pet. "Especially with the kitten."

"I still don't know how this is going to work. I barely keep up with the job and the kids as it is. Having two extra little mouths to feed…"

"Six-year-olds aren't known for taking good care of pets," she said, "but I think you'll get lots of willing help from those two."

"I hope so." Max leaned close to kiss her. "See you soon."

"Yes, soon," she said.

They'd agreed that Amber would be spending Christmas dinner with her family while Max hung out with the kids at home, enjoying a prepared Christmas dinner from Abbas' Grocery and watching his children playing with their new pets.

Amber waved as the car pulled away, missing them already. Stepping back inside, she tidied the house, preparing for the evening at her parents' home. A thought came unbidden: *Next year, I could have a family of my own.* It startled her so much, her knees grew weak and she had to sit. As she thought of what following Christmas might bring, she smiled, banishing any sadness she felt at letting Max and the kids drive away without her.

Chapter Twenty

M ax watched his children with a sense of satisfaction unlike anything he'd felt since that first day in the nursery. Kate played with her kitten—the name Koi had stuck—ignoring the minor bites and scratches. Will had kept Scoopy within arm's reach since the pup came out of the box four days before. That had led to some bedding changes and several short lectures about house- training the puppy including one more about overfeeding when the pup got sick again. Max knew he'd have to step in soon to make sure the dog had a chance of being housebroken, but he hated to interrupt this. It had been a long time since he'd seen Will this happy.

During the school vacation, Max still worked days. He did more work from home on days like these but went to the office for a few hours each morning. Will had to be forced to leave Scoopy behind during the hours he spent at Mrs. Larsen's. Otherwise, he had the puppy in his lap or by his side almost constantly.

Max checked the clock. "Getting close to bedtime, kids. Will, let Scoopy stay in his box tonight so we don't have to wash your bedding tomorrow. Deal?"

Will's face dropped. He pouted as he said, "Okay, Dad. If I have to."

"You need to for a while, son, until we get the dog trained."

"Then can he sleep with me?" Will brightened.

Max wanted to say no. His parents had never allowed dogs to sleep inside, let alone in the family's beds. Of course, Will's situation was somewhat different… "Yeah. Okay. After Scoopy is trained, he can sleep with you, or at least in your room. Good enough?"

"Yeah. Thanks, Dad!" Will hurried from the room with the puppy at his feet. That was one thing the pup hadn't had to be taught. He knew whose dog he was. Max watched them go with a warm, sweet feeling. The housebreaking could wait 'til tomorrow. He'd let them have tonight.

~

THE DAYS before school started again were always a pleasure for Amber. With the pressure off, she could use morning hours to catch up on necessary office work and spend afternoons with family and friends. She had just sent out a required report when her cell phone rang. Seeing Max's number, she picked up. "Hey there, Handsome."

"Hey to you too, Gorgeous." She could hear him juggling the phone. "What do you have going this evening?"

"Thought I'd warm a can of soup, sit in front of the fire, and read a good book. You?"

"I'm going to start housebreaking a puppy."

"You haven't started yet?"

"Well, yeah, a little bit. Here and there. Now and then. Will hasn't been willing to let go of the dog long enough for me to accomplish much. I've let him know we're getting serious about it this evening. Want to join us?"

"Sure. Housebreaking a puppy sounds like a wonderful way to spend the evening."

"Okay, now you're worrying me."

She chuckled. "Honestly, I can think of more fun things to do than housebreaking a dog, but I'd enjoy spending the time with you and the kids."

"Great. I'll take everybody out for dinner, so don't worry about that. We'll pick you up on the way home from Mrs. Larsen's place, say around three?"

She checked her watch. She'd have time to get her second report done and get ready before Max could get here. "Sure. That sounds good. See you then."

"See you then." Max clicked off.

By two-thirty, Amber sat in her living room, writing the last of the thank you cards she wanted to send to parents who'd helped with class Christmas parties. Max and the kids picked her up just after three and they grabbed a snack and picked up food for dinner before heading back to Max's. Will barely made it through the door before calling, "Here, Scoopy! Here, boy!" He went running to find the pup.

"Whew!" Amber cringed at the acrid stench of ammonia. "I'm afraid the place smells like an untrained puppy." Seeing Max's face fall, she added, "but it looks like everybody's settling in well." Amber stepped inside, waiting while Max took her coat and hat.

"The kids have hardly let those poor creatures alone," Max said. "Look. Kate is already settled in her favorite chair with Koi in her lap."

Indeed, Kate sat in the chair she preferred, the calico kitten in her lap jumping to catch a string she held in her fingers. Kate giggled each time the kitten made the leap.

"She looks happy." Amber settled in her own favorite spot at one end of the couch.

Max sat beside her. "I wonder where Will is. He's barely through the door most days before that pup is in his arms."

He barely finished his sentence when Will came running, tears streaking his face. "Dad, you've gotta come. Something's wrong with Scoopy."

"Okay, Son." He stood and offered Amber a hand, helping her to her feet. "We'd better check. I suspect the puppy is just sleepy. Will probably woke him out of a nap."

"He's still just a baby, after all. Babies sleep a lot." Amber followed Max down the hall. They entered Will's bedroom to find another foul smell and a scared little boy standing over the dog carrier that doubled as Scoopy's bed when he wasn't sleeping in Will's. "Look at him, Dad. He won't sit up and there's yuck all over him. I think he's been urping up stuff."

Max put his hand on Will's shoulder. "Let me have a look, son." Will moved back and Max moved forward...and gasped. Amber knew the problem was real the instant she heard that sound, but Max's voice was calm when he said, "Will, can you run to the bathroom for me? Dampen a washcloth and bring it to me. Okay?"

"Sure, Dad." Will ran from the room.

Max turned to her. "Can you look at this? Have you ever seen anything like it?"

Amber stepped forward. After Max's response, she expected something unsettling. Still, what she saw made her gasp, too. "Oh, Max. This is bad."

"Yeah. That's what I thought." He turned to take the washcloth from Will. "Thanks, Son. Can you bring a little bowl of water, too?"

"Sure, Dad. Is Scoopy gonna be okay?"

"We don't know yet, kiddo. Let's see what we can do."

Amber dropped her voice. "You're trying to keep Will out of the room, aren't you?"

"Out of the room and busy," Max answered, speaking quietly, "at least until we get this mess cleaned up." He began to mop at the carrier floor. "The puppy is lethargic. He's wagged his tail a couple of times since I got here, but he hasn't stood up even once." More quietly, he added, "He's been vomiting blood."

Amber nodded. "Yes, I can see that. I can't help thinking that's a bad sign."

"Yeah, very bad."

"I bought this little guy from a quality breeder with a clean reputation. A veterinarian Skye knows referred me and that vet gave this litter all their puppy shots. I'll go call the office and see if we can get an appointment for Scoopy to be seen today."

"Sounds good. Find something for Will to do while you're out there, okay?"

"Yeah. Will do." She met Will at the door. "Will, can you come with me into the living room? I'm going to call a vet and I want you next to me so I can ask you questions about how Scoopy normally does things. Can you do that?"

"Yeah, I guess. Can I go check on him first?"

She put a gentle hand on his shoulder. "Your dad is taking good care of him. I need you here right now, okay?"

"Yeah. Okay." Will took a deep breath, standing a little straighter.

"Thanks. You're being a great help." She scrolled through her contacts, found the number for the vet, and started to place the call. She quickly realized she'd need to get Will out of the room if she wanted to tell the whole truth. "Will, we'll need to tell them what kind of food Scoopy is eating. Can you get the package and bring it in?"

"It's heavy," Will said, "but I'll try."

"Maybe Kate can help you. Katydid, can—"

"Yeah. Come on, Will." The girl put down her kitten and joined her brother. Koi bounced along at their feet.

With the children out of the room, Amber called the veterinary office, explained who she was, and quickly detailed the puppy's symptoms. "There's a lot of vomit for such a little guy," she said, "and I'm surprised at how much blood is in it. No wonder he's lethargic."

The receptionist asked her to wait and went to speak with the vet. Amber thanked the children when they dragged in the huge bag of food and drew them both close while explaining that she was waiting to talk with the animal doctor. Of the two vets available, the one who answered was the young woman Amber had spoken with when she asked about the puppy, the one who had done Scoopy's latest vaccinations.

"Hello? Miss Reyes? I hear you have a very sick puppy."

"Yes," Amber answered, avoiding elaboration for Will's sake. "Can you work him in to the schedule today?"

"The good news is we'll be happy to see him if you can get him in before eight this evening. The bad news, I'm afraid, is very bad."

Amber looked at Will and tried to offer an encouraging smile. "Yes?"

"We've already seen two puppies from that same litter; both came in yesterday. We just managed to track down the source and figure out what happened. In fact, we were about to call you. We've been trying to reach everyone who has a puppy from this litter."

Amber stiffened. "What happened?"

"We had a parvo puppy in here just before that litter came in for their last puppy shots. We also had a new technician on duty that day, someone who did not know and apparently did not follow proper protocols when disinfecting the room before the healthy litter came in. The two puppies we've seen have parvovirus, although neither sounds as bad as the one you're describing. I'm afraid your little guy may be in serious trouble, but if you can get him in here, we'll do what we can."

"Thanks. We'll bring him right down." Amber clicked off.

Will gave her a resentful glare. "You didn't ask me any questions."

"No, you're right. I didn't need to. The vet thinks she knows what's wrong. She says to bring Scoopy right in. Can you and Kate wait out here while I go tell your dad about it? We'll bring Scoopy out and you can hold him in your lap on the way to the vet's, okay?"

"Yeah, okay."

"Why don't you go get a nice, fluffy towel to wrap him in?"

"All right." He started down the hall.

Kate whispered as she asked, "Is Will's puppy really sick?"

"I'm afraid so, honey." Amber gave Kate's shoulder a squeeze. Then she went to Max. She found him on his knees, holding the puppy in an old baby blanket. Scoopy seemed barely able to hold his head up.

Amber delivered the news about parvovirus and explained that she promised to bring the pup in.

"Parvovirus?" Max swore under his breath.

Amber said, "I've heard the name, but I don't know what it is."

"Not many dogs survive it." Max stood, his face like stone. His voice rose. "Amber, how could you? Surely you know better than to get Will a sick puppy!"

Amber took an involuntarily step back. "You think I did this on purpose? Give me some credit! I interviewed the vet that gave the shots. I interviewed people who'd adopted from this breeder before. Max, I did my full due diligence." She repeated what the vet said about a new technician and a parvo pup that came in just before Scoopy and his littermates got their last shots.

"I'm sorry," he said. "That was a rotten thing to say. I know it's not fair to blame you, but…well, you know what this is doing to Will." In an act of contrition, he drew her into a hug, which she stiffly accepted. He looked back at the inert form in the blanket. "We'd better see what we can do. If Will's puppy dies—"

"Let's not give up yet." Amber picked up the sad little bundle and led the way to the car.

186

MAX CALLED the veterinary office as they made their way to the valley, and the receptionist met them at a side door. As she let them in, she explained their strict protocol for dealing with contagious disease, including separating the sick animal from others in the waiting area. "We do all we can to avoid cross contamination," she explained. "Despite our best efforts, it sometimes happens, but we've never had a breach of sterile procedure this serious." With a look of apology, she said, "We'll do what we can for your puppy." She escorted them into an examination room. "The doctor will be in shortly."

Will put his face against the puppy's fur. "I want him to be all right."

"We all do." Max sat beside him, pulling his son close.

"He's really sick, Dad." Will barely held back tears.

"I know, kiddo." The poor pup wasn't even trying to wag his tail anymore.

The vet arrived then, introducing herself and asking for a quick rundown of the symptoms and when they started. "We don't know exactly when this all started," Max said, explaining how the puppy had been left alone all morning. "Will, was he fine when we left him this morning?"

"Not really. He was lying down and he didn't get up or anything. He hadn't been urping up stuff, so I thought maybe he was just sleepy."

Max said, "I guess it started earlier than I thought. Come to think of it, he vomited yesterday. I thought Will was just overfeeding him, but it could have been the parvo even then."

The vet said, "Let me take him into the back. We'll have a good look at him and run some tests. I'll be back when I know more." Before leaving the room, she turned, "Mr. Burnett, I assure you that we recognize our responsibility in this puppy's illness. There will be no charge and we'll reimburse you for the cost of the puppy as well."

"Thank you," he said.

The doctor nodded acknowledgment.

Max turned to the other worried faces. "We'll do everything we can to help Scoopy."

Kate sat next to him. "Daddy, can Koi get sick from what Scoopy has?"

"I don't know, sweetie," Max answered honestly. "I don't think so, but we'll ask the doctor when she comes back."

"All right, Dad." Kate curled against Max's side, making herself impossibly small. Max put an arm around her and held the other one out for his son. "Will?" He gestured at the space next to him.

Will shook his head. "I wanta stay here, across from the door. I wanta see him when the doc brings him back."

"Okay," Max answered.

They sat silently. The clock in the room ticked away seconds. Amber went to the magazine rack and picked up a recent edition of a children's magazine. "Come help me, Kate. We'll get this mouse out of the maze." Kate went to her and the two of them used a pencil to trace a route through the paper puzzle. Neither woman nor girl seemed involved in the effort.

Max looked at the clock again. Almost twelve minutes had passed since she left. Had the clock always been that loud?

The door opened and the doctor came in with Scoopy held gently in her hands. "The tests weren't hopeful," she said, putting the puppy on the exam table. "I believe we told you we've seen other puppies from this same litter. We have two in the back of our shop, in the area we call our hospital. They're receiving IV fluids and the best support we can give them. They're responding, and I think they have a chance. For whatever reason, this little fellow—did you call him Snoopy?"

"Scoopy," Will said.

"Scoopy," the doctor corrected. "Scoopy isn't doing as well. I don't think he'll make it. We aren't hearing bowel sounds, so it's even possible his intestine is necrotic. I fear trying to save him would only postpone the inevitable." She aimed a meaningful look at Max. Then to Will, she said, "In the meantime, your puppy is suffering. He's trying to be brave, for you, but he's in a lot of pain. The kind thing would be to let him go."

Will looked up at his father. "What does she mean, Dad? Let him go where?"

Max cleared his throat. "Will, honey, she means it would be best to put Scoopy to sleep."

"Then, when he wakes up, he'll be better?" The hopeful look on the child's face broke Max's heart. He knew kids had to learn about death sometime, but Will and Kate had already lost their mother. Why did it have to be this hard? He put a hand on Will's shoulder.

"When the doctor says 'put him to sleep,' she means give him a shot so he will go to sleep and not wake up again, ever."

Will's eyes widened in horror. "She's gonna *kill* him?"

"He's dying, son. The doctor will give him a shot to make it easier."

"No!" Will grabbed the puppy, holding him against his chest. "No, you can't do that! You can't kill my dog!"

Max took Will in his arms. "Will, it's the kind thing to do. Scoopy is hurting. He's dying, son. Let the doctor make it easier for him." Carefully, Max eased the bundle from Will's arms and handed the puppy to the vet.

"We'll make it quick," the vet said. "Would you like me to administer the injection here?"

Max looked at his son, who now lay sobbing on the bench. "No, best to get it over with." He let his eyes point to the back door.

The vet nodded and left the room. The terrible silence was broken only by Will's anguished sobs. Kate, quiet tears streaming, sat next to her brother, her hand on his back, comforting him with her presence.

Max looked to Amber. "I'm going to carry Will to the car. The doctor will have questions …you know, about things like…disposal." He gave Amber a pleading look. "Try to handle things in the most … distant sort of way." He hoped she understood. The last thing Will needed was to bring home a dead puppy. He picked up his son, hefting him into his arms. "Oh! Please ask if parvo can be spread to cats."

Kate nodded at Amber, her anguished eyes filled with tears.

"Come on, Katydid. Let's see if we can help your brother." Max carried Will out.

Chapter Twenty-One

The drive home seemed longer than the drive there. Will continued his hopeless sobbing, refusing every attempt to comfort him. Kate, who still sniffed and brushed back tears, kept a hand on her brother's shoulder. Amber did her best to fill the front seat with quiet talk, explaining to Max what the doctor had said about parvo, that cats had a different version of the virus so they couldn't catch it from dogs. "Koi will be just fine," Amber assured Kate, who managed a small smile as she nodded her thanks.

"I got a printout," Amber said, unfolding the pages. "It tells us everything we'll need to do to sterilize the...um, the infected area... before we bring another—"

"Not soon," Max said. "We should wait."

"Yes, of course, the doctor said to give it a while. Even with all the careful disinfecting, it should be several weeks before we bring... before we try again." She folded the papers and put them in her bag. "It was good of the doctors to waive the charges."

"The least they could do," Max said in a hard voice.

"I do hope those other puppies—"

"Amber?"

"Yes?"

"Stop, okay? Just stop."

Amber swallowed hard. She turned to look out the window, blinking back tears of her own. She had tried so hard to do something good and it turned out so bad. A memory popped into her mind, her father standing in the kitchen of her childhood home. She had complained about being the last one cut from the spelling bee and how the winner didn't have to spell the word she missed. She ended her tirade by crying out, "It isn't fair!"

Her dad took her hand. "Life isn't fair, *Chiquita*. The sooner you learn that, the easier it will be to carry on. Don't expect fairness, and you'll be okay." But why did a six-year-old have to learn it this way? Would her father say the same thing to Will? Her mental image of her father didn't answer, but she imagined him looking into the back seat with compassion.

Though the drive seemed interminable, they finally arrived in Destiny. Max said, "It's dinner time and I haven't planned anything—"

"I have everything for spaghetti and meatballs," Amber volunteered. "I think I've got the makings of a green salad to go with it, and I have a half loaf of French bread in the freezer. We can make garlic bread. Sound good?"

Max looked over the back seat. "What d'ya think, kiddos? Shall we have spaghetti at Amber's house?"

Kate spoke quietly. "I like pisketti."

Will didn't answer.

"Will? Do you think you can eat some dinner? Maybe spaghetti?"

"Not at *her* house." Will glared at Amber.

"Will! That's not nice. You need to apologize to Ms. Reyes."

"I won't!" Will shrieked the words. "I heard what you said. It's her fault! She got me a sick puppy. She knew he was gonna die!"

Max stopped the car at the side of the road and leaned over the seat. "Will, that's not true. Ms. Reyes tried hard to find you the perfect puppy. Nobody knew he was sick when she brought him home. Even the doctors didn't know he was sick. I shouldn't have said what I said."

"I don't care! It's still her fault."

Max toughened his voice. "Will, you need to stop this. It isn't Amber's fault and she's been very kind to offer us dinner at her home. Now you need to—"

"I'm not doing anything with her. Not anything! You always wanta be with her and not with us! I don't wanta be with her at all anymore."

"Will—"

Amber caught his hand. "Max, I think you'd better take me home. You and the kids can find something for your supper, and we'll talk again later, maybe in a day or two, after things settle down."

"Amber—"

"Really, Max. I think this is best. Will needs some time to get over this shock. Maybe we all do." She picked up her purse. "We're just a couple of blocks from my place. I'll walk from here. You can call me tomorrow."

"I don't want to handle it this way—" Max began.

Amber got out. Looking to the back seat, she said, "Will, I am deeply sorry about what happened to Scoopy. He was a great little puppy and I know you'll miss him. We'll all miss him."

Will turned away from her, burying his face in his arm as he began sobbing again.

Amber looked to Kate. "I'm glad Koi will be all right." Then to Max, she said, "Call me tomorrow?"

"Yeah," he said, "maybe tonight."

She nodded and began to walk briskly in the direction of her home, hoping Max couldn't see her own sorrow turning into sobs.

THE NEXT DAY, both Max and Amber left work early, but kept the children at Mrs. Larsen's while they met at the Burnett home. Max had asked Amber to read to him the vet's instructions for disinfecting his house, and Amber had volunteered to help, telling him she already had most of the cleaning items on her shelves. Max had just arrived when Amber pulled in behind him and began unloading gloves, cloths, two buckets, a new mop, and a gallon of chlorine bleach. Max hurried to help her carry it all. "Will we need all this?"

"We will if we're going to do all the cleaning the vet expects." Amber reached into the back seat and drew out a box full of sponges.

To Max, it looked like enough to scrub the whole neighborhood. "You have anything else in there?"

Amber looked at her stack of supplies, counting off items. "No, I think that's it."

"Should be." Max mumbled under his breath, but Amber's sharp look let him know she'd heard. He began lugging items to the front door. "I guess we should start in Will's room."

"Did Will ever take Scoopy outside?"

"No." Max paused while he thought carefully about the question, then shook his head. "No, I'm sure he didn't. The snow started again while we were at your house, and we had snow on the ground the whole time the pup was here. Will didn't want him to be cold."

"That's good. The doctor's directions say parvovirus freezes well. It would be late next summer before you dared have a dog in the yard if you had parvo out there. Scoopy was pretty much everywhere in the house though, right?"

"Right. Well, not really. Will had him in the living room, dining room, and kitchen. Then he spent most of his time in Will's room. I know he was in the kids' bathroom too. Will gave him a bath in the tub. I never had the dog in my room, though, and Kate didn't allow him into her room, either. She said she wanted Koi to have a place where the puppy wouldn't bother her by wanting to play all the time."

Amber smiled sadly. "The puppy and kitten really seemed to like each other."

"Yeah. I think they did."

"By the time I can get Will another pup, the cat will be too grown up to appreciate him."

"About that, Amber." Max straightened. "I don't know if we want to consider doing that any time soon—"

"It's okay, Max. We don't have to think about it now. It will be at least a month or more before you'll want to risk it anyway. Decisions can wait until then."

What Max didn't say was that Will wouldn't want Amber to be involved with another puppy. His resentment of her was completely unfounded, but it was as deep as the blue Pacific and nearly as wide. "If you'll hand me that bucket, I can get started in here."

Amber gave him a bucket and a mop, told him how to measure the bleach—one part bleach to thirty parts water—and turned him loose on the floors in the kitchen and dining room. "I'm going to start in Will's room," she said. "I'll wash all the bedding and rugs with bleach and mop the floor. Thank goodness these are all hardwood floors. Carpeting would be a nightmare." She started from the room but turned back. "Max?"

"Hm?"

"That carrier is part plastic, part fabric, and part plastic fabric. It would be very hard to disinfect. It's also stained. I'm planning to throw it away. I hate the waste, but I can't guarantee we can disinfect it adequately, and if we give it away, some other puppy could be infected—"

"No, I agree with your judgment. Put it out back by the trash cans and I'll break it down."

"Okay. Thanks."

For the next three hours, they worked, speaking only as needed to get the work done as they scrubbed, mopped, let dry, mopped again, washed, dried, and scrubbed some more. Whenever Max glanced at Amber, she was elbow-deep in a bucket or bent over a bed, tucking in covers over the freshly sprayed mattresses.

At a little before five, Amber declared they were done, "for now."

"Uh, what do you mean 'for now'?"

"I'm going to want to scrub all the floors at least once more, and items like the doghouse and leash and such—everything the puppy touched—will need another thorough disinfecting."

"Whew! You do take this seriously."

Amber stepped closer, laying her hand on his chest. "Max, I saw Will's heartbreak and I know he blames me. I can't let that happen again."

"That wasn't fair, and I know it's my fault. I blamed you in that initial outburst and Will has held onto that. It was an awful thing to say, and I've regretted it ever since. It wasn't fair."

"I know, but Will is only six years old. He isn't concerned about what's fair. His heart is broken, and I'm the obvious person to blame."

"I get it," he said, drawing her into a hug. He'd already decided not to involve her in getting the next dog, somewhere down the line. He needed to take care of Will, but he wanted to protect her too, even from the unreasoning wrath of his six-year-old. Aloud he added, "I love you."

She looked up, surprised, perhaps by his timing. "I love you, too, and I love your children. I want to see them happy."

"We'll make it happen," he promised.

Noting the time, Amber invited Max to bring his family to her

195

home for the spaghetti and meatballs they'd missed the night before. Max demurred. "Will's hurt and anger are still raw. It might be better to let that healing happen a little at a time," he answered. "Not force things."

"Okay. I understand. We'll let it go...for now."

As Max watched Amber drive away, he wondered how he could fix this. He loved Amber and wanted her in his life. But Will was his son, and his first responsibility was to him. He sighed and started for his car to pick up his children. He didn't like the doubts that swarmed about him as he drove.

DAYS PASSED and Will remained intransigent, refusing to have anything to do with Amber. Max tried talking him through his faulty thinking, but Will would not be reasoned out of his resentment. He remained convinced that Ms. Reyes was responsible for his puppy's death.

New Year's Day came and went, and school started again. Although Max and Amber made a few opportunities to see each other, the chances for Max to get away without the children were few. Amber realized how serious the situation was becoming when Mrs. Nguyen sent her son, Jacob, and Will to the principal's office for fighting, and Will refused to go. "Go ahead and call my dad!" he yelled, responding to the teacher's threat. "Make him take me home. Kick me out of school if you gotta, but I'm not gonna go see Ms. Reyes. I won't do it!"

When Mrs. Nguyen reported the situation, Amber asked, "Tell me about the fight."

She listened carefully, not surprised that the argument began when Will said he used to have a dog and Jacob doubted him. Flying into a temper, Will screamed, "I did too have a dog! Ms. Reyes got it killed!" and shoved Jacob to the ground. Jacob jumped up and shoved back.

"I need you to deal with this one on your own," Amber told the teacher. "Explain to them both that they are not allowed to shove and hurt each other. Then decide on appropriate discipline, and please call their parents as soon as you can. I'm sorry I have to leave it to you, but I think that's the best way to handle it."

Mrs. Nguyen said she understood, but as she left the office, Amber read the flicker of concern in Mrs. Nguyen's eyes. If she couldn't resolve this problem with Will, it would hurt more than her relationship with his father. It could make her ineffective as a principal, too. She resolved to discuss it with Max—as soon as possible.

After Mrs. Larsen picked up her after-school group, Amber called Max. When he didn't answer, she left a message. "Max, it's Amber. Call me. We need to talk."

Twenty minutes later, he called. "I'm sorry, babe. This is a bad time. Can we talk later?"

Amber sighed. "This can be put off, but not for too long. When do you think you can get back to me?"

"After five?"

"That will work but call me before you pick up the kids."

"This is about Will, isn't it?"

"I'm afraid so. The situation is becoming...untenable."

"How untenable?"

"His teacher sent him to the principal's office today, and he refused to come."

Max mumbled something incomprehensible. Amber suspected she was glad she hadn't heard it. "Okay, I'll call you." He clicked off.

Amber paced around her office, annoyed at her lack of ability to focus. As soon as it seemed appropriate to do so, she went home, leaving Liza to lock up. Once there, she began pacing again, working through what to say when Max finally called her.

He didn't call. Just after five, he came to her door.

"Max! I thought you were going to call me!"

"I thought so too. Then I started for home, got ready to pick up my phone, and realized my car was already finding its way here." Wrapping his arm around her shoulders, he led her to the couch. "Tell me what happened at school today."

Amber caught him up on the situation, starting with the argument between Will and Jacob that had ended in pushing and shoving and bringing him to the point when Will refused to visit the principal. "We may need to force this situation," she finished.

"I agree. Absolutely. But how?"

"Just put Will and me in the same room and insist that he talk with me. Things can't continue the way they are at school, even if I'm keeping my distance from him otherwise."

"I agree, but Will won't like being forced."

"Well, what we're dealing with now can't continue."

Max nodded. "You're right. Of course, you're right. When do you want to try it?"

"How about this evening? You do whatever you were planning for dinner, I'll eat here, and then I'll come to your place. When Will gets up to leave the room, you insist that he stay. Either that or let me follow him to his room."

"No, no following. His room is his sanctuary."

"Then he can't be allowed to retreat to it."

"I don't like this, Amber, but I'll see to it, even if I have to sit him on my lap."

"We could try to talk about this with Dr. Schafer. But I was hoping to see if between the two of us, we could make this happen."

Max stood. "I tried calling Dr. Schafer earlier today, but he's out of the office this week. We're on our own for a little while, anyway."

"Okay then. We'll give it our best shot."

"I'll call or text when dinner's over."

She walked with him to the door and gave him a quick kiss. "I'll see you then."

Chapter Twenty-Two

The scene proved to be even worse than Amber had feared. Max had to physically restrain Will, holding him in his lap to keep him in the room. Amber tried to draw close to him, to maybe hold his hands, but Will struggled when she approached. His anger frightened his sister into hiding. Max finally had to pull out the disciplinarian voice to say, "Will, sit still and listen to what Ms. Reyes has to say. You will talk to her and you will be a gentleman about it. I won't accept anything less. Do you understand me?"

"Yessir," Will answered, but he directed a withering glare at Amber.

Half an hour later, Amber wondered if they'd made any progress. Will still insisted that she was responsible for Scoopy's death, and he wanted nothing to do with her. What became clear as he talked was his jealousy of the time Max spent with her. "We don't do stuff just with you, Dad," he said finally. "Any time we do family stuff, she's always with us and she *is not* part of our family!"

"What if—" Max began, but Amber shook her head. Hard. Max got the hint. This was not the time for that announcement. "What if we do some family things together, just you and me and Kate?"

"Yeah," Will said. "Yeah. I like that, but I want to do *all* our family stuff like that, with just three of us."

"Will, that doesn't—" Max said.

Again, Amber cut him off. "Will, what happened at school today can't ever happen again. Not ever. What if I give you some time with just you and Kate and your dad and I stay away from your family activities, at least for a while? If I do that, can you agree to respect me as the principal of your school when we are there?"

"Yeah. I guess so."

Max said, "No guessing, son. This is important. Do you promise you will treat Ms. Reyes with respect when you are at school?"

Will hesitated, glared at Amber again, and said, "Yeah. I promise. But she's gotta stay away."

Amber said, "Thank you, Will. I believe we have an agreement."

Max said, "Yes, thank you, son. You can leave now if you want."

The words weren't out of his mouth before Will ran from the room, shutting himself into his sanctuary.

"That was awful," Max said. "I had no idea. Amber, I don't like you agreeing to stay away. It isn't right to let the kid blackmail us like that."

"I fully agree. We can't let a six-year-old start calling the shots for the people around him or making decisions about what's between us. Not for the long term, anyway. It isn't fair to us and it isn't fair to him to give him that much responsibility. But just for now, while he's still so hurt and so angry, this may be the best approach."

"I'll talk with Dr. Schafer about it on Wednesday next week."

"Good idea. Maybe I'll try for an appointment, too." She paused, looked around, and stood. "Since this constitutes family time, I think I'd better make myself scarce."

Max also stood, catching her hand, and gently drawing her to him. "Hug me first?"

She melted into his arms. "Oh Max, how are we going to work through this?"

"I don't know. But we have to. It isn't good for any of us to let this go on."

"I'd do anything if I could take it all back, make it just never happen." She took a deep breath. "That wouldn't fix everything, though. The jealousy would still be there."

"He seemed to be doing so much better for a time, not bothered by having you with us."

"Maybe it was always under the surface, but he didn't think about it much, until…well, until Scoopy died. He may always resent me for Scoopy."

"I don't know what to do about that, but I don't want to stop seeing you, either. You are way too important to me for that to happen."

"I feel the same way. Maybe we can get together in the afternoons once or twice a week? While the kids are still at Mrs. Larsen's."

"That's a possibility." He kissed her.

She melted into it. "I love you, Max. We have to find a way past this."

He nodded. "Yeah. Let me walk you to your car."

"Let me just go from here. You probably need to talk with Will, make some plans for family activities with just the three of you."

"Yeah. Okay." He frowned, an expression hard enough to rival Will's. "I hate this."

"Me, too." With a final quick kiss, she walked out, hurrying to her car. As she drove away, she could see Max closing his front door. She was struck with a sudden terror that she might never see him again. *Stop it, Amber,* she told herself. *This is temporary, all temporary.* Her self-talk did not stop the tears.

As she drove away, a part of her recognized this could be an end. If she didn't find a way to reconcile with Will, a wedding seemed highly unlikely.

AT THE BURNETT family's next appointment, Dr. Schafer took a long time with Will. He spent some time with Kate as well, and allowed a second full appointment for Max. When he had heard all three accounts, the therapist said, "Max, I don't know what to tell you. You are absolutely right that a six-year-old can't be permitted to make important life decisions for the adults around him, so the compromise you have going now should be temporary and must end as soon as possible. At the same time, I don't know when I've seen a child as angry as Will.

"If it were just the anger, I'd suggest pushing him into acceptance, not letting his fit of temper control the situation. But it's deeper than that. Will is distraught. I suspect the death of his puppy brought back all the grief he felt at his mother's death, grief he was too young to express then, really too young to accept." Dr. Schafer paused, tapping his pen on his chin. "I'll spend some time with Will, working on this, trying to help him bring his feelings to the surface. Until then, I don't know. The compromise may have to stand, at least for a while."

Max blew out a sigh. "I was hoping you'd have some answers. I don't see how we can go on like this, Dr. Schafer. Amber and I are in love. We want to marry, probably by summer. Right now, I have to sneak around just to see her. I feel like a teenager whose parents have forbidden him to see the girl he's crushing on, but I'm the parent in this scenario. It's all backwards!"

"It is. Completely. And I agree that we have to find a better long-term solution. Still, when I look at this from Will's point of view, he's a sad little boy who's grieving in ways he can't process. He needs to blame someone. If you were to force the situation with a wedding any time soon, he'd see you preferring her to him. Repairing that breach could be—"

"You don't have to go on. I get the picture." Max stood. "I hate this. I hate it! But I understand that I have to give Will a better sense of security. I'll need to invest some time in him, help him see how important he is to me."

"It's more than that." Dr. Schafer punctuated his statement by standing. "You need to let him know that he is of *primary* importance, that no one in your life is any more important than he is."

"But—"

"No buts, Max. In time, he can see that Kate and even Amber are just as important, but he needs to know, deep down where he lives, that no one counts *more* than he does. Right now, that's the critical point."

Max slowly began to nod. "I see that. I hate it, but I also get it. I'm the only parent Will has. He needs to know I'm willing to give him what he needs. He has to feel secure knowing I won't leave him."

"Exactly." Dr. Schafer opened his door. "We'll work on it."

"Yeah. Thanks, Doc."

"Thank me when we get somewhere." Dr. Schafer looked as despondent as Max felt.

Amber's visit went much the same way. By the time she left Dr. Schafer's office, she also realized how critical a turning point Will had reached. "Max's first responsibility is to those children," Dr. Schafer said as she stood to leave his office. "He can't let Will run his life or yours. At the same time, he has to make certain Will feels secure in his father's love before he alters the family dynamic. It's going to be a tricky balancing act."

"I understand," Amber said, but as she drove away, she wondered. Her head understood; her heart was not so certain.

The next week she and Max managed two late-afternoon visits, but Mrs. Larsen complained when he picked up his children later than usual. Twice. The following week, they saw each other only once. That and a few late-evening phone calls after the kids were asleep were all that tided them over. When their compromise was a month old and nothing with Will seemed to have changed, Max arranged for Luisa to babysit the children.

"Where are you going?" Will asked as Max prepared to leave.

"I have a d—a meeting."

"With *her*?"

Max felt his patience slipping. "Will, I'm a grown-up. I get to decide where I'm going and with whom. You don't decide that. I do."

"I don't like her."

Max bit his lip. "You've made that very clear."

"I don't want you to hang out with her."

"That's not your decision."

"I hate you!" Will ran to his room, slamming the door.

Max muttered a mild curse. He thought he should probably go after Will, hold him, and talk this out. He considered doing just that, but realized he was far too angry. If he went in there now, he'd likely lose his temper completely no matter how many promises he made to himself. And losing it wouldn't help either himself or his son. No. It was better to let Will sit in there and stew. They could talk tomorrow after they both had time away.

Luisa arrived, parking her bike on the front walk. Max tried for a pleasant smile when he let her in. "I shouldn't be too late," he said. "Kate's in her bedroom with her kitten. Will is having a temper tantrum in his room. I suggest you leave him there until he feels like coming out."

Her sympathetic smile reassured him. "No worries, Mr. Burnett. Go have a fun time. The kids and I will be fine."

"Thanks." He told her where he'd left snacks for the kids and headed out. He deliberately relaxed his fists as he went to meet the woman he loved.

~

THE CROWD at Broadway Louie's discouraged any serious conversation. "The spa must be doing well," Max said as he paid their dinner bill.

"Looks like it," she answered. "I'm sorry we couldn't talk, though. We can chat at my place."

"That may be the only time we get the chance."

Amber heard new and bitter anger. "I'm sorry, Max. I'm so sorry about all of this."

"It isn't your fault."

"I wish Will didn't think so."

At her home that evening, they talked, and they talked some more. Max detailed that evening's argument with Will and Amber sympathized. They analyzed the situation from every angle they could find. Neither could find a way to bring them past the current standoff.

"It's been long enough," she said, "for a new puppy, I mean. I can—"

"No." Max's response was quick. "If you get a puppy, he'll be sure it's going to die, too."

"Is it really that bad?"

"I'm afraid it is. It's exactly that bad. I don't know what to do anymore."

They talked through Dr. Schafer's advice to them both. Max said, "I don't know how to use advice like that. It's wrong to let a kid make decisions that govern the actions of the adults around him. That's too much responsibility to put on a boy his age."

"I agree."

"At the same time, I suspect he's right about Will's deep-seated feelings. He isn't just grieving the puppy; he's grieving his mother, too, and he doesn't know what to do with those feelings. Some part of him is also afraid of losing me and thinks that could happen if I stay with you." Max ran his hand through his hair. "I've been thinking about it. It's possible that Will doesn't want to get close to you because he feels it would be disloyal to her—to Isabel. Not that she ever worried about loyalty to him."

"Oh Max! I hadn't considered that, and I don't expect Will has either, not consciously anyway, but he could be feeling it." Sliding her arm through his, Amber said, "That may make it worse."

"What do you mean?"

"Whether he can think it through or not, Will is aware that his mother had other priorities that took her away from him. Now he sees the same thing happening with his father—"

Max got to his feet. "You're saying he thinks I'm deserting him like his mother did."

"I can't be certain that's what's happening, but it certainly seems possible."

"That could be part of the problem. Dr. Schafer suggested the same thing some time ago, but then things got better." He ran his hand through his hair again. Twice. "I'm sure that's part of it. I don't know what we can do about it, though."

"Maybe…" Amber paused, swallowing the emotion that threatened to dissolve her will. "Maybe we need to stop seeing each other, completely. At least, for a little while."

"Amber—"

"He has to feel secure, Max. That's more important than anything. We're adults. We can postpone our plans, but the situation with Will is now or never. He needs to know that no other priority is enough to take his father away from him. You're all he has."

"There's got to be another way."

"I want that more than I can say. I want us all to be a happy family, but I don't see that happening soon. If there were a better way, don't you think we'd have found it by now?"

He breathed out a sigh. "Maybe you're right," he said. "I hate it, but maybe you're right."

"I hate it, too." She leaned against him.

"Do you think we can rely on late-evening phone calls?"

"Maybe we need to stop those too."

"What do you mean?"

"You told me last week that your supervisor has started finding fault with your work, and you fell asleep on my couch the last time you came here. Maybe you need some time away from me to focus on your work and your family and to get some rest. These last weeks have been so hard, for all of us."

"Are you telling me you want to break this off?"

"No, I don't want to! But maybe we should take a break, at least for a while."

He furrowed his brow. "How long a while?"

"I don't know. Maybe if Will gets another puppy, maybe if he has time to adjust—"

"And what if that doesn't work? Are we going to let Will's problems break us up?"

"I don't want that either, but..."

Max shook his head. "You said *but*. Amber, I thought—" He picked up his coat. "I need to go."

"Max—"

"No, we're on or we're off. Looks like we're off." He opened the door. "I'm sorry it's come to this."

"Max, please listen."

"No need to explain anything. I get it. We're done." Max turned and strode to his car and drove away without looking back.

Amber sank to the floor as the tears overtook her. It was not supposed to happen this way. Yet a better solution still eluded her.

Chapter Twenty-Three

A week passed. Amber caught a glimpse of Max when he came to pick up the children on Wednesday afternoon, and she saw his car in town a couple of times, but silence reigned between them. Kate stopped her in the hall the following Tuesday to tell her Will had a new beagle puppy. "He said he didn't want it at first, but it's a really cute puppy. Will sleeps with him now, but Dad says they'll have to house-break him soon."

"What's his name?"

"Scooter. Will said it sounds kinda like Scoopy, but it's a good name all on its own."

"I agree. Tell Will I'm happy for him."

"Ms. Reyes? It's better if I don't talk to Will about you." Kate smiled sadly.

Amber wilted. She hadn't expected that. How bad did it have to be for a six-year-old girl to read the signals? She fought the impulse to lock herself in her office and have a good cry. Instead she wished Kate a good day and walked away, going back to her work. She was a professional woman on the job. Her personal problems had no place here. She repeated that mantra several times over the course of the afternoon. She had never believed Max would hold out this long.

Despite her attempts at upbeat self-talk, she mourned. She knew now that she wasn't ever in love with Chad. Her pride was hurt, but her heart wasn't involved. She'd felt sad and hurt over Chad, but she grieved for Max. Several fitful nights in a row had her taking over-the-counter sleep aids so she could stop recycling their last argument. When she recognized her mental turmoil was interfering with her work, she tried not to think about Max at all. That hopeless effort ended before it began.

She saw Will in the hall the next day. He'd left class on his way to meet his father for their therapy appointment. So far, Will had kept his promise to be respectful. She decided to give kindness a try. Smiling, she said, "Kate told me about Scooter. I'm happy for you."

Will bit his lip. "Thanks," he said, but he had to grind it out between his teeth. The look he gave her was venomous. Then he darted past her and hurried down the hall.

Amber caught her breath. It lodged somewhere in the center of her chest, provoking a physical pain. She retreated to her office so no one would see the look on her face or the tears that gathered in her eyes.

An idea had been rattling in her thoughts, and Amber decided to try it. Just because she and Max weren't dating anymore, that didn't keep her from being a good friend and neighbor, did it? Rationalizing the answer, she picked up her phone and sent Max a text:

Kate told me about Scooter. I'm glad.

Although she checked her phone frequently through the rest of the day, she was not surprised when she received no response. Max's silence broke the last tiny pieces of her fractured heart. There was no sign of it healing any time soon.

I must have looked at that text forty-two times today, Max thought as he picked up his phone. He read it again for the forty-third time: Kate told me about Scooter. I'm glad.

What was Amber up to? First she said they should take a break. Then she tried to walk that back and had let him know, quite clearly, that what she really meant was they were done. Hadn't she? She'd even pushed *him* into saying it! And now she was trying to pretend they were buddies and none of that ever happened?

He ran his hands through his hair and then stopped himself. If he didn't stop doing that, he'd be bald before he turned forty! He sighed, trying to remember, hoping to forget…

He'd examined their last argument so many times, he'd almost forgotten who said what. What he remembered, what he feared he would always remember, was the way she had looked at him when she said, "I don't want to, *but—*"

"But," he said aloud. "Amber, didn't you realize what you were saying with that one little word? It's over! By your own choice, it's over between us."

In therapy that Wednesday, Dr. Schafer asked if he wanted to talk. "No. Not now."

"It's obvious you're preoccupied with something. If I can help—"

"No. I don't think anybody can help me with this one." He'd lost a wife in Isabel. Now he'd lost a future wife in Amber. One day, he might have to figure out what was wrong with him that he couldn't keep a woman in his life, but not now. He was too raw now.

Dr. Schafer slanted a sideways look. "I haven't seen Ms. Reyes in here lately."

"No, and you won't be seeing her." That was Max's cue to leave. He started for the door.

"Is that what's—"

"Thanks for talking with Will. Next Wednesday then." Max could not get out of that office fast enough. Even herding both kids, he made it in record time. He had driven almost to the edge of town when Kate said, "Daddy? I miss Amber. I mean, Ms. Reyes."

Looking into the rear view mirror, seeing the dark look on Will's face, he said, "Let's not talk about her anymore, Katydid. You'll still see her at school."

"But—"

That word reverberated in his skull. He tried to keep his voice even. "No buts, Baby. Ms. Reyes isn't part of our lives anymore."

"Okay." Kate pouted. "But I miss her. Even if you don't!" Kate folded her arms across her chest and glared at his reflection.

Great. Now both kids were brooding. Kate scowled at him when he didn't see Amber; Will glowered when he did. And both kids needed to feel secure! There was no way Max could win. A few minutes later, he got Will talking about how they were training Scooter. As they approached Destiny, he said, "What do you think about sandwiches from Joe's for dinner?"

"Great!" Will said. "I want the ham and cheese."

"How about you, Kate?" He looked at her in the rear view mirror. "What do you want?"

Kate gave him a resentful glare. "I want Ms. Reyes."

Stuck for any kind of answer, Max chose silence.

ANOTHER WEEK PASSED. When Max arrived at school the next Wednesday, he found Amber waiting.

"Will and Kate are just inside the door," Amber said. "I have them waiting with a classroom aide."

"Why, Amber? What's the point of this...this ambush?"

"Ambush?" Amber felt the word like a physical blow.

"Whatever you call it. I don't see why you keep pushing this."

What she thought was, *I've texted you once in weeks. Now I'm speaking to you for the first time and I'm pushing? Get over yourself!* What she said was, "Mr. Burnett, we both live in this very small town and your children are in my school. We need to at least be civil with one another."

He started to speak, then stopped. He dropped his eyes, looked up again. "You're right, Ms. Reyes. We can be civil."

"Good, because there's a spring parent night coming next week. I hope you'll be here, and I very much hope we can speak *civilly* in front of the rest of the town, or at least those who come."

He nodded. "I believe we can do that."

"Good. That's all I had to say, so let me wish you a good visit with Dr. Schafer. Tell him I said hello."

"Yeah. I'll do that." He paused. "He'll be happy to hear. He's been asking—" Perhaps he saw the pleased look that brought to her face. His own expression soured. "I'll tell him."

"Thanks." Amber tried not to think about how good—how really, really good—Max looked. She forced a smile. "I'll send out Will and Kate."

"Good." He turned his eyes to his cell phone.

Taking the hint, Amber walked as quickly as she could manage back into the school. "Kate, Will, your dad is ready to go now."

"Thanks, Ms. Reyes." Kate touched her hand as she went by.

Will said nothing, but marched past with his eyes down. When he was almost through the door, he turned. "Yeah. Thanks." Then, as if that had exhausted his patience, he ran for his father's car.

Amber didn't know whether she felt better or worse as she trudged back to her office.

WITH PARENTS' night coming, Amber had reasons to stay late at school, avoiding long evenings alone at home. Wherever she looked in her living room, kitchen, or dining area, she saw Max. It was as if the ghost of Max still inhabited her life. She'd already scrubbed out the ghost of Scoopy, disinfecting her whole home since the puppy had been there first before he went to the Burnetts. Now she tried to banish memories of Max just as thoroughly. She especially avoided her favorite place on the couch. She could almost see the indentations from the last time Max sat there. She wondered if this was some early indication of insanity and pictured herself asking Dr. Schafer.

She found it easy to imagine the therapist's response: "No, Amber. You're grieving the death of a personal relationship. That may be a form of insanity, but it's usually temporary."

They'd had too many ghosts, too much grieving. Way too much! Max for his marriage and his wife. Will for his first puppy. Both children for the mother they never really had. Amber for Max and the kids. And earlier in her life, her family's grief for her Aunt Donna, for the horrible things Sunny and Skye had experienced, for Skye's difficulties... Way, way too much grief! Amber resolved to move on, to put those months of being with Max behind her. But how could she when they were both right here in Destiny? She couldn't avoid him. How could she pretend to feel nothing, to treat him and his beautiful children as neighbors and nothing more?

That blasted inner voice of hers answered that she'd have to find a way. Either that, or she'd better start looking for a job elsewhere.

She shook her head, hoping to banish that voice once and for all, knowing she would never succeed. Mumbling to herself, she mused, "Maybe I will have to start looking for another job. Destiny isn't exactly full of eligible men and the one I want—" She deliberately stopped that thought. Chad had left her because she wouldn't give up Destiny. Now she was considering giving up Destiny because Max had left her. Wasn't that some fine irony!

On Friday, two days after she spoke to Max, she decided to try one more time with a different approach. She sent a text:

Max, I'm miserable. I regret what I said. Can we talk? Please?

She waited eagerly, checking her phone every few minutes for a response. When midnight came without a reply, she finally realized she had his answer.

Looking at his phone just before midnight, Max tried to form a response. What kind of game was Amber playing, anyway? He read her text one last time. She was miserable, huh? He'd see her miserable and raise her two more. Max hadn't thought he'd ever hurt like this again. This was almost as bad as losing Isabel! He growled out a rough curse, something he'd never allow his kids to say, and deleted the text.

Amber looked at her calendar. Had it really been a month? Well, almost a month. Sometimes it felt much longer. She told herself she needed to prepare to see Max next Tuesday at parents' night. Even a glimpse of him when he picked up the children that Wednesday had given her such a rush of mixed emotions she'd sequestered herself in her office for the next half-hour. Next week, she'd be seeing him in front of other people, folks who knew they had dated and weren't anymore. She'd need to keep her cool. Well, she could try anyway.

The final bell rang, freeing the children. Looking out her window, Amber saw the cars crowding in. Looked like the teacher on duty could use some help. Pulling herself together, Amber walked out to the drive-through space just as Will and Kate arrived. "Hi, Will. Hi, Kate."

Kate beamed. "Hi, Ms. Reyes."

Will said nothing. Then he mumbled, "I thought Mrs. Larsen would be here."

"I'm sure she'll be here soon."

Will looked up sharply but said nothing and turned back to the drive-through. He saw Mrs. Larsen's van at the same moment Amber did. "Look, Kate! There she is."

Mrs. Larsen drove into the pull-through, but the lane closest to the curb had no empty space. "She'll need to come around again," Amber said. She put a hand on Kate's shoulder and the other on Will's. He looked up, frowning, but didn't pull away.

Kate spoke. "Dad says we get to go to another party at the Reeds' tomorrow. Will you be there, too, Ms. Reyes?"

Amber had been planning to attend the Reeds' party. The Daughters of Destiny were in town and a rumor had gone around that they planned to sing at their parents' party. Yes, Amber expected to be there; she just hadn't expected to see Max. Well, it would give her a chance to try out her acting skills before parents' night. "Yes, Kate. I plan to be there."

Kate said, "Will's mad 'cause Dad says he can't swim, that it's not a swim party."

"Your Dad's right. It's too cold for swimming now—"

"But the pool's heated!" Will flushed red as he realized he'd just spoken to Amber.

"Yes, the pool *is* heated," Amber said, keeping her voice even, "but the air around the pool is not. Besides, the Reeds get to decide if they want people swimming in their pool or not. In this case, they've been kind enough to invite us all, but they've made it clear this is not a swim party."

"I still wanta swim," Will grumbled.

Mrs. Larsen made her second orbit and stopped at the curb.

"See you tomorrow!" Kate chirped as she got into the van.

Will said nothing, but he didn't glower. Amber watched the van pull away. She'd been excited about the Reeds' party. Now she didn't know what to feel. She sighed. What else was new? She turned and went back to her work.

Chapter Twenty-Four

"Get ready, kids. We're going to a party!" Max wished his heart was in it, but Kate had told him Amber would be there. That alone made for a pretty good buzzkill. He'd have to pretend they were nothing more than good old pals, and he'd have to do it in front of curious neighbors.

"I'm gonna wear my swim trunks under my jeans," Will said. "That way, I can swim if they say it's okay." He looked defiant, as if daring his father to argue.

"There's no point, kiddo. The people who own the pool have already told us they've winterized it. They don't want anyone to swim now and you can't expect them to change their minds."

"How come Kate is taking so long? Is she getting her swimming suit on?"

"Girls like to dress up for parties, Will. May as well get used to that now. They all want to look especially pretty for a party."

"Well I don't care about lookin' pretty, but I wanta swim, so I'm gonna wear my swim trunks. And I'm gonna bring Scooter too." Will looked even more defiant.

"No Will, you are not. We're taking the three of us and the big salad we bought at Joe's. We'll also take our picnic dishes. That's *all* we are taking."

Will slunk into his room, mumbling under his breath.

Max congratulated himself on winning that round. Will was getting his way entirely too often. But Max didn't see Will pulling on his jeans over his swim trunks, and he certainly didn't see him sneak out to the car, putting Scooter into the trunk.

AMBER DRESSED WITH CARE. If the town was about to see her as the scorned and rejected woman, she at least wanted to look desirable, like maybe someday someone would want her. She squelched the self-pity before it could take over, glad she'd remembered the frozen fruit salad Will was so crazy about. She'd made lots of it. He might have a tough time resisting, even if he knew she made it. She found a smug satisfaction in that.

She put on the new pantsuit she'd purchased just for this occasion rationalizing the expense since she'd use it for school board meetings and other occasions. She'd get full value out of it, even when she had to take it to the valley to have it cleaned. She'd had more trouble justifying the new pumps—red ones, to match the color-block in the suit coat. As a final touch, she wound bits of hair into tiny braids and used them to hold back her glossy mane. She admired the finished product in the mirror, thinking, *Bite me, Max Burnett. I look darn good and you'll regret being so quick to push me out of your life.*

An hour later, she stood at one of the long tables in the Reeds' outdoor kitchen, her fruit salad tucked into a fridge, while she watched the entrance to the yard, wondering when Max would appear. Then he came around the corner. She looked back to the two town council members beside her, embroiled in a spirited discussion about how best to capitalize on the influx of health spa visitors. Although she'd lost track of the conversation, she nodded along, pretending to listen.

Max and the children approached, and others greeted them. When the council members both spoke, Amber smiled, hoping it looked genuine. "Good to see you, Max, Kate, Will."

"Hi Amber," Max said, quickly looking away. To the group, he said, "Is it almost time for food? Or should I put this salad in the fridge?"

"Fridge!" Several people called out.

"Hi, Ms. Reyes." Kate came over, taking her hand, laying her head against Amber's leg.

Will stood where he was, but said, "Hi" before following his father. Half-way to the refrigerators, he broke off. "Wait! I forgot something." He took off running the way he'd come.

Max strolled to the other side of the table to join a discussion on the big game the next day. Amber heard him join in, commenting that his

216

team wasn't playing, but stating a preference anyway, now and then glancing to where Will had gone. That's why he was looking when Will came in with—

"Will, I told you not to bring that puppy!" Scooter romped happily by Will's feet as the boy approached, defiant look firmly in place.

"Scooter gets tired of stayin' home when we do fun stuff, Dad. It's not fair!" Will glared at his father, defying him to say or do anything.

Max grabbed his son by the arm, angry enough to hurt him, but making a point not to. "Will, come with me," he said. Amber watched as they walked several yards away. She pretended to examine a poinsettia the Reeds had planted in a pot they'd brought outside, allowing her to get close enough to eavesdrop, but still she heard little. She did hear Max say, "You are getting away with entirely too much. We'll have to talk about this," but when they walked back to the group, the puppy still played at Will's feet. Uncertain what that meant, she blended back into the group. It hurt to realize that what went on between Max and his son wasn't her business anymore. Maybe It never had been. Not really.

Amber pretended to be involved in various conversations, speculating with others about whether and when the Daughters of Destiny would sing, all the while keeping an eye on Max and the children. Greg was there with Paris. She envied their relaxed camaraderie.

The sad thought came that she and Max could have been like that, but maybe that was fantasy too.

She spotted Kate and Will playing with the other children, almost all of whom seemed enthralled with the puppy. At least Scooter was having fun.

The two Reed families began setting out the food, and people gathered at the tables. Amber helped by carrying salads and side dishes and inviting the children to get in line. She put a large spoon into a macaroni salad, took a step back to look at it and ran into—

"Oh hello, Max." He looked as surprised and uncomfortable as she felt. She scrambled for a topic. The weather was always a safe topic, right? "What do you think of our spring-like day?"

"I remember this weather." He looked around as if he could see the temperature and wind speed. "There's always a bit of false spring before the last of the winter storms." He stepped away. "Too chilly to swim, though." He smiled, as stiff a smile as she'd ever seen. Then, "Will! I told you not to wear the swim trunks. We're not swimming today. Where are your jeans?"

"Over there on the chairs." Will, Scooter in his arms, pointed.

"Go put them back on, young man. Now."

Glowering, Will walked toward the jeans. When Max turned back to the other men, Will sidled toward the other children, still in his swim trunks. Amber watched, knowing matters with Will were getting seriously out of hand. Max might have noticed, but he didn't look in Will's direction. The situation had spun out of control, but it wasn't her place to intervene.

People began serving food, and Amber took her place in line. For a moment, she forgot about Will's defiance while she walked along the table, chatting with others and pretending to have an appetite. But a few minutes later, seated at a table with two members of her school board, she found herself defending a new policy her school was trying to improve classroom management. She dived into the discussion, realizing only sometime later that she hadn't thought of her situation with the Burnett family for all of fifteen minutes. She was even enjoying the food for the first time in a while.

She looked around again and spotted Max at a table with the Salvador family, Kate by his side. She scanned the area, trying to spot Will. Other children sat with their families. Where was Will Burnett? That's when Scooter started barking hysterically.

Her instincts kicked into high alert. Something was wrong.

Someone at the next table said, "What's wrong with that dog? Can somebody shut him up?" She heard someone else mumble, "It's just plain rude to bring a puppy to someone else's party." Another said, "I'm sure Max didn't intend that. His son sneaked the dog in." Amber didn't hear anything more as she hurried to the side of the pool where Scooter was jumping and barking.

All it took was a split second: Will was in the deep end, under water, terrified eyes looking up, his hands clawing at the slick pool wall as he tried to jump to the surface. Amber ran to the edge preparing to jump in but tripped over a garden hose and fell forward into the water.

She struggled to right herself and grabbed Will around the waist, hauling him to the surface. Moments later, they broke through and she swam to the pool's edge, keeping Will's head up as he gasped for breath. Then he began to wail.

The crowd, alerted by Amber's splash, came running. Max pushed through and reached down, taking his son from Amber's arms. With a grunt of pain, she grabbed the side of the pool as several hands pulled her up so she could sit and catch her breath.

A cacophony of voices surrounded her as everyone seemed to have a comment or question, but it was all background buzz to her own thoughts. Will was okay. He was all right. What if Scooter hadn't been here? What if she hadn't heard him? The what-ifs almost overwhelmed her.

Behind her, she heard Will's voice. "I almost drowned-ed! I was really, really scared, Dad. I thought I was gonna drowned!"

She heard Max murmur, "You scared me too, son. Are you sure you're okay?"

Will answered. "Ms. Reyes pulled me up. I couldn't breathe, but she—" The next came out garbled as Will sobbed again and the Reeds suggested Max and the kids go inside for a while.

At her side, Amber heard the concerned voices of Greg and Paris as they helped her up. Only then did she realize she'd ruined her new business suit, her hair dripped onto the tiles at poolside, and her new red pumps were a mess. So much for looking desirable! She half-laughed half-snorted as her feet touched down.

"Ow!" The moment she stood on her right leg, it warned her not to do that again.

Holding her under one shoulder, Greg said, "What is it?" The urgency in his voice reminded Amber that she'd just been in a life-threatening situation. The combination of adrenaline and pain had her trembling, knees weak.

"My right leg. It doesn't want to hold me."

Greg leaned down, looking at her damaged leg. "I'm not a doctor, but—"

"I am." Carl Fuentes stepped up. Amber immediately recognized him, both as a friend and classmate from years ago and as a physician at County Hospital. He squatted next to her. "How does this feel?" he said, gently squeezing a specific place on her right leg.

"Ow!"

"That's what I thought. We'll need x-rays, but I think you may have a fracture."

"How could I have a fracture? That doesn't make sense." Then the pain kicked in full force.

Paris lifted the garden hose. "It looks like she may have tripped on this."

"I tripped on something," Amber said. "I tried to dive, but something caught my ankle and I fell in. I must have hit my leg against the side as I fell."

Fuentes answered, "That's about the only thing that makes sense."

Pain and unexpended adrenaline caused Amber to shake, but she was still worried about Will. "Carl, did you check on Will, the little boy—?"

"I checked him out," Dr. Fuentes interrupted her question. "He's going to be okay. Other than having the scare of his life, he's going to be fine. I told his father to call me if something changes. In the meantime, they have him wrapped in warm blankets in front of the fire."

"Thank you," Amber said. Her teeth had begun to chatter.

"You're the one we need to thank, Amber," Paris said. "You saved Will's life. You're a hero."

"I'm not."

"You most certainly are," Paris shot back.

Amber choked down tears and Paris hugged her while Greg and Dr. Fuentes tried to keep the pair of them from toppling over.

The next minutes blurred by as an off-duty police officer volunteered his patrol car to drive her to the hospital. Dr. Fuentes asked to ride along. Others began helping to move things out of the way or wrap Amber in towels or help in whatever other ways they could think of. Before she knew it, Amber sat in the back of a patrol car with her leg up, roaring down the hill, red lights and siren announcing an all-out emergency, whether it really was or not.

GLANCING AT HIS SPEEDOMETER, Max dialed it back. No point in his having an accident on the way to the hospital. He lowered his speed to some ten miles over the limit.

He'd spent a frightened hour making certain Will was okay, bundling him up and getting him home, but even then, he took Luisa Salvador with him to babysit, knowing what he needed to do as soon as he had Will settled. He just didn't know quite how to do it. Until he entered the emergency room, it hadn't occurred to him that he had no legal right to be there.

"I'm here to see Amber Reyes," he announced when he finally burst into the ER.

The straight-faced man behind the front desk asked, "Are you family?"

Max swallowed. "Yes, um, yes, I'm her husband."

The man screwed up his face in a tight-lipped stare, looking Max up and down. "I'll see if you can go back."

"You do that. I'll wait right here."

The man disappeared into the curtained-off area.

ON THE GURNEY in her small exam room Amber overheard the conversation. She heard Max say, "Yes, I'm her husband." In that instant, she knew they'd be all right. Happy tears began to form.

"Miss? Are you in pain?" The nurse, who was checking her blood pressure, looked at her in concern.

"Yes," Amber answered, "but it's better now. Really, I'll be okay." The shakes had worn off. As long as she didn't move too much, she could manage the pain. She'd still be glad when the doctor okayed a shot of something.

A man stuck his head in through the curtains. "There's a guy out here who says he's her husband. He wants to come in, but I don't have any record of a husband."

"Please, let him come in." Amber attempted a smile.

The nurse nodded. The man nodded back. In less than a minute, Max stood at her side. To the nurse, he said, "Is it okay if I take her hand?"

"Just so long as you stand on that side of the bed. And you'll need to get out of the way quickly if we ask you to move."

"Gotcha," Max said. Gently, he took Amber's hand in his. "How are you doing?"

"I'm going to be fine now that my *husband* is here." She couldn't help smiling. "Ouch! I'll have to learn not to move that leg."

"Then don't move it," he said. "Don't do anything that hurts." He lifted her hand, tenderly kissing her fingers.

She spent a few seconds looking into his face, loving him with her eyes. "Thank you for coming, Max. Thanks so much. I didn't think you would."

"Of course, I would." He looked meaningfully at the nurse. "I'm your husband."

She smiled again. "How's Will?"

"He's okay, cold and penitent, but he knows how much danger he was in. He's really doing great, thanks to you—" Max cleared his throat and blinked several times. "You saved my son's life," he rasped. "You're the one we're all worried about."

"Don't be worried. I'll be up in no time. I have to host parents' night next week."

"No, you won't," the nurse said. "I'm not the doctor here, but I can almost guarantee you'll be off your feet for a while."

"I'm sure that's not necessary. It's just a bump. I'll be ready to go in an hour or two."

"I appreciate your diagnosis, Dr. Reyes." The nurse looked amused. "But I'd like to hear what the doctor on duty has to say."

"That would be me." Dr. Fuentes joined them, dressed in the standard-issue lab coat with a stethoscope around his neck and a clipboard in hand. "Ms. Reyes, you will likely be with us overnight. After that, you'll need to stay off your feet for a week at least."

Chapter Twenty-Five

D r. Carl Fuentes held out his hand and Max took it. "So you're Amber's husband now?"

Max flushed. "Um, it's new. We only recently got married."

The doctor gave him a look. "You can drop the fiction. It's just us now, but I'm curious. Last I heard, you weren't even dating." He looked first at Max, then at Amber.

"That's true, Carl." Amber managed a smile. "But please, can Max stay anyway?"

The doctor dropped his voice. "You don't tell, and I won't either." He winked.

Max breathed out a relieved sigh. "Thank you. Very much. Now, what can you tell us? How's she doing?"

Dr. Fuentes flipped through his notes, methodically detailing what he knew so far. "We've checked her out. There's no head trauma, so I've okayed pain medication—"

Amber interrupted. "Thank you! I'm looking forward to that."

"A nurse should be in with that any minute." He looked back at his notes. "Amber, you've sustained some other bruising and minor abrasions, but our only real concern is that leg—"

"It's broken?" Amber and Max asked it simultaneously.

"We don't have x-rays yet. We'll have a technician in here with a machine any time now. Palpation suggests a fracture in the fibula, possibly in the tibia as well. Even if there is no break, the soft tissues have sustained a pretty good whack—"

A young woman poked her head in. "Ready, Doctor."

Fuentes nodded. "Amber, this is Lucy, our x-ray tech." He spoke to Max. "We'll need to step out of this space while she shoots a picture." He winked at Amber. "Don't forget to smile."

"You're funny." Amber smirked. But she remembered to add, "Thanks, Carl."

"All part of the job," he said, and stepped out.

"I'll be right back." Max leaned down for a quick, barely-there kiss.

Two hours later, she lay in a real bed in a room on the second floor. The injection had relieved her pain, but she'd been admitted while the orthopedic surgeon decided if the fibula fracture needed anything more than a boot.

Max, unable to stay during the x-rays and subsequent exam, used the time to pick up the kids, feed them Joe's Sandwiches, and bring them to the hospital. Giving Amber a quick kiss as he entered, Max presented a bouquet of daffodils. "The kids wanted to see you."

Amber couldn't resist. "And you, Max? Did you want to see me, too?"

"I can't stay away from you. I know you wanted it to be over between us but—"

"Wait. *I* broke us up? That was your idea. You're the one who said, 'We're done.'"

"You thought *I* wanted to break up? No, you're the one who said…" He stopped abruptly, cutting off the thought. "I don't know. Maybe I'm not remembering it correctly. If I screwed up again, I'm sorry, but Amber, I can't let you go. If you want me, I'm yours."

"I never thought I'd hear you say that. Max Burnett, you know I want you." She reached out, touching each of the children. "All three of you."

Will didn't cringe at her touch, but he didn't respond, either. Then he breathed a long sigh and looked at his father. "Dad? Can I talk to Ms. Reyes? Just me and her?"

Max's face showed his surprise, but his voice remained even when he answered, "That's fine, Will. We'll wait in the hall. You let us know when you're ready." He took his daughter's hand. "Come on, Katydid. Let's give Will some space."

"Okay." Kate began humming as they left the room.

Will stepped closer. "Ms. Reyes, I'm s-sorry," he said, and then he was sobbing, his face down against her side.

"It's okay, sweetie." She stroked his hair. "You don't have to say anything…"

"Yes, I do!" Then he calmed his voice. "I been really awful to you, for a long time. Today, you saved my life!" He sniffed. "I was so scared and I coulda drownded and then you jumped in and you got all wet all over and ruined your good clothes, and hurt your leg, but you got me out so I could breathe again, and all the time, I been so awful—" He burst into sobs again, putting his head down at her side.

"Will? Will, honey, look at me."

Will sobbed harder, burying his face in the bed covers.

She felt so sorry for this sweet little boy. His effort to hate her had hurt him badly. "Will, please look at me."

He slowly lifted his head.

"Will, I love you."

"No. You can't. I been so mean…"

"Yes, you were mean, but you didn't mean all the things you said. You wanted to have your dad with you, and I understand that." Her vision blurred with tears. "I love you and Kate so much that I would never want to come between you and your father. Do you understand that?"

Will nodded. "Yeah, but you love Dad, too. Don't you?"

Amber ruffled his coppery hair. "You are a very smart little boy."

"Dad loves you too. I heard him say it."

"I know he does, and you're right. I love your father very much."

"But you stayed away from us 'cause I was mad."

"Yes, I did. I love you too, Will. I didn't want to hurt you."

Will ducked his head, bit his lip. "What happened to…that wasn't your fault. Kate said so. She got real mad at me. She said I gotta stop blaming you."

Amber made a mental note to thank Kate. "No, it wasn't my fault, but I'm sorry anyway, deeply sorry. I wouldn't have hurt you like that for anything."

"Kate wants you to be our new mom." His face crumpled. "She's still real mad at me."

"What do you think about that? Would you like me to be your new mom?"

"I got so mad at you when Dad was spending all that time—"

"I know you did. I'm sorry you were hurting."

"…but Kate said if you're our mom, Dad won't have to leave to see you, and you'll be there to love us, too."

"I'd like that very much. Would you?"

"I didn't think so, not at first. But Kate made me think about it." He sounded sheepish when he said, "You can be our new mom if you want."

Amber stroked Will's curly hair. "Do you know that Scooter helped to save you?"

"Yeah!" Will perked up. "Dad told me how Scooter ran and barked and stuff."

"He's the one who let me know you were in trouble. I'd like to come over and thank him, if you don't mind."

He lowered his eyes. "Yeah. I'm sorry I been so mean. I was mad about Scoopy, and I was mad at…lots of people, I guess. Maybe everybody. But I'm not mad no more."

Amber hesitated, and then said what she'd been thinking. "Will, I want to ask your father to marry me. Will you give me your permission?"

Will's eyes widened. "Then you'll be my mom? And you'll live with us?"

"Yes. If it's okay with you and Kate, I'll ask your dad about it when he comes in."

Will didn't answer, but he nodded vigorously and hugged her with both arms. When he did speak, he said, "I know it's okay with Kate. She's been telling Dad to 'pologize and get back together with you. I guess she was real mad at him, too"

Amber couldn't help grinning. "I'm pleased to hear that. Not that Kate was mad, but that she approves. Now, will you ask your father to come back in, please?"

Will grinned, nodding like a bobblehead. "I'll get 'im right now!" He ran from the room. Amber could hear him in the hallway: "Dad, Ms. Reyes wants you to come in now. She's gonna ask you to marry her!"

Amber laughed. Then she smiled through happy tears as Max

approached the bed, smiling as hard as Will. "My son says you want to propose."

"Your son is right. Max, regardless of how it happened, whichever one of us caused the break-up, it was a terrible idea. I don't ever want to be that far from you again. Not from you or your beautiful children, either. Max Burnett, will you marry me?"

"Yes. Absolutely yes! But when you're feeling better, let's do this right. You know, me down on one knee, complete with a ring."

"You can if you want to, but it isn't necessary. Just promise me if we have another misunderstanding, you'll never be much farther away from me than you are right now." She grasped his hand tightly.

"That's a wonderful idea." He leaned in for a kiss, keeping it light to avoid bumping her leg and causing pain. "Amber?"

"Yes, Max?"

"I'd suggest we drive to Reno tonight if I thought it was a good idea. As it is, we need you to feel better first, and I'm guessing you'll want some time to plan."

"We did Sunny's wedding in three weeks," she said.

"Yes, but you don't want to limp down the aisle in a boot." He paused, looking thoughtful. "I don't want to wait until summer, either. What do you think of spring break?"

"That's about eight weeks if I count correctly. I should be running circles by then. Yes! I like spring break."

"I do too. Even if you aren't running yet." He leaned in for another kiss.

"Daddy?" Kate stuck her head in, looking from one adult to the other.

"Come on in, Katydid. Will, you too. Ms. Reyes and I have decided we want to be married. What do you think of that?"

"Yay!" Kate jumped up and down.

Will looked from one to the other and began nodding. "Yeah, that's good. Dad?"

"Yes, son?"

"Is it okay if I call Ms. Reyes Amber now?"

"At school, you'll still need to call her Ms. Reyes, okay? The way Jacob calls his mom Mrs. Nguyen when they're in class."

"Yeah. Okay. But when we're at home?"

Amber took Will's hand. "When we're at home, you can call me Amber." She paused. "Or if you want... Will, would you like to call me Mom?"

"Yeah. I think I like that. Thanks...Mom."

Amber drew both children close.

"I like it too. I love you, son." She looked at Kate. "I love you too, Katydid. So much."

Kate snuggled against her. "But you love my daddy more, huh?"

"I love you all. More than I can say."

Max joined them for a group hug.

Epilogue

Sunny stuck her head into the classroom where Olivia fussed over Amber's hair. "Everything's ready in the chapel," she reported. "How are we doing here?"

Amber responded with a grin. "It seems only a short time since I was saying that to you."

"It hasn't been long," Olivia said. "Just a few months."

"Imagine!" Sunny said. "Max was here, among our guests, when Evan and I were married, and none of us knew him then."

"Still, we've known each other longer than you and Evan did when you married. Even if you don't count the years he lived next door."

"You're a great couple."

"There." Olivia put one final tweak on the floral ring in Amber's hair. "I believe we're ready."

Sunny asked, "Should we tell the organist to start?"

Olivia looked at Amber, who answered, "Yes. Please. We've waited long enough. Two months ago, I told Carl Fuentes that my visitor at the ER was my husband. It's time Max made an honest woman of me." She winked at her mother.

"Come on then," Olivia said. "Let's go meet your bridegroom."

The women took their places, ready for the ceremony to begin.

A Message to YOU from the town of Destiny

I hope you enjoyed *Amber in Autumn*, *the revised and refreshed third book in the Seasons of Destiny Series*. Please consider rating and/or a reviewing it. If you'd like to stay up to date on my books and find out about upcoming releases, contests, giveaways, and more, please sign up for my newsletter at susanaylworthauthor.com. Thanks for reading. May you find your own Happily Ever After.

Warmly,
  Susan

Keep Reading for A Sneak Peek of *Winter Skye*, the fourth and final book in the Seasons of Destiny Series, where you'll get to know Skye Ray, a graduate student and talented artist, who meets and falls in love with fellow artist, Peter Koury. Together they will face their own unique challenges on the road to love. You'll also get to attend Amber and Max's wedding where you'll see Paris and Greg, and Sunny and Evan again. Everyone will be there in *Winter Skye*.

Sneak Peek

Winter Skye

Seasons of Destiny Series Book 4

First there were voices—sounds, really, with no individual words. Then she began hearing people call to her, but everything around her remained dark. Gradually even the darkness cleared, and she saw faces in a circle around her head: the student who walked over with her, the man who shooed her out, a couple of others she didn't recognize, and Pete. "Ohhhh," she moaned, putting a hand to her forehead. "What happened?"

Everyone tried to explain at once. Then she heard Pete say, "You fainted."

"That's ridiculous," she heard herself say, although she didn't remember thinking it. "I never faint."

"Well, you did this time," the older man said. "If you just lie still, we'll get an ambulance—"

"No!" The strength of Skye's voice surprised her. "I don't need an ambulance. I promise I'll be just fine." To prove it, she forced herself into a sitting position. The action caused her to feel woozy again, but she persisted. Slowly, her fuzziness cleared. "It was just a combination of the heat and hunger. I…I skipped lunch." *And breakfast. Did I eat last night? I can't remember.* "Just give me a minute to clear my head and I'll be on my way."

The older man said, "Well, I don't—"

He was interrupted by the student who walked with her. "I got that glass of water you asked for."

The man took the glass and offered it to Skye. "Here. Drink up. We'll see how you're feeling in a few."

Skye drank, first just a few swallows. Then she realized how desperately thirsty she felt. *When was the last time I had a drink of water?* The only water she could recall drinking since leaving home that morning had been a sip here and there from a water fountain. *I guess I need to start paying more attention.*

She finished the water and thanked everyone around her. Then she stood, reassuring the group that she'd be fine on her own.

"Are you certain?" the older man asked.

"Yes, I'm sure."

She heard Pete say, "I'll stay with her until she's stable."

"I'll take care of your station," the student offered.

"Thanks, Emily," Pete said. He gave the student a few quick instructions.

"Will do," Emily answered, beaming at Pete as if the king had granted her a boon by allowing her to clean up after him. "You take care," she said to Skye as she left.

The older man asked Pete, "You sure you can handle this?"

Pete, or Jamison, or whomever, answered, "Don't worry, Al. I've got this."

"Okay then." Al, still sounding doubtful, left them standing in the hall.

Pete said, "Come on, stalker. I'll drive you home."

Skye let Pete lead her behind the Hot Shop to a small, sleek pick-up truck. He opened a door. "Get in."

Meekly, Skye obeyed.

He closed his door, turned on the A/C, and said, "Okay, explain yourself. What was that all about?"

With a few conscious minutes behind her to consider the possibilities, Skye offered the best explanation she had. "I guess I *was* stalking you, but not in any negative kind of way."

He frowned, his expression skeptical.

"What I mean is, I was...curious. Since I saw you at that AA meeting, I've wondered why you didn't come back. Then, when I saw you again at the Soho show, I also saw your work. One artist to another, I'm impressed. When the student in the metals forge mentioned she thought you might be working in the Hot Shop, I followed along. I wanted to see what you do." She offered a pleading look. *Please accept that. I don't want to dig any deeper.*

"You're interested in my *work*." He practically sneered as he drew out that last word.

"Well, yeah. I saw you at the Soho Gallery at the show we both did—"

"Wait. You had work there, too?"

Now she was the one who frowned. "Of course. What did you think I was doing there?"

"I assumed you were one of the student helpers."

Now she was the one to sneer. "Oh, that's truly flattering."

He had the grace to look embarrassed. "I know you weren't the trash artist," he said. "He had the space right next to mine."

Skye, who'd tried to control her amusement at "trash artist," allowed a smile. "No, I'm not the trash artist. Incidentally, I feel the same way about his work."

"Not much to brag about, is there? I wonder why the professors included him?"

"Dr. Weems suggested they wanted to include several different media. Maybe they thought this guy's work might interest someone. Do you know if he sold a single piece?"

"I think maybe one or two. Not much, though. But you weren't me and you weren't the trash dude. That leaves four possibilities. Which are you?"

"I had the space in the room on the south, back corner."

He closed his eyes, apparently visualizing the space. "You had the garden paintings? And the sculptures?"

"Yes. That's my work."

His expression changed. "You're Skye."

She sat straighter, surprised he knew her name. "Guilty as charged."

"Vickie is one of your top advocates."

Does he mean Professor Weems? "You call her Vickie?"

He smiled. "When I first came back to grad school, it wasn't easy. I kept calling her Dr. Weems, just as I always had. After the first couple of weeks, she said, 'You're a teacher and colleague now, Pete. Call me Vickie.'"

"Then you're Pete here, too. Not Jamison Peters, but Pete."

He blushed, his cheeks reddening slightly. "My name is Peter James Koury. Professionally, I'm Jamison Peters."

"But you're Pete at AA meetings."

He acknowledged that with a twist of his lip. "Yep. There, too." He started the ignition. "Well, now that we've cleared that up, is it true you haven't eaten all day?"

"Honestly, I've been working like crazy to meet a big deadline and I don't remember the last time I ate—at least, not more than a breakfast bar or an apple."

"I can fix that." He maneuvered the truck out of the parking lot and into traffic.

"I haven't told you where I live yet. Where are we going?"

"Don't worry. I'll see you get safely home." He grinned. "In the meantime, I'm taking you to dinner."

Dinner? Mr. Gorgeous is taking me out for a meal? I don't even remember what I'm wearing! She examined her ensemble: strategically distressed denim jeans and a linen blouse in a rich salmon pink that highlighted her dark complexion. *Did I put on earrings?* She touched her lobes and fingered the tiny pearl-like drops, one of her go-to pairs. She sighed, brushing her hair behind her ear. *I could look worse. Good thing I stopped at the forge coming from the gallery and not the studio.* She imagined having these same conversations while splattered in various colors of paint. The image made her cringe. *Lucked out with that one!*

Pete stopped at a local place that catered to students. It offered fresh, house-made soups, salads, and sandwiches using what it claimed were all-natural ingredients, that were both healthful and organic. They also offered "artisan" coffees and a tea bar featuring kombucha.

"Trendy," Skye said when Pete opened her door.

"Very trendy," he answered. Then, with a shrug, "I just like the food."

"Good enough reason to come here." She swayed slightly.

He caught her arm to steady her. His brow furrowed in concern. "You okay?"

She nodded. "I will be. I just need to eat."

"Then let's get you something." He took a step, preparing to lead the way.

She tried to follow him, but swayed again.

"That's it," he said. "Don't get the wrong impression here, Skye, but I don't want to pick you up off the floor again." He put his arm around her waist. "Lean into my shoulder."

She leaned in and instantly felt a full-body buzz, reveling in the warmth of his touch. Maybe it was the combination of the lack of food, the heat, and the nearness of a very desirable man. Whatever it was, Skye felt herself losing consciousness again. "You smell like glass," she heard herself say, her voice far away as she sagged against his side.

I hope you enjoyed this little sneak peek of
Winter Skye

Please visit susanaylworthauthor.com for more.

Books by
Susan Aylworth

The Rainbow Rock Romance Series [available in eBook]:
Welcome to Rainbow Rock, Arizona, a quaint small town nestled in the striped hills of the Painted Desert region, where every rainstorm brings a rainbow and every heart is filled with hope and love. Meet the McAllister family—brothers Jim, Kurt, Chris, sister Joan, and their beloved widowed mom, Kate. Follow each of their stories as they find love under the high desert stars. Get to know the McAllisters' friends and neighbors in Rainbow Rock and enjoy more heartwarming romances in this wonderful and memorable close-knit community. Each story may be read separately but there is great enjoyment in reading them in order.

Over the Rainbow: **Prequel**
Joan McAllister never imagined a world without her larger-than-life father. After his sudden death, she is overwhelmed with sorrow, harrowed up by guilt, and coping with her father's dying wish: helping her mother run the family farm and care for her three younger brothers. To complicate matters, Joan is attracted to a man she met at her father's funeral. How can she be thinking of romance when her life is in turmoil?
Bob Riley sees in Joan the woman he has always wanted. Even though they met under somber circumstances, there's nothing somber about his feelings. Bob knows he and Joan have much in common, and he's pretty sure she's attracted to him, so why does she keep pulling away? Come to Rainbow Rock, Arizona, and learn what awaits Bob, Joan, and the rest of the McAllister clan in *Over the Rainbow.*

Ride the Rainbow Home: **Book 1**
In time for her ten-year class reunion, Meg Taylor is lured back to the

tiny town in northeastern Arizona where she suffered through high school. Overweight, step-daughter to the principal, she was anything but popular. Now she's slim, attractive, and accomplished—and still wary of all she knew then.

Except for Jim. "Little Jimmy" McAllister was one of her two best friends. Ten years have changed him, too. (No one calls him "little" anymore!) He always cared about Meg and seeing her again only enhances those feelings. He wants her to stay, permanently, but Meg, the daughter of a serial-marrying mom, can't imagine herself in "happily ever after." What will it take to change her mind and bind her heart to his?

At the Rainbow's End: Book 2

Alexa Babbidge is about to hit it big as a Hollywood scriptwriter—if only her car will cooperate. Stranded near Rainbow Rock, Arizona, she is rescued by Mr. Could-Be-Right. Too bad she isn't looking for romance! But she is looking for a job, at least until she can reschedule her meeting in movieland.

Kurt McAllister is looking for a scriptwriter, not a wife. But Alexa fits easily into his video production company, and almost as easily into his life. As they work together, taping a documentary about Navajo weaving, he longs to persuade her to stay.

Gold beckons at the end of the rainbow, and Alexa, who has seen too much of poverty, can't resist its pull. Kurt longs to hold her, but at what price? As their time together draws to a close, each must decide whether it is wealth and fame or love and family that await them *At the Rainbow's End.*

Don't Promise Me Rainbows: Book 3

When faced with a birthing emergency in his prized breeding stock, pig farmer Chris McAllister calls the local veterinarian for help. He expects the wiry, middle-aged man his family has long trusted, not a petite but tough young woman whose edgy personality could qualify her as an Amazon queen from Greek mythology. Even so, he can't avoid a magnetic attraction to the pretty, red-haired vet.

Beneath her composure and stiff professional demeanor, Sarah McGill hides deeply painful secrets. She's only returned to Rainbow Rock for a short time, filling in for her dad while he recovers from a nasty knee injury. The last thing she needs is some cute cowboy stirring up trouble, digging for answers, making her feel emotions she hoped never to feel again.

When a project for the Navajo Nation throws them together, Chris and Sarah must decide whether they can risk their hearts to promises that come without guarantees.

A Little Night Rainbow: Book 4

Max Carmody was married once. It wasn't pretty. Now he finds himself stuck for the summer with a thirteen-year-old daughter he barely knows and a sister who will take her in, but not unless he comes with her. Marcie tells her dad she wants him to marry again, but the last thing this Mozart-loving-car-parts manufacturer needs is romance. In fact, his ever marrying again is about as likely as finding a rainbow in the night sky.

Cretia Sherwood was married too, and it definitely wasn't pretty. She is finally healing and regaining some independence after years of struggling to raise her kids on her own. Now that her daughter Lydia is thirteen and her son Danny is eleven, Cretia can take a breath and focus on making sure she can give her kids everything she didn't have growing up. The last thing this Mozart-loving mom needs is to lose her new-found independence to a man. When her daughter asks her if she would ever consider remarrying, Cretia replies—when she sees a night rainbow in the sky.

When love brings them a rainbow, both Max and Cretia have to choose between the security and safe routines of their present lives or a leap of faith, betting on the future.

Note: This book introduces thirteen-year-old Lydia Sherwood whom you'll meet again in *Always a Rainbow* (Book 7); thirteen-year-old Marcie Carmody whom you will meet again in *The Promise of Rainbows (Book 8),* and eleven-year-old Danny Sherwood whom you will meet again in *Once in a Rainbow (Book 9).*

A Rainbow in Paradise: Book 5

Eden Grant vowed never to go back home. A painful childhood growing up in Rainbow Rock made Eden swear off marriage and a family of her own. With a successful childcare business in Phoenix, Eden can lavish all the love she has on the children of others. But when her best friend, Sarah McGill, asks her to be her maid of honor, Eden makes the trip home to Rainbow Rock for Sarah's wedding. What Eden doesn't count on is her immediate attraction to the best man. Logan Redhorse might be the best man at his friend Chris's fairy-tale wedding but holding Eden in his arms feels like his very own paradise. How can Logan reconcile his immediate attraction to Eden with the promise he made? An attorney for the Navajo Nation, Logan vowed to his ancestors and descendants that he will marry a desert child, a daughter of *Dinehtah*.

How can Eden and Logan reconcile their differences to embrace a future that could bring them both a love beyond paradise?

The Trouble with Rainbows: **Book 6**

Joe Vanetti was deeply in love with his late wife, Roberta. Even thinking of another woman feels disloyal. Although his romantic life ended with Roberta's death, he still has their children to raise. He's returned to Rainbow Rock so they can grow up close to his family. The last thing he's thinking about is dating, but when Joe runs into Angelica DeForest, the former "Ice Queen" from high school, he can't help but wonder at the change in her.

Despite a successful career as a violist, Angelica DeForest lives a lonely life. Painfully awkward and socially inept, she's spent her adult years caring for aging, bitter relatives. She promises herself she will try to be bolder, to reach out to others and maybe even (gasp!) socialize. She certainly doesn't intend to begin with Joe Vanetti, the high school Golden Boy who was always so perfect, so far above her, no matter that he's even more handsome now than back in high school.

A promising future beckons, if they have the courage to banish the ghosts of their past.

Always a Rainbow: **Book 7** (New to the series)

When a handsome Air Force pilot comes to her rescue in a tricky situation, Lydia Sherwood never expects to see him again—and certainly not on the operating table where she's about to assist in emergency surgery. He's come to the rescue again, hailed as a hero, but has suffered life-threatening injuries as a result. Lydia's admiration for pilot is almost as great as her attraction.

Drake Westcott is riding high—literally. Near the top of his class at the Air Force Academy and a standout in pilot training, he's flown some of the nation's fastest, highest-soaring airplanes. Only the U-2 remains, and Drake has sworn to fly "the dragon lady." Now that dream is gone, as is the life he had planned.

Lydia and Drake are on different trajectories with a world of obstacles ahead. Their mutual attraction is strong, but how can it overcome all that separates them?

The Promise of Rainbows: **Book 8** (Formerly: *Return to Rainbow Rock*)
Eleven years have passed since Marcie Carmody left Rainbow Rock for the big city, starry-eyed and eager to build her future. She found love with a struggling law student—or thought she had. When her boyfriend's rejection also leads to the end of her job, she limps home, dejected and ashamed, fearing harsh judgment from her family and community. Finding unexpected acceptance, Marcie also lands a new job in the law offices of Logan Redhorse, working with a new associate. On hyper-alert to make sure she exceeds expectations, she calls the police the moment she sees a man in a hoodie rifling through Logan's files.

Ryan Fields needs a new start. His wife has left him for a man she met in an online role-playing game and has taken his sons with her. Ryan is experienced in native law, having practiced with a Sacramento firm, and the position with Redhorse sounds like a perfect fit. He does not expect to be picked up as a burglar on his first visit to the office, thanks to a nosy redhead. No way does he want *her* as a legal assistant!

But Marcie's apologies and her office skills are real, and Ryan decides to give her a try, firmly ignoring the glimmer of attraction that hovers any time she draws near. Both Marcie and Ryan have wounds to heal and obstacles to overcome. Surely, they aren't ready to find new love, but Fate, and Love, may have other plans.

Once in a Rainbow: **Book 9** (Formerly: *Danny's Girl*)
Running from a man who has threatened her life, Manon DuPre fears even slowing down, let alone stopping, but the Arizona Highway Patrol disapproves of her speed. How can she persuade the handsome trooper that she needs his help, not an arrest?
Raised by a drunken abuser and a terrified mother, young Danny Sherwood grew up to be a protector. Maybe that's why he's such a dedicated patrol officer. When he stops a dangerous speeder on the Interstate, he doesn't expect a beautiful, terrified woman, who claims to be fleeing a killer.
As the community of Rainbow Rock rallies to help, how can Manon and Danny embrace a joyful future when they still must face their difficult pasts, and a potentially lethal threat?

Chasing Rainbows: **Book 10** (Formerly: *Roman's Holiday*)
Roman Kincaid has it all: a meteoric rise to fame and fortune as a country-pop performer and now, as an A-list Hollywood celebrity. He also has a demanding agent driving him to exhaustion. Depleted and dispirited, Roman takes an impromptu holiday, disappearing into Arizona's high desert. A chance encounter leads him to Lottie Beale's café and pie shop.
Lottie Beale is humming along to one of Roman's new releases when the man himself walks through her door. Keeping her cool, she serves him as she would any customer, but his presence fills her with happy thrills—and terribly unhappy memories. She has her own reasons to hide.
Roman's offer to travel with Lottie as his guide sounds like an awkward come-on when Lottie first hears it, but he swears he'll be the perfect gentleman and she easily reads his need for friendly, undemanding companionship—a need she understands too well. Their road trip takes them to well-known places like Mesa Verde and the Four Corners monument, and to less famous sites only the locals know.
It also takes them on a journey of self-discovery as each comes to terms with where they've been and where they want to go. Can a famous star and a small-town pie maker find common ground?

Anything is possible in Rainbow Rock, romance capital of the great Southwest.

An Unexpected Rainbow: **Book 11 (Formerly:** *A Monumental Love*)
An unexpected romance might have the power to heal the past. Roxelle McCann is eager to meet the family of her roommate and "frenemy," Kyra Redhouse, so she takes a mini vacation to the Navajo Nation. Roxelle expects to find out more about Navajo language and customs and to be awed by the beauty of Monument Valley. She does not expect to find love among the monuments. The man she meets offers both a tender reminder of the past and a surprising possible future.

SEASONS OF DESTINY ROMANCE SERIES [in eBook and paperback]

Welcome to the small town of Destiny, California, where love blooms all year and the bonds of family and friendship last forever. The Seasons of Destiny series features four sweet and clean romances that will warm your heart based in a former Gold Rush community that you'll want to visit again and again.
Each story may be read separately, but there is great enjoyment in reading them in order.

Paris in the Springtime: **Book 1**
After false accusations lead to the loss of her job, Paris Cutler returns to the small mountain town of Destiny, CA to crash and regroup at her grandmother's. When she runs into her former high school crush, Greg Frantz, Paris begins to feel like a smitten kitten. Greg can't get Paris out of his mind. How can he convince her to make Destiny hers?

Sunny's Summer: **Book 2**
Sunny Ray arrives in the small town of Paradise to document the survivor stories of the Camp Fire, the deadliest in California history, for her graduate thesis. Her empathy enables her to connect with the community and to help the survivors heal, except for Deputy Sheriff

Evan Millett. Evan's anger and pain run deep and Sunny is determined to find out why.

Amber in Autumn: **Book 3**

Amber Reyes loves her job as the elementary school principal in Destiny, California. When two new kids begin struggling, Amber steps in, not realizing their father is her childhood neighbor, Max Burnett. Max is also suffering, wounded by a disastrous marriage. How can Amber help Max's troubled twins and heal Max's heart so he can love again?

Winter Skye: **Book 4**

Skye Ray and Peter Koury are drawn together by their joint love of art and a determination to turn pro after they graduate from college. But it's their shared education from the school of hard knocks that threatens to shatter their dreams. With Christmas break around the corner, can they mend the broken pieces of the past and build a bright future together?

CHRISTMAS TOWN ROMANCE SERIES [available in eBook]:

Welcome to Christmas Town, officially known as Bedford Falls, CA— where the spirit of holidays are celebrated all year long, and where a wholesome romance is just around the corner. This sweet and clean small-town romance series will make you want to curl up by a cozy fire with a mug of hot chocolate and a plate of freshly baked gingerbread cookies. Enjoy Christmas year round and make Christmas Town your destination for Holiday romance reads.
Each story may be read separately but there is great enjoyment in reading them in order.

A Joyful Eve in Christmas Town: **Book 1 (formerly *Joy Comes to Bedford Falls*)**

A new job brings Claire Reiser to Bedford Falls, California, a Sierra resort village widely known as Christmas Town because it celebrates the Holiday Season year-round. Claire arrives just days before Christmas, reconciled to spending the holiday alone.

Ben Scarge is also new in town, whisked in to manage the estate of his late Uncle Simon, a curmudgeonly miser who puts Scrooge to shame. Like Claire, Ben knows no one and anticipates a lonely holiday. Then a furry visitor delivers a gift neither Claire nor Ben will ever forget.

St. Nick Comes to Christmas Town: **Book 2**

Kiley Ross postponed her dreams of a university degree for many years, but she's ready to tackle it now, including the newswriting lab class taught by grad student Nick Santino. Nick's class challenges Kiley in every way. Trouble is, Kiley can't seem to stop thinking about her movie star look-alike teacher outside the classroom.

Nick Santino knows better than to become involved with a student, especially in his first class as a teaching assistant, but he can't help his attraction to Kiley; she captured his attention on Day One.

Kiley and Nick are coping with the rules and getting through the term. When circumstances throw them for a loop, how will they deal with the fall-out?

Kisses and Kittens in Christmas Town: **Book 3**

Amanda Velasquez is weary of attending her girlfriends' weddings when she can't even get a date. Is it her fault she's tall and built more like her linebacker dad than her runway model mom? Marco Fuentes admires the striking woman whose quest for good health brings her to the gym where he lifts weights. A mutual attraction draws them together, but their pride and prejudices keep tripping them up. Can a basketful of abandoned kittens help them choose snuggling over sparring?

Mischief and Mistletoe in Christmas Town: **Book 4**

Emily Draper and Carl Fuentes can't possibly fall in love. New career opportunities have them both contemplating major changes, and they both know the odds for long-distance relationships. How can the magic of Christmas and a cute kitten called Mischief make their future warm and bright?

Holly and Hearts in Christmas Town: Book 5

Bethany Sheridan has created a comfortable life for herself and her disabled daughter, Gracie. But with the daily demands of her work, her pet fostering, and caring for Grace, Bethany has no time to date let alone fall in love. Richard Hale has just landed a new job with a load of responsibility. He has always relied on a stable routine to manage his severe stutter. But his life turns upside down when he meets the lovely Bethany. How can a wheelchair-bound Cupid, a sweet-but-confused service dog, and an adorable puppy called Holly turn their awkward meeting into a second chance romance?

About the Author

Susan Aylworth loves "travel, great music, and perfect raspberry jam" and claims addiction to "words in almost all polite forms." Her first book, started when she was nine, "was a rip-off of *Black Beauty*. I wrote eight whole pages!" For her fifth-grade career day, she stated her ambition to become "a rich and famous author." Years later, she is pleased to have achieved the 'author' part of that goal.

Susan enjoys researching backgrounds and careers for the characters in her novels. "It's one way to live many lives all at once." She lives in northern California with her writer husband, Roger. She has also lived on the East Coast and in the Navajo Nation, the setting for several of her novels. Like most women of her generation, she wishes the kids would visit more often.

She loves hearing from readers. Reach her at susan@susanaylworthauthor.com. You may also sign up for Susan's newsletter at her website: susanaylworthauthor.com. Follow Susan on BookBub for updates on new releases. Like Susan's Facebook author page, www.facebook.com/Susan.Aylworth.Author, and/or follow her on Twitter @SusanAylworth. "If you enjoy my books, please tell everyone you know: friends, relatives, neighbors, the person who delivers your mail, people you meet in line in the grocery store, everyone!"

www.ingramcontent.com/pod-product-compliance
Lightning Source LLC
Chambersburg PA
CBHW020058180626
46812CB00006B/2380